I0748427

IRRECONCILABLE

The Dragon Oak Sagas

Book 1

BRADLEY F. BURTON

Irreconcilable is a work of fiction. All names, characters, places, and incidents are a product of the author's imagination and fabricated without malicious or deceitful intent. Any resemblance to actual people (living or dead), or localities, is completely coincidental.

Published by B-Squared Enterprises, LLC

Editing/Consultation: Paula F. Howard, AHA Publishers.com
Illustrations by Ray Martin,
Fine Art Pixel Painting by moc.das@gmail.com
Illustrations Design by Bradley F. Burton (B2urton)

ISBN: 9798992488166 (Paperback)

PRINTED IN THE UNITED STATES OF AMERICA

DEDICATION

Deb Burton

Beloved Wife and Muse

Thank you for your encouragement and support.

and

John Tierney

Long Time Friend

To our childhood adventures that honed my penchant for storytelling.

Table of Contents

Heed This Warning

ou are no doubt familiar with the adage that those who refuse to learn from their past are doomed to repeat it.

With that maxim in mind, I have written this first book of The Dragon Oak Sagas entitled. . .

Irreconcilable.

Be mindful of the lessons provided herein, before going forth . . . into an uncertain future.

Hereafter penned by my own hand,

Conrad Nightingale

PRELUDE

DESTINY BE DAMNED

"Helping those who can't help themselves, and everything that comes with such a daunting responsibility, is out of your control. It is simply part of your destiny."

While I meant to ease the weight of Johnathon Alcott's obligation to help others, apparently, it accomplished the exact opposite.

"Destiny be damned! There is only one master of my life, and that is me!" he replied. Taking a deep breath, then exhaling slowly, he dismissed my counsel with a wave of his hand. "I no longer choose to walk this path. I will hear no more on the matter."

It was a foolhardy statement made by a proud man under considerable duress. He would soon learn that one's fate is – inevitable.

Conrad Nightingale

PROLOGUE

IRRECONCILABLE DIFFERENCES

Spring, the season of renewal wherein winter discards its snowy shroud allowing both Mother Nature and the human spirit to be born anew. Nowhere in Calvendar is this transformation more evident than among the gently rolling hills of the Kenosha Plain, a region of abundant and undeniable beauty. Every spring this prairie becomes a spectacle for the senses. Patchwork fields of colorful wildflowers dot the hillsides; their seductive scents wafting upon gentle breezes through a sea of velvet green grass. It is a special time in a unique place where one's focus on life's more arduous demands freely gives way to troubled thoughts.

But alas, one cannot hide from reality forever, and all too soon, this transitory refuge fades like a dream . . . dawn's magenta light splits the distant horizon, marking the beginning of a new era for some, and the end for others. Trumpets blare and drums hammer, shattering the peaceful night. It is a call to arms . . .

(So writes Conrad Nightingale)

"The Cleanse," a great civil war to determine humanity's cultural and political destiny has begun.

Covered in filth and blood, Walter Bembridge was hardly recognizable. Unlike the other Overlords of Calvendar, the battered Lord Bembridge was never one to command from a safe distance. Always in the thick of the fight, he was a renowned warrior — a champion of the people.

Now safely back at the Preservation Coalition's Headquarters, with the last of his vitality spent, unable to stand of his own volition, he slumped to his knees. Whether out of fear or respect, nobody approached to assist him as he stared blankly across the expanse of death and destruction.

The sights, smells, and sounds of the armed conflict lingered. Thousands of bodies, professional soldiers and civilians alike lay scattered about the battlefield. The dead were now forever mute, while the mortally wounded, still in the final throes of passing, wailed in anguish as impatient vultures ripped the flesh from their dying bodies.

Colorful standards of the Preservation Coalition flapped in the breeze, announcing a rapidly approaching storm. The nauseating stench of war was carried on the wind. Lord Bembridge did not seek shelter but rather remained transfixed. He watched as the coming rain extinguished distant fires across the battlefield. He watched as small crimson tributaries merged downstream into a bloody torrent.

Then the storm caught up to him, and dark rolling clouds burst open as he lifted his face skyward, as heavy droplets of rain poured down, attempting to cleanse away any physical remnants of war.

But not everything was so easily made right. With time and proper care, eventually all his cuts and bruises would heal.

however, he knew from experience that the psychological wounds of battle never mend.

Raising his bloodied sword toward the heavens, he tried to yell above the howling wind and pounding rain. "Was there no other way?"

There was no response, though it didn't matter, for it was a rhetorical question. The answer was stretched out before him. When confronted by irreconcilable differences, there is no place for compromise, and mercy is a sign of weakness.

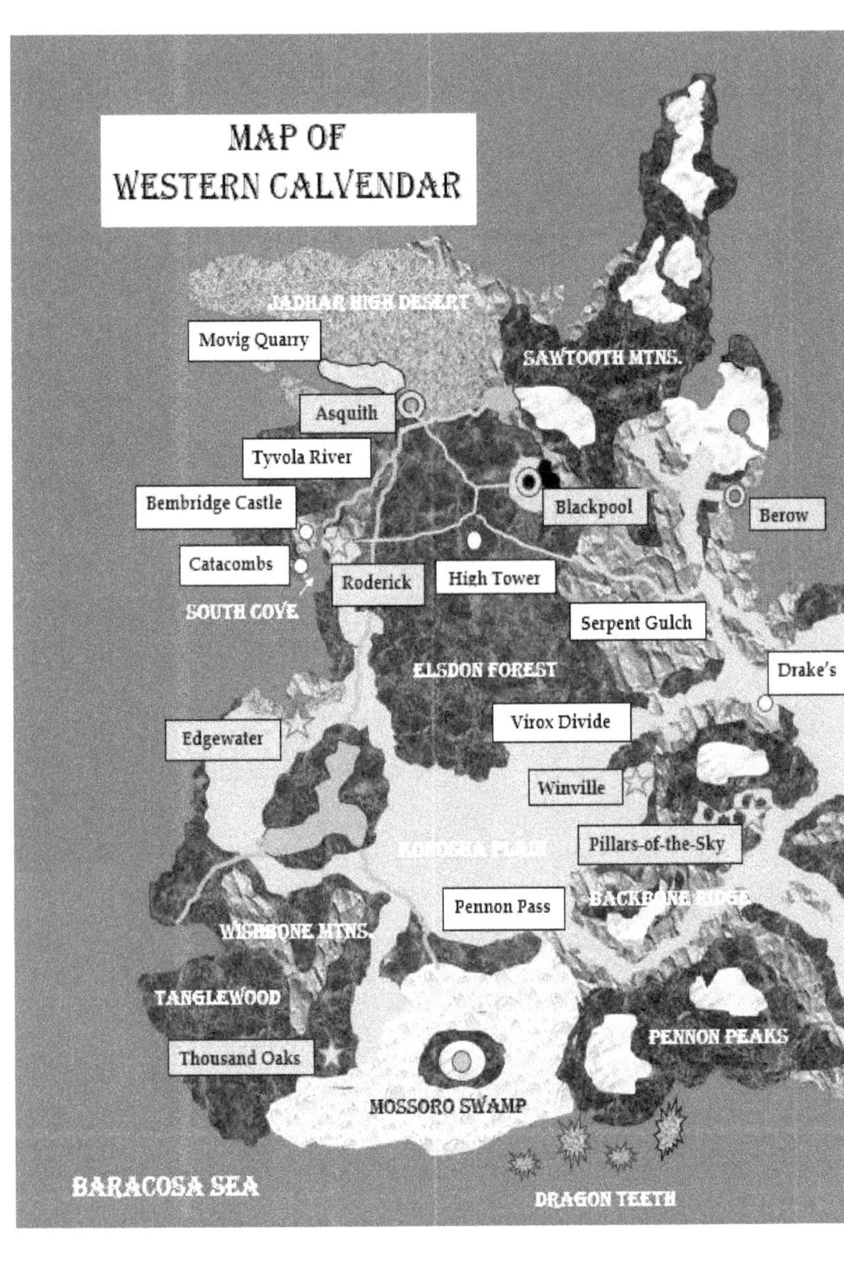
MAP OF
WESTERN CALVENDAR
JADHAR HIGH DESERT
Movig Quarry
SAWTOOTH MTNS.
Asquith
Tyvola River
Bembridge Castle
Blackpool
Berow
Catacombs
Roderick
High Tower
SOUTH COVE
Serpent Gulch
ELSDON FOREST
Drake's
Virox Divide
Edgewater
Winville
Pillars-of-the-Sky
Pennon Pass
BACKBONE RIDGE
WISHBONE MTNS.
TANGLEWOOD
PENNON PEAKS
Thousand Oaks
MOSSORO SWAMP
BARACOSA SEA
DRAGON TEETH

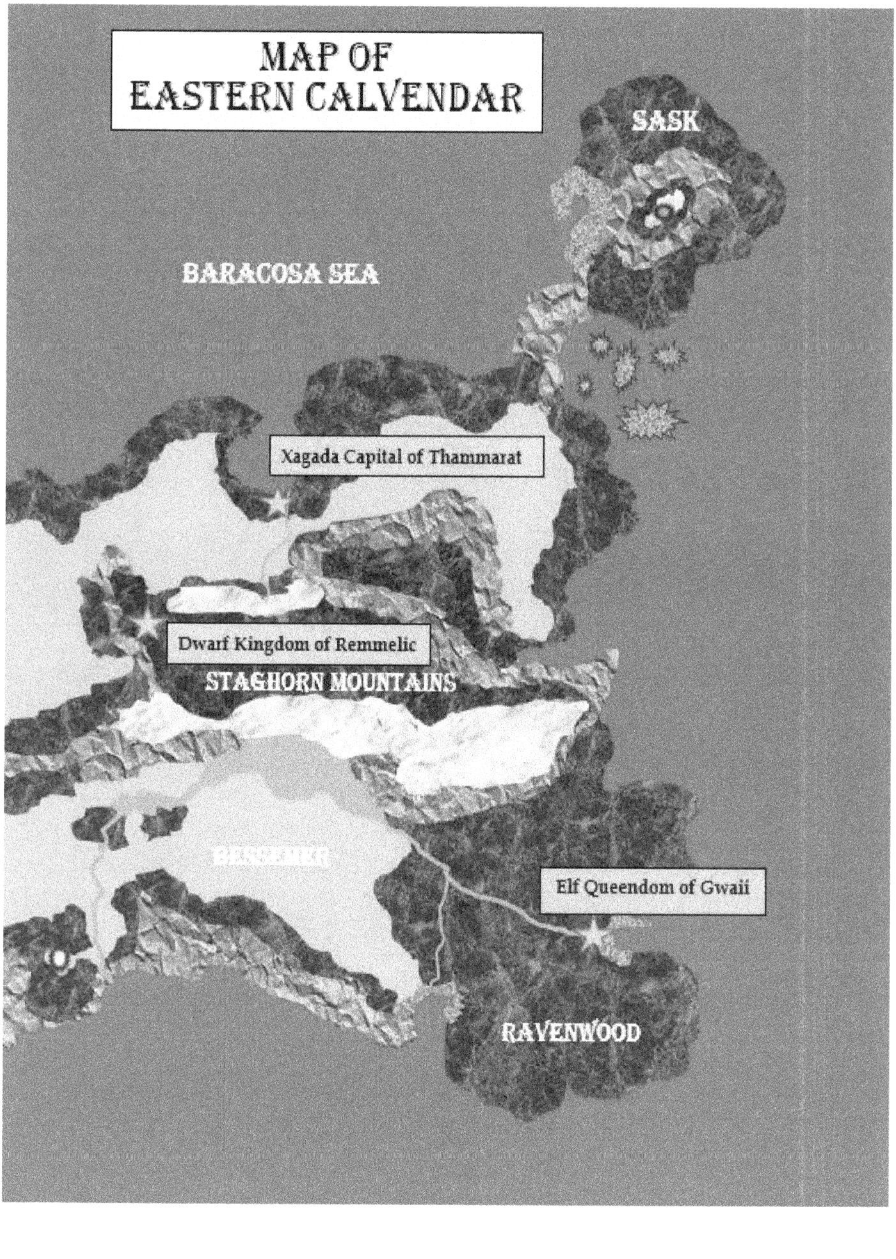

MAP OF EASTERN CALVENDAR

SASK

BARACOSA SEA

Xagada Capital of Thammarat

Dwarf Kingdom of Remmelic

STAGHORN MOUNTAINS

Elf Queendom of Gwaii

RAVENWOOD

CHAPTER 1

TURNING THE PAGE

For generations, the Alcott family has faithfully served the House of Bembridge. Johnathan Alcott's father, grandfather, and great-grandfather had each risen to the highly respected position of Chief Game Warden, stewards over thousands of hectares of prime fishing and hunting grounds. Naturally, everyone assumed that Johnathan would follow in his forefathers' footsteps. However, he chose an entirely different professional path...

(So writes Conrad Nightengale)

It would be one of the most memorable times in Johnathan Alcott's life, for on this evening, Lord and Lady Bembridge were hosting a ceremonial dinner to honor his retirement. Some were attending the occasion to express their sincere admiration and thanks for his service, while others came just to be seen, offering perfunctory speeches and halfhearted congratulations. Regardless of their motives, he wished his parents were still alive to witness how much he had accomplished.

Since he was a boy, Johnathan had performed various jobs for the House of Bembridge, and as he grew with proper guidance, so had his responsibilities. From his humble beginnings, through hard work and dedication, tonight Johnathan was retiring with honors as Commander of the Ranger Regiment at forty-five years of age, an accomplishment for which he was about to be rewarded beyond his own expectations.

As the celebration progressed, so did the merriment. Once the guests were happily occupied, Lord and Lady Bembridge whisked Johnathan and his companion, Ingrid Cooper, into the High Counsel Chamber adjacent to the Great Hall. A guard was posted at the door to ensure they would not be disturbed.

Lady Bembridge's eyes were filled with an inner glow of gratitude as she spoke. "John, over the years, you've attended many celebratory functions. Tell us, how does it feel to be the guest of honor?"

A stoic man by nature, Johnathan blushed slightly. "Reluctantly, I admit that sometimes being the center of attention can be quite agreeable," he chuckled. "Seriously though, Ingrid and I can't thank you enough for your hospitality." Ingrid nodded in agreement, squeezing Johnathan's arm as she beamed with pride.

Lord Bembridge turned and quietly walked over to the credenza. Upon it lay a silver box which held a rolled parchment tied with a red ribbon. "Well, John, you deserve far more than a dinner party for your many years of loyal service, which is why we want to give you this token of our gratitude." He presented it with a flourish.

Johnathan removed the ribbon, unrolled the parchment, and started reading. Discerning the true meaning of the document made him weak in the knees, and he had to lower himself onto a nearby chair to keep from falling.

"That's not exactly the response we expected," said Lord Bembridge. "Are you okay?"

"Ye . . . yes," he stuttered. "I just need a moment to collect myself."

Taken aback by Johnathan's reaction, Ingrid insisted on knowing what was happening.

Lord Bembridge attempted to put her at ease. "No need for concern, my dear. The document that John holds is a Deed of Ownership to a small parcel of land on one of my hunting reserves. In addition to the land, there is a modest lodge that might serve nicely as your home. Amanda and I hope it will give you both a boost in your new lives."

Motioning for Ingrid to take a seat next to Johnathan, Amanda interjected. "Perhaps a little background story will help you understand, Ingrid. When John, Walter, and I were children, we often accompanied our fathers on their hunting expeditions. While they were out pursuing quarry, we three stayed behind, exploring and having adventures of our own. Every time we visited this particular reserve, John would proclaim without fail that it was the most wonderful place in all Calvendar," Amanda smiled. "Do you recall that, John?"

"I do, and it is a declaration I still hold firm today. However, this is far too much. We can never repay you for such generosity."

"Ahh, but that's the nice thing about a gift: repayment is neither expected, nor required. May you both enjoy a happy and thriving retirement," replied Lord Bembridge.

The four embraced with genuine affection for one another before returning to the party.

***

The celebration continued late into the evening, and everyone seemed to enjoy themselves until even the heartiest attendee succumbed to the need for sleep. However, such was not the case for Johnathan and Ingrid. Back at the Ranger Regiment's Officer Quarters, they snuggled under a feather comforter, too excited to close their eyes as they recounted the night's festivities.

"I had no idea you had so many friends," said Ingrid.

"I think most people were there to partake in the free food and wine," Johnathan responded.

"Nonsense. You don't give yourself enough credit, John. Many people admire you; I know Lord and Lady Bembridge certainly do."

"The three of us have held a special bond since childhood, but the love they showed me tonight … Well, I'm simply at a loss for words." Ingrid gave Johnathan a gentle hug. She understood what he couldn't express.

"I can't wait for the morning so I can show you our new home. I know you're going to love it as much as I do."

"I'm sure I will, but is there any chance we can catch a few hours' sleep before starting the next chapter of our lives?"

A few hours' sleep was all Ingrid got because Johnathan was up banging around at the crack of dawn. "Good morning, sleepyhead," he greeted her when she appeared. "The horses are saddled, and I've packed enough food and drink to hold us for a couple of days. Are you ready to go?"

Ingrid balled her fists, and her face turned a bright red. "**UGHHH!**" came the prolonged groan.

The two had been together long enough for Johnathan to know exactly what that meant. "Right. I'll wait while you get ready. No hurry, take your time."

Ingrid wheeled about and went back into the bedroom without so much as another sound.

That was a close call, Johnathan thought.

Thirty minutes later, Ingrid found Johnathan standing outside with the horses. "Good morning," she smiled while handing him a muffin and cup of tea. "I don't suppose you've bothered to eat?" Johnathan sheepishly accepted the breakfast. "As soon as you finish your breakfast, we can head off to the property."

"Albem," he mumbled while cramming the food into his mouth.

"What?"

Johnathan swallowed hard, "'Albem.' That's what I named the new farm. It's a combination of Alcott and Bembridge. Do you like it?"

Ingrid mounted her horse. She pursed out her lower lip and replied softly, "I thought you might name it after me – 'Cooper Farm.' That has a nice ring to it, don't you think?"

I've stepped into it again, and the sun is barely up, he thought. "Well, yes, I guess."

"You guess?

"No, I'm sure of it. 'Cooper Farm,' it is."

"Too late. Besides, 'Albem' is the perfect name." He could hear Ingrid laughing as she trotted off. How she loved to tease him.

***

After a short ride out of the city of Roderick, they crested Hardgrove Hill. Below them lay a hundred prime hectares of pastures and woodlands fed by Brookstone Creek. It was as beautiful as Johnathan had described. However, what really caught Ingrid's eye was the sturdy-looking structure made of hardwoods cut from the property. Off she galloped, slapping the reins across her horse's flank, with Johnathan following close behind.

Once she reached the lodge, Ingrid dismounted her horse in one fluid motion. Running up the porch steps, she grabbed the doorknob, only to find the door locked.

"Please tell me you remembered the key!"

Meandering close behind, Johnathan patted his body up and down. "The key? Where did I put that thing?"

"John!"

"Oh, so now you're the one in a hurry," he laughed.

"**JOHN**," she repeated sternly; it was clearly a warning.

"Okay, dear."

Johnathan unlocked the door, and Ingrid entered, bumping him aside as she stepped over the threshold.

"Oh my," she said in amazement. "I envisioned a tatty old cottage that wreaked of tobacco and spilled mead, but this is really quite tasteful." Ingrid plopped herself down on one of the overstuffed chairs next to a large stone fireplace. Dust billowed up to meet her, and she coughed slightly. "Still, the place could stand a thorough cleaning." There was no arguing with that observation. "I'll bet this is where the men gathered to formulate strategies and swap yarns about the hunt while you children eavesdropped from the loft overhead," she said, pausing slightly before continuing, "I can sense the joy in this house, John." Within a second, she was back on her feet again, continuing to explore. Ingrid called out from another room, "What will we ever do with all this space?"

"I'm sure we'll find good use for each room," John called back. "But you haven't seen the best of it yet. Come into the kitchen."

As she entered, Ingrid could hardly believe her eyes. There in the sink was a pump. She drew the handle several times, and clean, cold water began to flow freely. She laughed gleefully, dipping her fingers beneath the faucet of running water.

"It's called 'indoor plumbing'," Johnathan said. His heart was full to see her so happy. Then he noticed

movement outside the kitchen window. The stable door was closing slowly. Ingrid saw it, too. They fell quiet.
"Is anyone else supposed to be here?" she said softly. "No." Johnathan pulled his long knife. "Stay here."

Johnathan approached the stable cautiously, his knife held forward, ready to ward off any attack. Kneeling close to the door, he could hear whispering.

"She's just a child, Marc, she doesn't understand."

"Do what you need to, but keep her quiet," a male voice said. *"We'll move on at nightfall."*

The barn door flung open, flooding the inside with sunlight. They saw a silhouetted figure of a tall man holding a wicked - looking weapon at the threshold. Inside, the family of three backed themselves deeper into the corner. They were trapped.

"I don't understand either," Johnathan said, responding to what he had overheard. "Come outside."

Sheepishly, all three figures obeyed the big man's order. From the kitchen window, Ingrid saw what was happening and went outside to join them. "Who are you, and what are you doing here?"

"My name is Marc Kershaw. This is my wife, Alison, and our daughter, Cora. We mean you no harm, and we'll just be on our way if it's all the same to you." The three started to move slowly away from Johnathan and Ingrid.

"No, it's **NOT** all the same to me," Johnathan said. "Now I know who you are, but you haven't explained why you're hiding inside my stable."

The man and wife exchanged sideways glances but gave no further response. Ingrid could sense they were genuinely scared, so she tried to alleviate the situation by speaking directly to the little girl.

"How old are you, Cora?"

The girl was not shy and shot up four fingers.

"Oh my, four years old! Why, you're practically full grown." Cora beamed. "Are you hungry?"

Cora nodded.

"Come with me."

The girl readily accepted Ingrid's outstretched hand, and the two walked into the house as though nothing out of the ordinary was happening. Apparently, Ingrid and Cora had reached an understanding even though questions still lingered with the parents. Johnathan sheathed his long knife and gestured Marc and Alison toward the house.

Retrieving the provisions Johnathan had packed for himself and Ingrid, he spread them out to share with the strangers. The three devoured their share of the meal as if they hadn't eaten in days. In truth, they had not.

Once their hunger was quelled, the questioning resumed, albeit in a gentler manner. "You don't appear to be thieves," Johnathan said. "Are you ready to tell us how you came to our house?"

Immediately, Marc protested, making it clear they had never stolen anything in their lives, but he was still reluctant to answer any questions. "Thank you for your kindness," he continued. "Perhaps there is some chore I can do to repay you, and then we can be on our way."

"That won't be necessary; you're our guests," Johnathan said. "Besides, it looks like you could use some rest, especially your wife and child. Stay here and get a good night's sleep."

It sounded more like a command than an invitation. Eventually, Marc and his family settled down, even though it was difficult to relax for the remainder of the day. Marc kept a watchful eye on Johnathan as he wasn't sure whether Johnathan's kindness had any alternative motive.

That night was a completely different experience. It had been a long time since Marc and Alison lay on a fathered mattress under warm blankets. Before long, they fell into a deep sleep and woke up the next morning much later than they had intended.

Cora was nowhere to be seen, and Alison panicked, as any mother would until she heard her child's laughter coming from another room. Upon closer examination, she found Cora in the kitchen playing with Ingrid and Johnathan. Seconds later, Marc followed Alison into the room.

"Good morning," Ingrid greeted them. "I trust you both are well rested?" Cora ran to hug her mother, who lifted her gently and returned the embrace. "I can offer only a meager breakfast as we are low on provisions. Perhaps, Marc, you can accompany Johnathan to the city for supplies?"

"I'm sorry, that won't be possible. We must be on our way," Marc replied abruptly. Everyone went quiet.

Alison looked from one to the other, then spoke in earnest to her husband. "Marc, Johnathan, and Ingrid have shown our family nothing but kindness when they had no reason to do so. They deserve an explanation. You need to regain your trust in people."

Marc paused before responding. "All right, you've been pressing us for an explanation, so here it is . . . We cannot return to Roderick because we are wanted criminals. Our lives are no longer our own."

"And what, pray tell, are your crimes?" Johnathan asked.

"Putting our trust in the wrong people." It was an unwarranted jab. Alison dropped her head, and Marc immediately felt ashamed.

"Marc, please," implored Alison.

Marc sighed deeply and reluctantly started their story, "Alison and I met one another while in the service of others. Provided it was honest work, no job was beneath our status, and we toiled every day from morning until night with not much to show for our efforts. Then, one day, the gods blessed us with a child." Marc looked at Cora and smiled. "Alison was working the fields when she gave birth and was back working the next morning. However, now, with the added burden of caring for a child, the pace was unsustainable. Alison grew ill. Although I took a second job, the doctor, medicine, and daily costs just to survive were more than I could handle. Soon, I found myself having to borrow money that I couldn't repay. After some time, I was brought before the local magistrate, who informed me that my debt was shared by each member of my family, including the infant child. Our futures were all but sealed – Debtor's Prison, and we were not alone."

"That's when our benefactor stepped forward, Chancellor Nigel Oswalt. He was in court that day, buying up selected debts for pennies in exchange for two years of indentured servitude. He sweetened his magnanimous offer by separating out a small portion of land, saying we could establish a community and grow our own crops during off- hours. Naturally, those selected jumped at the opportunity. However, the reality was quite different. Time off for working our fields was scarce, and the land was rocky and bare, lacking sufficient water."

"Nevertheless, by working together, we managed to scrap out a meager crop and then came the surprise — taxes. We all thought it quite suspicious that Chancellor Oswalt had neglected to inform us of the pending taxes", he said sarcastically. "Of course, the Chancellor was happy to cover the tax burden in exchange for additional years of servitude. In truth, we had been tricked into a never-ending cycle of indentured servitude, and those who refused to continue found themselves sold to the slave market at Berow, a fate worse than Debtors Prison."

"Not much of a bargain," Ingrid said. She gazed sympathetically in Alison and Cora's direction.

"No, not much of a bargain — AT LEAST NOT A FAIR ONE. So that is why you found us hiding in your stable. Better to take our chances as fugitives than exist another day living in a corrupt society where noblemen and slavers profit off the desperation of the poor."

"Perhaps," Johnathan said, "but a life on the run is difficult enough by yourself, let alone with a family."

"And a life without my family is no life at all," responded Marc.

"It doesn't seem right," Ingrid said. Can we do anything for them, John?"

"Unfortunately, Ingrid, what is right and what is fair aren't always the same thing in the eyes of the law. I'll think upon the matter and try to come up with an idea. I suggest you all make yourselves at home. Please finish the food and drink. As for me, I have a full day ahead in Roderick. I'll be back with provisions as soon as I'm able."

Mounting his horse, Johnathan trotted off toward the city. As he rode off, Marc turned to Ingrid. "I know who your husband is, and I suspect the Commander will be returning with more men."

Ingrid looked at him for a long moment, clearly perturbed. "In the short time I've known you, it is obvious you speak before thinking of the consequences of your words. If you truly knew my husband, you would know two things for sure: first, he doesn't need any help taking you prisoner should he want to, and second, justice runs deep within his core."

Marc didn't mean to appear ungrateful, but he could only look back at Ingrid with uncertainty.

***

Upon arriving in Roderick, Johnathan went straight to the magistrate's office, where he had the records produced for Marc Kershaw's original sentence and subsequent sale into Chancellor Oswalt's service. He also reviewed the most recent documents that sold Marc and his family to Taraz Surat, an Orc Slave Master. The paperwork verified Marc's story and the obvious injustice. *This is exploitation at its worst and needs to be rectified*, thought Johnathan.

With determined strides, Johnathan found his way to a seedier part of the city, where he found Taraz Surat sitting at an outdoor table preparing his recent acquisitions for their march to Berow to be sold as slaves.

SNORT ... "Commander Alcott, what you want," HARRUMPH ... Taraz Surat grunted, barely lifting his head up to make eye contact. Taraz Surat was scrawny and fouler than most, even by orc standards.

"Marc Kershaw and his family, I want to buy them." Taraz Surat scanned over his ledger sheet. SNORT ...

"Happy to sell, but no have them — yet." HARRUMPH ... A twinkle could be detected in his beady yellow eyes.

"Don't worry yourself about the details. Write up the Bill of Sale."

SNORT ... "Negotiate, first." HARRUMPH ...

"No negotiation. I'll pay you exactly one sovereign more than you paid Chancellor Oswalt. And don't try to cheat me! I saw your paperwork in the magistrate's office.

SNORT ... "One sovereign profit. You joke!" HARRUMPH ... Johnathan Alcott wasn't laughing when he bent closer, holding the orc's gaze.

SNORT ... "I sell man and woman." Taraz Surat began drooling down his chinless neck. "Girl stays with me." HARRUMPH ... Taraz Surat grinned a crooked smile that spoke volumes more than his broken attempt to communicate. Instantly, Johnathan Alcott was enraged. He grabbed Taraz Surat by his protruding lower tusks, jerking him to his feet.

"Now I'll give you half of what you paid Chancellor Oswalt and spare you the beating of your life, you **CHILD-MOLESTING PRICK**!" He slammed the back of the orc's head into the stone wall to emphasize his point. "Write up the Bill of Sale while you can still hold an ink quill!" Johnathan ordered.

***

After concluding his business with the Orc Slave Master, Johnathan set about gathering provisions before returning to Albem Farm.

Ingrid, Marc, Alison, and Cora greeted him on the porch steps as he rode up in a new wagon full of supplies.

"Looks like you had a productive day," Ingrid smiled.

"Quite productive." He returned the smile. "And look, I've made a new friend along the way." Johnnathan held forth a beautifully dressed doll.

Cora excitedly accepted the doll, looking as if she couldn't believe it her good fortune. She had never had anything before to call her own.

"I'll bet you're all hungry. I brought plenty of food and drink. Marc, how about helping me unload the wagon while our wives prepare a meal."

Once the ladies were out of earshot, Johnathan informed Marc, "Your debt has been settled. You and your family are free to go where you wish. However, I would like you to stay."

"I don't understand."

"I have no skill in farming, but I'm a quick study and hard worker. If you agree to help me get the farm up and running, you can stay in the caretaker quarters above the stable free of charge. In addition, I'll give you twenty percent of the harvest to do with as you please. What say you?"

"Why are you doing this?"

"Because I need help, and it is the right thing to do."

Marc's head sank. "I'm sorry, I've misjudged you," he mumbled.

"Does that mean we have an agreement?"

"Yes!"

"Good, then go help the wives start a cooking fire. Here's a piece of kindling to get you started." Johnathan handed Marc a piece of paper.

"I can't read. What does it say?"

"It's the Bill of Sale for you and your family. Burn it."

CHAPTER 2

TOO HIGH THE PRICE

The wheels of justice turned quickly for Tobias Rycroft, unquestionably Calvendar's most notorious criminal. Less than a week had passed between his capture and sentencing: a life of solitary confinement within the dungeons of Blackpool Penitentiary. It is a most fitting end for a truly despicable human being. At the stroke of midnight, the so-called Xagada Butcher was placed within a prison transport wagon and spirited out of the city of Roderick without so much as a single tear shed on his behalf…

(So writes Conrad Nightingale)

Adjacent to the castle's courtyard, set back among towering hardwoods, sits a large stone building used to accommodate the Impregnable Guard, an elite league of hardened veterans sworn to protect the House of Bembridge with their lives. Within the bowels of this barrack is a space dedicated to a half dozen jail cells used to hold prisoners awaiting trial or for their subsequent transfer to Blackpool Penitentiary, should they be found guilty. Tonight, these cells were empty except for one lone prisoner.

Clouds danced across the night sky as the moonlight flickered through the tree limbs, casting lace-like shadows about the courtyard; a silhouetted figure rapped upon the barrack's door. A guardsman came to the nearest barred window and peered through the thick leaded glass, looking for verification. The cloaked stranger pulled back his hood, exposing his unique features; it was all the confirmation required. A moment later, a screeching sound pierced the silent night as the heavy wooden door swung open on iron hinges. First to step through the doorway with short swords already drawn were two guardsmen; a prisoner, his arms and legs impaired by shackles, walked slowly behind, followed by two more guardsmen at the ready.

Without formality, Tobias Rycroft was handed over to the Blackpool Penitentiary Sentries, known throughout Calvendar as the BPS. The squad was made up entirely of bohkors, a no-nonsense race that held tightly to its traditional values. One of the sentries crept up behind Rycroft and deftly slipped a spiked collar on a long pole around the prisoner's neck, assuring maximum control without getting too close. The harness would be released only after the prisoner was safely within the transport cage. Despite such dire circumstances, Rycroft smirked as though incarcerating him was nothing more than a temporary inconvenience — a look that didn't go unnoticed.

One huge bohkor with a menacing demeanor dismounted his pale stallion, a large horse of equal stature to its rider, and shuffled toward Rycroft. Unable to bend his right knee from a previous battle injury, the bohkor's approach was announced by the scraping sound of his metal-braced boot scuffing along the cobblestones. Once opposite, the bohkor and his prisoner looked one another up and down with an almost palpable revulsion.

Although the alliance between the human and bohkor races went back more than a century, there were enough physical distinctions to exacerbate unfounded stereotypes, such as the bohkors' proclivity for indiscriminate acts of aggression. Typically, bohkors were more substantial in height and weight than their human counterparts. Salted hair and dark lips provided a distinct contrast with their ashen skin, while pupilless black eyes made it difficult to determine their actual point of focus. Yet, despite these fearsome characteristics, bohkors were usually slower to provoke and much less aggressive than their human counterparts.

However, there was no mistaking this unusually large bohkor's intent as he loomed over Rycroft. Attired in the traditional BPS uniform, his dark leather breastplate was covered by a red cloth sash bearing a black scorpion. The numerous diagonal stripes below the scorpion identified him as the ranking non-commissioned officer.

The bohkor's lip curled in disgust as he broke the awkward silence. The cadence of his voice was slow and deliberate.

"I am Master Sergeant Ramson; my friends call me 'Ram.' However, you are not my friend and never will be; therefore, you shall address me as 'Sir.'" Ramson emphasized this point by jamming his thick index finger into Rycroft's chest. "As for you, from this moment forward, you no longer have a name and shall simply be referred to as 'Lifer 005,' an identification that indicates you are part of a distinct group of inmates that shall never be released back into society."

Rycroft didn't respond but continued to grin and stare back into the bohkor's lifeless eyes. Ramson paused momentarily, cocking his head slightly as though he was perplexed.

"I'm not sure you grasp the gravity of your situation, so let me try to enlighten you further. You have been stripped of all human rights by order of Lord Bembridge. Solitary confinement awaits you at Blackpool Penitentiary. Don't despair; you will always have a roof over your head, a bit of straw for bedding, water, and somewhat edible food scraps." He stopped talking long enough to assess the effect of his words.

"Think about it, Lifer 005; you'll never have to cut your hair, shave, or bathe again for the rest of your life. Other than the ghost of your victims, no one will ever bother you while you wile away the days and nights contemplating your heinous deeds. That is, except for me — I promise to visit you on every anniversary of your incarceration, if for no other reasons than to remind you of the time you've lost while confined within the dungeon of Blackpool Penitentiary and, of course, to beat the shit out of you," Ramson chuckled. "It will be interesting to see how long it takes until you're driven completely insane."

The realization of what his future held was all it took to swipe the smirk from Rycroft's face. Nevertheless, trying to appear unaffected, Rycroft blurted out, "I'm not afraid of you, kory!"

"Perhaps not now," the big one said, "but I assure you that you will rue the day when you hear me standing outside your dungeon door. Oh, there's one last thing before we go – Do you understand that referring to a bohkor with that vulgar slang word 'kory' is the most offensive term you can use? If you're not careful, it's liable to get you a good crack alongside your skull. "

Master Sergeant Ramson motioned the sentry holding the pole harness to get the prisoner on board the transport wagon. As the sentry pushed the yoke forward, spikes poked at Rycroft's soft neck, causing him to wince. He offered no resistance. Once locked safely inside the cage, the driver released the wagon's brake, and without further ado, the squad of six sentries and their prisoner took the road east out of the sleeping city.

***

After several uneventful hours, Ramson felt comfortable enough to stop and rest his men. They made camp, tethered the horses, built a fire, and settled down for the remainder of the night.

At dawn, the camp stirred awake; an uneasy feeling permeated the air. The dense morning fog made seeing more than a few feet impossible, but the BPS sensed they were no longer alone. Master Sergeant Ramson ordered the sentries to break camp and move out immediately. Everyone was on edge, that is, everyone except Rycroft. The sentries strained their eyes and ears, looking and listening for anything unusual, and then they became aware of the sound of additional hoofbeats alongside them. One by one, strangers appeared out of the mist like phantoms, a dozen hooded men on horseback.

Readying for a fight while assuring a hopeful Rycroft he would be the first to die, Ramson grabbed his mace, and the sentries followed his lead, drawing their weapons.

That's when the nearest mystery rider called out, "Ram, hold fast! There's no need for hostility; it's Ben Higgins!"

As Master Sergeant Ramson's eyes adjusted to the defused light, he recognized his former colleague, Higgins, with whom he shared a brief past as a young soldier in Lord Bembridge's cavalry unit.

"Men, stand down," he immediately ordered.

Higgins now wore a forest green cloak attached by a silver leaf brooch, the insignia of a junior officer in the Ranger Regiment, a unit highly trained in stealth maneuvers. Although relieved they weren't under attack, the surprise still perturbed Ramson, and his curt response made that clear.

"I'm transporting a prisoner, Lieutenant; this is neither the time nor place for an unexpected reunion. Explain yourself and be quick about it."

"Since you insist, Ram, let's get down to business. Lord Bembridge considers your prisoner a high risk, so he thought it best that you have an escort as far as the turnoff to Blackpool. We've been with you since the prisoner exchange in Roderick."

So, you've been with us throughout the night, thought Ramson, *probably treating this prisoner transfer as a mere training exercise. Am I supposed to be comforted by your presence?* Ramson's jawline tightened, and he pursed his lips together, looking as though he was fighting back the words he wanted to speak, "The BPS is quite capable of transporting this prisoner on its own," was all he said.

Lieutenant Higgins stiffened both his body and his resolve. "It's not your call, Master Sergeant. As the ranking officer, I'll hear no more of your protest. The Rangers shall ride with you, so make the best of it. Am I clear?"

Ramson's eyes narrowed, and he began to squeeze the handle of his mace repeatedly as though he was being personally challenged, but then he thought better. "It seems I have no choice in the matter, so your assistance is appreciated, Sir. Just try to keep up," he responded contemptuously.

Hardly a word was spoken for the remainder of the day as the BPS and its Ranger Regiment escort made their way through Elsdon Forrest. When occasional wayfarers were encountered along the route, they gave a wide berth to the heavily guarded prison transport wagon. Much to everyone's relief, the day remained uneventful.

The next day, after a somewhat meager breakfast, the combined troops set out into ever deeper woodlands. When the sun reached its apex at noon, they arrived at the turnoff to Blackpool Penitentiary.

"Well, Ram," Lieutenant Higgins chuckled, "as always, your gift for gab made what could have been a tedious journey almost bearable. But sadly, this is where we must part,"

"I detect a bit of sarcasm, Ben," Ramson said. "Perhaps the next time I'm in Roderick we can put this incident behind us over a pint of ale. You're buying, of course." Then, with cursory waves, the BPS and the Ranger Regiment separated at the crossroad, and each went their way.

***

Ten miles west of Blackpool Penitentiary, the main road cut through a stretch of densely packed shade plants under towering ancient hardwoods. The spiderweb of overhanging branches brought a welcome relief from the hot summer sun. It also turned the road into a dank pathway with only intermittent shafts of light poking through the treetop canopy.

Master Sergeant Ramson ordered Corporal Vox, one of the more experienced sentries, to drop back and ride sweeper while he took point. They were moving cautiously along the moss-covered trail when Ramson signaled the troops to stop. The coachman immediately set the wagon's brake.

The usual chorus of birds and sounds of small creatures scampering about had ceased, and the silence was disconcerting. The BPS held their place, awaiting the Master Sergeant's next order. But the momentary delay proved fatal.

An instant later came the distinctive whistle of a bolt in flight and the audible thud of an arrow as it pierced the coachman's leather breastplate. The remaining sentries attempted to draw their weapons while frantically swinging their horses about, searching the woods for adversaries, but to no avail. Multiple arrows of hidden assassins quickly struck them down.

By the time Corporal Vox closed the gap to give aid, all his brothers-in-arms lay dead. Vox immediately turned toward Rycroft, trying to stab him through the cage bars. The first thrust was a near miss as Rycroft scrambled into the far corner. The second thrust would have found its target, but it never came.

Ramson's steed broad-sided Vox's horse at full gallop, sending Vox and his horse to the ground. Ramson dismounted much quicker than one might think possible due to his injured leg and closed the gap on the semi-conscious corporal, who stared up befuddled. Without a word, down came Ramson's mace, smashing Vox's head asunder.

The waylay was over in seconds. Four assassins came out from hiding. They were indistinguishable from the surrounding woods; exposed parts of their bodies were covered by dirt, and their clothing was camouflaged with fern branches. Everything had gone as planned, yet Rycroft appeared highly irate.

"Get me the fuck out of this cage!" he screamed. Ramson tossed one of the men the keys. As soon as Rycroft was out of the cage and free of his shackles, he rushed Ramson, grabbing him by the collar and locking him so tightly that his knuckles began to turn white. He spit through clenched teeth as he spoke, "You seemed to be enjoying yourself a little too much the past couple of days! If you expect to get paid, it would be best to remember who's **REALLY** in charge."

"Believe me," Ransom snarled back, "nothing is enjoyable about dealing with you. Even so, I've upheld my part of the bargain. As for your less-than-hospitable treatment, it was necessary for me to treat you like the reprobate you are to avoid unwanted scrutiny. Any special treatment was out of the question, especially when the Rangers unexpectedly joined us. Besides, need I point out that I not only led my comrades into this ambush but also saved your pathetic life by slaying a close friend." Ramson leaned close, "Just don't mistake my lust for gold as loyalty to either you or your Xagada cause."

"Oh, we both know why you're here, and it has nothing to do with gold," Rycroft said. The two were sharing a secret.

"You better start thinking, Rycroft, and save the bravado for later because you're not in the clear yet. The way I see it, you have only three choices: one, you can continue along the road to the very doorstep of Blackpool Penitentiary; however, considering this atrocity, I doubt you'll live to serve your sentence. Two, you can turn back to Roderick and try your chances with the Impregnable Guard, but again, I believe your life would be forfeit. Or three, you can shut the fuck up and let me get you safely to Jadhar as we previously agreed.

"It makes no difference to me, but choose quickly, for we're running out of the precious daylight needed to make good on our escape. It won't be long before the BPS has search parties roaming the countryside, and since I'm the only one here who knows BPS tactics, you'll still need my help to get to the high desert in one piece. Now take your hands off me before I break them off and leave you to fend for yourself."

Rycroft slowly let his grip slip while holding Ramson's gaze. The two found themselves in a stalemate, but both knew this was a fragile truce.

Regaining his composure, Rycroft tried to make light of the confrontation, not wanting to lose face in front of his men. He rolled his head and shoulders, feigned a stretch, and let loose a thunderous fart. It broke the tension, and the men dissolved into laughter.

"Ahh, now I feel much better. Days confined in a small cage have me questioning myself. Of course, we need to stick with the original plan. Still, there's something I must do before we depart."

"I told you we don't have time to waste," objected Ramson.

"And I TOLD you, I'm in charge! Drag the dead kories into a single line over there," he commanded his men. "As for you, Master Sergeant, feel free to let your friend lie where you left him, but bring me his sword."

Once gathered, Rycroft hacked the feet off each corpse, carefully placing them alongside the heads of their respective bodies. Ramson averted his eyes in disgust; this situation was far more than he had bargained. When the last sentry was adulterated, Rycroft ordered his men to mount the BPS horses.

"**NOW**, we're ready to go, Master Sergeant, lead on."

Turning off the main trail, Ramson kept the afternoon shafts of sunlight to his left, guiding the band north as they weaved through the dense woods. All was quiet until curiosity got the best of the youngest hooligan, Jason Sinclair, and he asked Rycroft, "Why did you cut the feet off the corpses and place them by their heads?"

"It's a way to warn any pending search parties to think with their heads before following with their feet. Besides, it gives me pleasure to defile the bodies of dead kories."

Rycroft glanced over to catch Ramson's reaction, but the large bohkor wasn't listening. He was thinking back to where it had all started and lamenting what he had done:

> *It was little less than a year ago when a lone bohkor walked into Tobias Rycroft's place of business. The bohkor stood out of place among the established clientele, not just because of his race but also because of his size. As several bouncers moved to eject the enormous bohkor, Rycroft waived them off, instead approaching the hulking figure himself.*
>
> *"We don't get many of your kind in here." Rycroft had to move close and raise his voice above the din to be heard. "What exactly are you looking for: a night of unlimited*

drink to drown your sorrows, a chance to fatten your purse at one of our games, or perhaps something more personal?" Rycroft was adept at reading a tell and detected a slight response at the last suggestion. "Is there a type of woman you fancy: tall, short, fat, thin, blond, brunette, or fiery redhead? I can get you whatever you desire." Rycroft did his best to follow the bohkor's blank black eyes as he scanned the room, stopping on one of the service boys mopping slop off the floor. "Ahh yes, that also can be arranged for the right price. . ."

"Price is not the issue. Can you be discreet?"

"Discretion is the cornerstone of my business. Let me show you to one of our more private rooms." The upstairs rooms were little more than lightly partitioned cells with a single candle and straw mattress on the floor. The entire place reeked of vomit and piss, but it would have to do.

While Rycroft settled in his guest, he had several of his men scouring the city for the bohkor's horse and belongings, anything that might shed some light on his identity.

The servant boy didn't know what was happening when he was presented before the bohkor.

"I'll leave you two alone. Be sure to see me later so we can settle, and don't even think of running out unpaid." Rycroft exposed his hidden Xagada dagger to emphasize his point.

The bohkor grunted his acceptance as he pulled the frightened child closer. It would be the first and last time the boy had such an encounter – in this case, a deplorable and demeaning experience. While transfixed in the throes of passion, the powerful bohkor attempted to muffle the boy's cries, pushing his face into the mattress, inadvertently suffocating him. Although unintentional, one could say it was a merciful death.

Rycroft and several armed men burst into the room; he had been watching through a small hole strategically placed in the thin wall. "Well, it seems we will have to renegotiate our price, Master Sergeant Ramson." Rycroft had discovered the identity of his newest stooge.

I have slipped from the path of righteousness and fallen into an abyss of despair, a pit blacker than the tar at Blackpool Penitentiary. In doing so, I traded a life of honor for a moment of debauchery and became the very kind of monster I've sworn to punish. If I had even an ounce of integrity left in my body, I would kill all these bastards and finish myself off for good measure.

"Do you think that will stop the BPS from hunting us?" asked Jason.

"I don't know. What do you think, Master Sergeant Ramson?" Rycroft was pressing the matter, trying to reestablish his dominance.

"I doubt it will even slow them down," Ransom answered, slowly turning his head and glaring at Rycroft. "You know what else I think? – I think you're a rabid dog, totally void of humanity."

"What would a bohkor know about humanity?"

"I don't have to understand humans to know right from wrong any more than I have to break my arm to know it will hurt."

"I don't have to understand humans to know right from wrong," mocked Rycroft. "Do you hear this piece of shit, men? I'm getting lectured on the virtues of humanity from a child-raping, murderous, kory traitor." Once again, tension permeated the air.

"I suggest you shut the fuck up, kory, before I make you eat your teeth."

Master Sergeant Ramson was seething as he silently led the others on for several hours until it was too dark to see. Ransom reined in his horse and said, "We'll make camp here for the night."

"We'll stop when **I SAY WE STOP**," Rycroft countered. "Can't be much further out of these woods."

"Perhaps another few hours, but I can't see in the dark, and without sunlight to navigate, we could end up circling back the way we came. I told you earlier that there was no time to waste. I hope that message you had to leave behind won't end up being the death of us all."

Rycroft relented and gave orders to make camp. When the horses were hobbled, the men grabbed a quick bite before bedding down next to the warm fire, except Master Sergeant Ramson, who kept to himself.

As the last of the embers cooled down, young Jason approached. "Are you asleep, mister?"

"That's close enough, boy. What do you want?"

"Just thought I would give you some friendly advice — you're messing with the wrong man. Tobias is dangerous, and if you keep getting under his skin, he's liable to scratch if you get my meaning."

"Am I supposed to be scared, boy? That piss-ant couldn't take me down with all of you as backup."

"I'm just saying that you underestimate him at your peril. He hasn't lasted this long by fighting fair. Besides, he has more men at his disposal than the four of us."

Ransom looked at the boy to take his measure. "I'm puzzled, boy. Why would you waste your life following the likes of that scum?"

"I wouldn't have a life if not for Tobias. He found me cold and hungry on the streets of Thammarat. He gave me shelter, food, and protection. I owe him."

"We all owe him, yet I've realized far too late that my payment outweighs any benefit of the bargain."

From a short distance away, a voice called out. "Jason! Better move back from that, kory. He likes young boys," Rycroft snickered in the darkness.

CHAPTER 3

OVERRIDING CONSIDERATIONS

A remarkable community leader and formerly a decorated officer in Lord Bembridge's Ranger Regiment, the need to serve others with humility and honor runs deep within Commandant Bozwell Knoggs. This loving husband and father to five has a genuine zest for life. Notwithstanding, his ordinarily exuberant mood can instantly change to that of a stalwart officer and woe be to anyone who fails to follow his orders...

(So writes Conrad Nightingale)

The prison transport wagon was due before high noon today, and it was nearing the dinner hour. Knoggs sat behind his desk, unconsciously drumming his fingers, trying to occupy himself with tedious paperwork. Abruptly, he slammed his hand down. "Ogden, get in here!" Captain Cil Ogden, second in command at Blackpool Penitentiary, rushed in from the adjacent office. "Get my horse ready. I'll need enough provisions for a three-day journey and let my wife know I'm leaving. Also, get me five men, and be sure my son is one of them. It's time he is given an assignment outside the walls of the prison. I want to be riding within the hour."

"Sir, with all due respect, it isn't necessary for you, the Commandant, to lead a search party. I can assign it to someone else."

Knoggs rose slowly from his chair, pressing his knuckles into the desktop as his jaw tightened. He didn't have to say anything – the glare said it all.

"Sir, the men will be ready in half an hour, and I'll see that Mrs. Knoggs is notified immediately." Captain Ogden wheeled on his heel and dashed out of the office.

***

Just before dusk, the search party of six rode through the gates of Blackpool Penitentiary, a maximum-security prison surrounded by massive granite walls, three feet thick and thirty feet high. Built like a fortress, the prison is a bastion for housing Calvendar's worst criminals with only one objective

– to punish the guilty. There is no place behind these walls for hope or rehabilitation.

Commandant Knoggs' plan was simple: retrace the route the prison transportation wagon should have taken and look for anything unusual. The sun was waning when the search party approached the edge of Elsdon Forest. Although every moment was critical, Knoggs knew that it would be too difficult to track anyone through the murky woodland without sufficient sunlight. He couldn't afford to miss a single sign.

"We'll set up camp here. Privates Arn, Shriv, and Knoggs check everything within a two-hundred-yard perimeter and gather enough firewood for the night while you're out. Corporal Hirth, locate a vantage point. You will take the first watch. Sergeant Rivka, I want the watch rotated every three hours. Nothing gets into or out of the forest via this road without my authorization. Is that understood?

"I suggest everyone rest when they can, for tomorrow will be a full day."

STANDOFF

Rycroft's small band of degenerates were up at dawn but they couldn't move out until sunlight pierced the canopy. Once on their way, as Master Sergeant Ramson had predicted, it took about three hours before they broke free of Elsdon Forest at one of the only spots safe enough to cross the rushing Tyvola River. Now, the only thing between them and a successful getaway was a small farmstead... (So writes Conrad Nightingale)

"There's another place to cross about three miles downriver," informed Ramson. "By deviating slightly from our course, these settlers won't even know we were here, so they will have nothing to say when they undoubtedly get questioned by the BPS."

"What's the fun in that?" replied Rycroft.

"If that means what I think, I'll have no part of it," Ramson said. He'd had enough of needless butchery.

"On the contrary, you're already a part of it." Rycroft had anticipated this moment. He quickly yanked a crossbow from one of his men, aiming it at Ramson. "In case you haven't already guessed, I **HATE** kories. They're untrustworthy by nature." The bowstring hummed as the bolt was released, finding purchase in Ramson's good knee. The once highly decorated Master Sergeant of the BPS clutched his leg and screamed in pain. "Looks like your days of walking are over," laughed Rycroft.

"Now, no more delays! We've got a farm to visit."

FOLLOW THE EVIDENCE

As soon as the first sunbeams streaked through the trees, the BPS were ready to enter Elsdon Forest, anxious to get on with the search. For the first hour, the troop rode quietly, led by Commandant Knoggs . . .

(So writes Conrad Nightingale)

There was no sign of life when the Commandant spotted the horseless prison transport wagon. However, Knoggs wasn't taking any chances. Signaling his men to dismount, he ordered them to flank the wagon, keeping low in the thick undergrowth. When he saw the men freeze in their tracks, Knoggs drew his battle-axe and cautiously entered the ambush site, ready for whatever waited. There, his worst fears materialized right before his eyes. Displayed in a line lay the bodies of the prison escort detail. Their feet had been hacked off and placed alongside the heads of each respective corpse, a crude Xagada warning not to follow.

All but one sentry approached closer to the scene and gathered around the bodies of their fallen comrades. Rawl Knoggs stood off to one side, wanting to keep his distance from the carnage. The inexperienced private had never seen the aftermath of such heartless savagery and couldn't help but retch. Commandant Knoggs understood what Rawl felt and walked over to comfort his son.

"I'm sorry, Father," Rawl said, hanging his head like a shamed puppy.

"Nonsense. No apology is necessary."

"What type of person desecrates the dead in such a manner?"

"Some people are born without a moral code of conduct, while others are driven insane for reasons known only to the deities. This is why Blackpool Penitentiary exists, to imprison and punish those who take their madness out on the innocent."

"I truly want to follow in your footsteps, Father, and serve the BPS with honor, but I don't think I can ever get used to such violence."

"Nor should you, Rawl, for your virtue is what separates you from the criminals and psychopaths we incarcerate."

Commandant Knoggs bent closer, looking Private Knoggs straight in the eyes. "Listen, son, a life serving in the BPS isn't for everyone, but know this: you are a better man than me. No father can be prouder, regardless of your chosen occupation."

Rawl looked up at his father and managed a slight smile.

"Now gather yourself," Knoggs said, placing a compassionate hand on his son's shoulder. The two returned to the other sentries, which had moved over to the undisturbed body of Corporal Vox.

As Commandant Knoggs began to speak to his men, he pointed out pertinent parts of the terrain.

"Look closely at the ground. The ambush site reads like an open book. As we rode in, the first set of tracks we encountered was that of Master Sergeant Ramson's huge stallion. Ramson was riding point. Corporal Vox rode behind the patrol as sweeper. Ramson must have ordered the prison transport wagon to stop and hold its position, as evidenced by the fact that the wagon's brake is engaged. None of the sentries' weapons were drawn. That indicates they did not realize an attack was imminent until too late. Most likely, concealed assassins on both sides of the path caught the sentries in a deadly crossfire.

"Observing the onslaught from a distance, Vox drew his sword and rode to the rescue of his brothers; however, he and his horse were both knocked to the ground right where we stand. His horse scrambled and regained footing, but Vox met a swift end."

"What force could have taken down both horse and rider?" asked Private Arn.

"Getting broad-sided by another horse at full gallop. It's a cavalry battlefield tactic that would be known to a veteran like the Master Sergeant," Commandant Knogg's answered.

"It's a battlefield tactic known to many veterans whether they have served in the cavalry or not. Are you suggesting Ram killed Vox?" challenged Sergeant Rivka.

"I'm not SUGGESTING anything, Sergeant. I follow the evidence, even if it takes me somewhere I'd rather not go. Look closer around Corporal Vox's body. Do you see the marks left on the ground?" Commandant Knoggs pointed out several spots in the dirt. "You're all familiar with Ramson's dragging boot mark. However, you don't see any other footprints around the body.

Not to mention the condition of Vox's smashed skull. The mace is Master Sergeant Ramson's weapon of choice. In my opinion, Ramson signed his part in the ambush with Vox's blood."

"If your assessment is accurate, that would mean that Master Sergeant Ramson is a ..."

". . . TRAITOR." Knoggs finished Rivka's sentence. "With the help of our traitorous brother and Rycroft's henchmen, the most wanted outlaw in Calvendar made good his escape."

"But escaped where?" Corporal Hirth inquired. "We met nobody on the ride in, and returning to the city of Roderick would be suicide for Rycroft."

"Look over there at the trampled underbrush. There's no attempt to hide their tracks. They turned straight north through the woods. I suspect they are heading for Jadhar, and if they make it to the high desert, they could easily disappear into that unforgiving landscape."

"What are your orders, Commandant?" inquired Sergeant Rivka.

"We load our brethren into the transport wagon. Rawl, you'll hitch your horse to the wagon and take our brothers back to Blackpool Penitentiary for a proper burial. Private Arn will accompany you. The rest of us will track these sons-of- bitches to the underworld, if necessary."

"Send someone else back to Blackpool," Rawl pleaded. "I want to come with you. I'll be all right. I promise."

"Private Knoggs, I wasn't inviting a debate. You will do as I order as long as you wear that uniform and are under my command. If you can't tell an order from a request, I'm sure I can find a jail cell where you can contemplate the matter. Will that be necessary?"

"No, Sir!" came Rawl's immediate response.

"Tell Captain Ogden that I want the fallen buried with honors. Also, tell him to prepare several cells in solitary confinement for Tobias Rycroft and his thugs, who shall be captured and brought to Blackpool Penitentiary."

That afternoon, while there were still several hours of light, Commander Knoggs, Sergeant Rivka, Corporal Hirth, and Private Shriv began tracking the criminals.

CHAPTER 4

BITING THE HAND THAT FEEDS

At the northern border of Bembridge Province, across the mighty Tyvola River that carves a deep gorge from the snowcapped Sawtooth Mountains to the Baracosa Sea lies the end of civilization. The high desert of Jadhar is a land of sharp contrast, where sweltering days give way to frigid nights. Suitable for little more than tumbleweeds, here only the most destitute attempt to scratch out a life from the parched earth. They survive their meager existence, wanting little more than what their labors may produce and being left alone. Yet, even in this desolate land, peace is a tenuous commodity that comes at a high price…

(So writes Conrad Nightingale)

There are very few areas along the Tyvola River where the water runs both slow and shallow enough to cross safely. Stinson's farm is located near one of those spots. Rycroft and his men rode directly toward the farm with the wounded Ramson in tow. Strangers in these parts are rare but are generally not cause for concern. Usually, they would stop just long enough to trade or share a meal, then be on their way.

Upon seeing the riders' approach, Farmer Stinson and his twin boys walked forward to extend a greeting. "Well met, friends. You look in need of rest and perhaps a meal?" Rycroft's men slowly surrounded Stinson and the boys.

" A hot meal and some fresh ale would be most welcome indeed," replied Rycroft. "Unfortunately, we have no money to pay. How about a trade?" Rycroft dismounted his horse and approached Stinson. Then, Stinson noticed the brawny bohkor hunched over on his horse with an arrow protruding from his knee.

"No offense, but you don't appear to be traders."

"No offense taken." Rycroft's voice was calm and condescending. "Let me save some time by being candid. We are outlaws on our way to our hideout in the desert and require supplies. **YOUR** supplies, to be exact. But before we get to business, how about that hot meal?" Rycroft gestured toward the house, and Stinson and his boys timidly led the way. Looking over his shoulder, Rycroft ordered some men to tie Ramson to the porch post. "Use that string of barbed wire lying against the fence. Tie him good and tight. I don't want him crawling off."

Joined inside the house by his wife, Stinson and his family watched as Rycroft and his men had their fill of mutton stew and ale. After letting loose a crude burp, Rycroft wiped his mouth on his sleeve and leaned back in the chair. "Where are my manners? We've taken advantage of your hospitality and never properly introduced ourselves. I am Tobias Rycroft, and my companions are Brice Bowmont, Tucker Kinsley, Riley Albertson, and, finally, young Jason Sinclair. As for that disgusting kory tied up on your front porch, he is Master Sergeant Ramson of the Blackpool Penitentiary Sentries; however, he prefers to be addressed as 'Sir.'" Rycroft let out a belly laugh. "Sorry, it's an inside joke. And you are?"

Having become aware of the kind of men before them, the Stinson family was scared for their lives. Nobody responded, instead, they huddled in fear.

"No answer?" Rycroft smiled. He looked around at his men. "Well, no matter; I simply thought you would like to be introduced to your executioners." Rycroft jumped to his feet, flipping over the table. "Time for some fun, boys!"

In their state of merciless rage, nobody noticed the little girl with straight raven black hair and icy blue eyes peering through the window.

She stood still as a statue, watching through the windowpane, never diverting her sight from the carnage.

COME OUT – COME OUT

A murder of crows darted over the tiny farmstead, beckoning the riders. Conducting themselves with military precision, riding in single file, they traversed the rocky hillside with purpose, each vigilantly scanning the terrain for anything unusual. As they drew closer, you could see the red sashes bearing black scorpions across their leather breastplates — the insignia of the Blackpool Penitentiary Sentries. Stopping just outside of bow range, the leader, whose sash and rank were trimmed in gold braid, signaled the others to gather around him...

(So writes Conrad Nightingale)

Corporal Hirth was the first to state the obvious. "There's something amiss here, Commandant. We've made no attempt to hide our presence, yet nobody from the house has come out to greet us, just the damn crows screeching overhead."

"Agreed," replied the Commandant. "The question is, who awaits us inside?" Knoggs took another quick scan at the scene before continuing. "Only one way to find out for sure – weapons at the ready." The sentries immediately drew their swords. "Lord Bembridge wants the fugitive delivered to Blackpool, and frankly, so do I." Knoggs gave the others a sly smile. There was no mistaking his intent. "Go check the surroundings. Keep your wits about you and your eyes wide open. Remember your fallen brothers and stay cautious, for we hunt scum that would rather ambush us from the safety of blinds than confront us directly in hand-to-hand combat. Under no circumstances shall anyone enter the house without my expressed command."

"You heard your orders!" barked Sergeant Rivka, and off they rode.

The troops darted about looking for hiding places while never taking their eyes entirely away from the tiny house of stone and thatch. Then Knoggs noticed his men pull someone out of hiding. He spurred his horse into a gallop to quickly join them. As he drew closer, he saw a little girl biting, scratching, and kicking to be free; she fought like a rabid animal. Knoggs dismounted while gesturing to the sentry to release her. Once loose, she settled down immediately and stared in defiance as the commanding officer approached. Knoggs lowered himself to one knee as if speaking to one of his children. They looked at each other silently until Knoggs broke the silence.

"Am I the first bohkor that you have seen?" The child nodded her head in the affirmative. "I guess I must look scary. My wife says I'm ugly even by bohkor standards." One of the sentries started to laugh, and Knoggs shot him a glance that made him swallow his laughter. The girl giggled, having found the whole exchange amusing. Knoggs countered her giggle with a wide grin.

"My name is Boz; what's yours?"

"Eleanor."

"Is that what your friends call you?"

"No, just Ellie."

"I would like to be your friend. May I call you Ellie?" The girl shook her head yes. "Ellie, have any strangers visited you in the past day?" The girl hesitated then shook her head yes, again. "Are they still here?" This time, the girl shook her head no. "Is your family inside the house?" Ellie leaped into Boz's muscular arms. Hugging his neck tightly, she began to cry. "It will be okay, Ellie, but I need to go inside and see for myself. You stay here with Corporal Hirth." Eleanor didn't want to let go, but Boz gave her that reassuring grin and a pat on her shoulder.

The corpse of Master Sergeant Ramson, still tied to the porch post, greeted him as he approached the house. Ramson's pants had been lowered, his testicles removed and stuffed inside his mouth. Whether death came from suffocation or bleeding out was irrelevant: both methods were painfully slow and psychologically agonizing. It was a very deliberate killing usually reserved for rapists. Knoggs barely acknowledged the heinous act, for in his mind, Ramson had received the fruits of his betrayal. The young girl's family and why they had not come forward was of far more importance. As Knoggs stepped into the house, he stopped in his tracks. It was mayhem, sheer brutality for the sake of cruelty itself. Eleanor's family lay about the place, each tortured before dying a senseless death. On the far wall, smeared in the blood of one of the victims, the words **DON'T FOLLOW!** Knoggs looked over to Sergeant Rivka, who also stood transfixed.

"Sergeant Rivka . . . **RIVKA**!"

Sergeant Rivka snapped out of his trance. "Sir?"

"See that the family receives a proper burial before returning to Blackpool. Debrief Captain Ogden. I'll report the matter directly to Lord Bembridge. I'll also be taking the child with me. Advise Captain Ogden to notify Lord Bembridge by carrier pigeon that I am on my way."

"We're within a day's ride of hunting down the sons-of-bitches that slaughtered our men and this poor family, and you want to call off the search?" Rivka questioned.

As the ranking officer, Knoggs owed it to his men not to let emotions get the best of him. He also owed it to the child to see that she gets the help she badly needs. "Rest assured, Sergeant, Rycroft won't escape justice, nor will he evade the BPS's wrath. But for now, I'm confronted by moral imperatives that cannot be ignored. The men need to mourn their brothers, and this child needs the type of help bohkors can't render.

"What about Master Sergeant Ramson?" asked Rivka.

"Leave him for the crows."

DISTURBING NEWS

Once at Bembridge Castle, Commandant Knoggs and the child were taken directly to Lord Bembridge, joined by Chancellor Oswalt. Lord Bembridge asked his wife to care for the girl while he was debriefed...

(*So writes Conrad Nightingale*)

"Firstly, I wish to extend my condolences for the loss of your men, Commandant Knoggs. Their families shall want for nothing. My treasury is there for support. See to that personally, Chancellor Oswalt. Secondly, thank you for bringing the child here. Rest assured; she will be given the proper care."

"Thank you, Lord Bembridge."

"It's the least I can do."

"Is there any chance Rycroft will try to get back to Roderick? Do you think Lord or Lady Bembridge could be in danger?" asked Chancellor Oswalt.

"It's hard to say with a bastard like Rycroft, but you might want to post additional guards for the next few days."

"A proper precaution. Thank you again, Boz. I know you have pressing matters back at Blackpool. Get some food and rest, and please be safe on your return journey," Lord Bembridge said. Commandant Knoggs was being graciously dismissed.

Knoggs hesitated, "Forgive me, my Lord, but what about Rycroft?"

"I have underestimated Rycroft, but nothing has changed. I want him to serve his remaining days within the confines of Blackpool Penitentiary under your watchful eye. We will resume the search at the proper time." Commandant Knoggs bowed and left the room.

Lord Bembridge also dismissed the Chancellor and went to share the news with his wife. The child finally fell asleep in Amanda's lap as she gently stroked her hair. The two spoke in whispers so as not to disturb her. "I feel somewhat at fault. I should have had the Rangers escort the BPS all the way to Blackpool Penitentiary."

"That may have appeared demeaning to the citizens of Blackpool," suggested Lady Bembridge.

"Perhaps, but the sentries and the girl's family would still be alive."

"You can't know that for sure. So please don't add this to your list of burdens."

"Well, we need to do something other than wait. Any suggestions?"

"I think it's time to reach out to Johnathan."

CHAPTER 5

SUMMONING HELP

The sign hanging over the gate to a hundred prime hectares of woodlands and pastures read 'Albem Farm', a retirement gift from Lord and Lady Bembridge for Johnathan Alcott's years of faithful service. The past couple of years were challenging but ultimately rewarding, and with the help of their new friends, the Kershaws, the farm was already making a profit. Life was good for Ingrid and Johnathan, but little did they know how quickly that would change compliments of one notorious reprobate, Tobias Rycroft…

(So writes Conrad Nightingale)

Although it was mid-summer, Johnathan wasn't going to put off stockpiling firewood while waiting for cooler weather. He had been splitting logs for several hours under the blazing sun when Ingrid stepped out of the house onto the front porch.

"You need to stop, John. We've got enough firewood for the next six months. Besides, it's time to get cleaned up; dinner is almost ready." It wasn't a request. Johnathan glanced in her direction, and his heart skipped just as it had when he first laid eyes on her many years ago. Diminutive but forceful, she stood her ground, her head held high, her arms akimbo, as if daring him to challenge her. She was a handsome woman with imposing features. Sun-streaked auburn hair framed the angular shape of her face, with bright green eyes that made it nearly impossible for Johnathan to turn away once she caught him in her gaze. Without further words, she whirled around and walked back into the house. Johnathan mumbled a response, sauntered over to the creek, and submerged a bucket. He poured the cool, refreshing water over his head, rinsing the grime away from his tall, lean, muscular body. Stoic by nature and physically powerful, it's best to give this former commando plenty of leeway, for he can be dangerous if provoked, and from the look on his face, something was about to happen. Moving toward the house with determined strides, he entered, grabbed Ingrid from behind, and spun her around until they were face-to-face. He gripped her arms firmly so she couldn't wriggle away. Bending down close, she could feel his warm breath on her neck as he whispered.

"Will today be the day that you make me an honest man? **Marry me!**", he demanded. "Think carefully before you answer. I'm tired of the waiting game, so choose your words wisely; they could be your last."

There was no hesitation; Ingrid looked her aggressor straight in the eyes and answered resolutely.

"I don't think today will work for me. Try asking me again tomorrow." She giggled as Johnathan swept her up off her feet; their lips met in a long, passionate kiss. Though no formal ceremony ever memorialized this blessed union, never has there been a more perfectly matched couple.

The two finished their evening meal and were snuggling up before the fireplace when Johnathan put a finger to his lips. Men were approaching the house. He leaped to his feet and, moving swiftly, unsheathed his long knife. Flinging open the door, the intruders found themselves looking directly at Alcott's blade, and just as suddenly, behind them, came the menacing growl of Alcott's constant companion – a nearly extinct and extraordinarily large kolgarr.

"It seems you men have a choice; either I cut your throats, or Adak tears them out." To emphasize his point, Alcott stroked the razor-sharp blade down his forearm, shaving away the hairs with no effort.

"What shall it be?"

"Commander Alcott, pray you and your animal hold fast! We mean no harm. We are here by order of Lord Bembridge. He requires an immediate audience."

"No need to address me by rank, Sergeant. I've retired my commission and no longer jump simply because Lord Bembridge requests it. So, we're back to our standoff; try to take me if you dare.", he challenged. Adak moved extremely close to the soldiers, sniffing up and down their backsides. The kolgarr's neck hairs rose in response to their fear.

Alcott's response was highly unexpected, so other than exchanging dumbfounded glances, the soldiers stood frozen in place, unsure what to do next. Even together, they were no match for Alcott, let alone his kolgarr, and they knew it; that's when Ingrid intervened.

"John, stop frightening those boys. If Lord Bembridge sent for you, you must go, and that's all there is to it."

"Of course, I'm going. Adak and I were having a little fun."

Ingrid noticed a wet pant leg on one of the younger soldiers. "It seems not everybody appreciates your sense of humor. Now you and Adak stop playing and make haste."

***

Soon after the ill-timed interruption, Alcott found himself inside Bembridge Castle, escorted down a long hallway by two officers of Lord Bembridge's highly respected Impregnable Guards. The dimly lit hall was bracketed every five feet by two bodyguards, twenty in all, who in turn came to attention, allowing the three to pass unchallenged. Alcott had been summoned before Lord Bembridge on many occasions, but never this late in the evening and never to the Lord's personal chamber; obviously, this meeting was of great importance.

Chancellor Nigel Oswalt stood in front of the chamber door, holding up his right hand and effectively blocking further passage.

"Wait here while I announce you." His harsh tone and mannerisms made it clear that he would be obeyed. He quietly disappeared inside. A moment later, the door opened.

"You may enter now." As Alcott entered and Oswalt departed, the two bumped against each other as they passed. It was a childish gesture but one that spoke volumes; these two men were not fond of one another.

Lord and Lady Bembridge's private chambers are, in essence, a sanctuary within the castle's northeast tower consisting of a central gathering room, Lord Bembridge's study, and their bedchamber. The gathering room is large enough to accommodate dining and living areas; along its eastern wall, a bank of windows offers a commanding view over the rugged cliffs down to the harbor below. Alcott surmised that Lord Bembridge's private study was to his immediate left.

"Please come in." Lady Bembridge beckoned Alcott, and he took a few steps into the gathering room. Lady Bembridge stood before the windows, etched in the moonlight, dignified and elegant as always; at her side clung a disheveled young girl whom Alcott did not recognize.

He acknowledged them both, bowing slightly, "Good evening, my Lady, and to you as well, Miss." The girl didn't reply, burying her face into the folds of the Lady's night dress.

"It's all right, Ellie. This man is a trusted friend here to help us. Thank you for coming, John." The frightened girl exposed one icy blue eye, still unsure what to make of this towering man.

"Jonathan, so good of you to visit me at this hour." Lord Bembridge stepped forth from the adjacent study. Ever the diplomat, Lord Bembridge made it sound like he had extended an invitation to Alcott rather than a command to appear. "Come in. I have something of grave importance to share."

Then, turning to Lady Bembridge, he said in a comforting voice, "Please excuse me, my dear, John, and I must speak in private." Lord Bembridge motioned Alcott into the study and quietly closed the door behind them. Whatever he had to say, he did not want to be overheard.

"Can I interest you in a glass of wine?" The question was merely a courtesy, and Alcott respectfully declined. "Then we shall get right down to the matter for which I called you." Lord Bembridge took a seat and motioned for Alcott to do the same.

"Last month, a most despicable transgressor named Tobias Rycroft was brought before me to answer for numerous crimes against the good citizens of Bembridge Province. Murder, rape, arson, robbery… the list of charges read on and on, almost appearing to have no end. Nevertheless, despite these numerous atrocities, the trial was over quickly, for the evidence of Rycroft's crimes was overwhelming, and he offered no defense on his behalf. Standing on their merit, many of these heinous acts would warrant a swift execution; however, before I could pronounce the sentence, Chancellor Oswalt asked me for a brief recess.

"While behind closed doors, Nigel made a case that it would be too merciful to end Rycroft's life quickly under the executioner's axe. Alternatively, he proposed that Rycroft spend his remaining days in Blackpool Penitentiary, wherein he would have ample time to reflect upon the misery he had caused so many innocent people. I must confess I was intrigued by the idea of this degenerate living a very long life with no chance of parole, and where better to serve out his sentence than at a prison run by intransigent bohkors.

"Accordingly, I rendered my verdict without further delay. Tobias Rycroft was sentenced to a life of solitary confinement at Blackpool Penitentiary."

"It sounds to be a just sentence," Johnathan said. "Although I have never crossed paths with Rycroft, I know of his notorious reputation. He is ruthless even by Xagada standards."

Lord Bembridge nodded in agreement and continued, "Indeed, the Xagada lack any moral compass, and their abhorrent behavior grows more loathsome with each passing day; however, that is a matter for another discussion. My immediate concern remains with Rycroft – you see, he has escaped."

A moment of silence ensued as Johnathan took in the whole meaning of Lord Bembridge's statement.

"Escaped? Do you know how?"

"When the prison transport wagon failed to arrive at Blackpool Penitentiary as scheduled, Commandant Knoggs took a small detachment of sentries to investigate. According to the Commandant's accounting, the prison wagon had been ambushed in Elsdon Forrest, less than a half day's ride from the prison. His investigation concluded that the patrol was led into the ambush by one of his own, Master Sergeant Ramson," Lord Bembride explained.

"However, the carnage didn't end at the ambush site. Rycroft and his gang bypassed Blackpool, heading directly north toward the high desert of Jadhar. Commandant Knoggs and his men pursued the fugitive for better than a day when the troops came upon a small farm along the Tyvola River. The Commandant sensed something was seriously wrong when he saw crows circling in tight formation over the farmhouse.

"When Knoggs entered the house, he beheld a gruesome sight that nearly made him vomit. The farmer was tied to a chair with barbed wire; his eyelids had been removed so he couldn't look away as his family was tortured and slaughtered in front of him. The farmer's wife had been nailed through her hands face down on the kitchen table, where she endured repeated rapes before having her throat slit. Twin teenage boys had nooses tightly placed around their necks and were forced to watch while balancing precariously on a single stool. They slowly strangled to death when they finally slipped from their shared perch. Eventually, the farmer was released from this living hell when Rycroft eviscerated and strangled him with his entrails.

"Perhaps the worst thing about this atrocity was that it was witnessed by the small child you saw with Amanda, a young girl left alone in shock to fend for herself. John, this was an act of mayhem for no purpose but to terrorize anyone who dares to pursue Rycroft," Lord Bembridge said. He looked straight into Alcott's eyes, lowering his voice as if to emphasize the following words.

"I'm sorry to call you back from retirement, old friend, but you're the only one I can trust to complete this mission. John, I appoint you High Marshal and charge you to capture and deliver Rycroft to Blackpool Penitentiary, where he shall serve his sentence. Here is your warrant."

Alcott opened the parchment that announced his appointment and described his immediate responsibility:

Arrest Warrant

Let all know that having been tried for capital crimes against the good people of Bembridge Province and subsequently sentenced, Tobias Rycroft is a fugitive from justice. Accordingly, High Marshal Johnathan Alcott has been assigned to bring said fugitive to Blackpool Penitentiary, wherein he shall serve a life sentence in solitary confinement. Anyone aiding or abetting Tobias Rycroft shall be summarily found guilty at their peril.

Let it also be known that High Marshal Alcott acts on behalf of the undersigned and is authorized to use his sole discretion when executing all matters relating to this Warrant.

Signed and Sealed,

Lord Walter Bembridge

"Take as many men as you need to accomplish the task and use whatever means necessary, but it is imperative that Rycroft be brought back alive and serve his sentence as an example to those that pursue evil. Regarding any of Rycroft's accomplices, whether they remain alive or not is up to your discretion."

"There is no need for extra men; they'll only slow me down. I'll travel alone and leave tomorrow as soon as I gather the necessary provisions. Please send word and let Commandant Knoggs know I'm on the hunt; he'll know what to do at his end. I won't fail you or the girl."

As Alcott exited Lord Bembridge's study, he noticed Lady Bembridge cradling the little girl in her arms while humming softly; he caught his breath at the thought of what she had endured.

***

It was late in the evening when Johnathan got back home. He found Ingrid asleep in front of the fireplace; the last of the fire's embers bathed her face with a soft glow. She awoke to find him standing next to her, and as usual, she got right to the point. "I know that look on your face. When do you have to leave?"

"Not for a few more hours; let's go to bed."

"Poor dear. You must be exhausted."

Johnathan smiled, "I didn't say anything about going to sleep." He effortlessly cradled Ingrid, carrying her off to the bedroom. She felt safe in his embrace, wondering how such a powerful person could be so gentle. He pressed his manhood against her passionately, and she responded willingly.

Dropping all pretense, they delved into one another's most intimate regions until the final crescendo rendered them exhausted and unable to continue the dance. Still entwined, they fell into a deep and peaceful sleep.

CHAPTER 6

COMING TO GET YOU

The morning light found Johnathan already outside preparing for his journey. After listening to Lord Bembridge's explicit debriefing of Tobias Rycoft's escape and the effect it was no doubt having on the little girl, Eleanor, he was now very anxious to start the manhunt. *(So writes Conrad Nightingale)*

Ingrid strolled up, kissing his cheek. "Did you manage to get any sleep last night?"

"Not much, and yet somehow, I feel rejuvenated."

Ingrid began to rub against him. "Well, can I get you some breakfast or . . . anything else . . . before you leave?"

"You're not playing fair." Johnathan gave her bottom a friendly slap.

"I just wanted to remind you what's waiting for you when you return home."

INHOSPITABLE

Johnathan Alcott had never seen Tobias Rycroft, so with only his name and a description, he set out to investigate the ambush site before following the trampled brush north toward the high desert of Jadhar, Rycroft's last known destination... (So writes Conrad Nightingale)

Most people would avoid the inhospitable wilderness of Jadhar at any cost, but not society's miscreants who seek refuge in this desolate wasteland. Occasionally, these cockroaches scurry out from hiding just long enough to wreak havoc before retreating into the shadows of the rugged terrain.

Unfortunately for Rycroft, there wasn't anywhere in Calvendar that Alcott wasn't prepared to go. Alcott had been trained to track since childhood, and he possessed a unique set of skills for an assignment like this, and without a doubt, Rycroft would be captured. Even so, Alcott couldn't shake the feeling that finding Rycroft would be easy; bringing him back alive may prove more difficult.

Several days into the search, the sky was a vivid robin egg blue, void of clouds. It would be a brutally hot day, especially in the high desert. Attempting to conserve energy, Alcott kept his palomino at a slow but steady pace. He had trained Tess since she was a foal; she was not easily startled, was sure-footed, and as fast as lightning when given the rein.

Tethered behind Tess was a pack mule carrying an assortment of supplies, including iron shackles and weapons that may be needed in a serious encounter. By noon, the desert air shimmered, hovering above the cracked, baked earth, distorting the horizon. Through the haze, Alcott thought he could make out a single structure in the distance. He dismounted and knelt in the shade of an outcropping of boulders, concentrating and squinting to bring his vision into focus. A moment later, he felt the hard steel against his back.

"Don't move, not so much as a twitch if you know what's good for you." Alcott didn't appear startled for a man caught off-guard; his breathing remained steady, and he held the distant horizon in his gaze as if utterly unconcerned with the assailant. "Only two kinds of people come this far into Jadhar – those running and those chasing. Which might you be?"

Alcott responded in a quiet, steady voice, "I advise you to drop that knife while you still can."

"Bold words," he spat. "Are all humans so arrogant, or are you unique?"

As if on cue, a threatening snarl came from above. Adak stood atop a large boulder, hackles up, ears lowered, and lips curled back, bearing its massive incisors.

Immediately, the dagger dropped to the ground. "**CRUX**! Where did that bloody hellhound come from?" Adak jumped off the boulder, knocking the intruder onto the ground with a glancing blow. Before he could regain his footing, the kolgarr was upon him, licking his face like a sugar block. "Okay, all right, let me up! Good dog… get back now."

Alcott reached down, grabbing the bohkor's hand and helping him to his feet. "I keep telling you, Boz, Adak is not a dog; he's a kolgarr, and you should know by now he is never far from my side."

"Dog? Kolgarr? All I know is they both have four legs and a tail."

"That's like saying bohkors and humans look alike because they both walk upright, albeit some bohkors drag their knuckles when walking." Alcott chuckled.

"I know you think you're being funny, John, but sometimes your sense of humor goes too far."

"That's what Ingrid tells me."

"She's a smart woman, other than her momentary lapse of judgment when she settled down with the likes of you."

"Ouch, now that's just cruel, Boz." They had a good laugh and exchanged hugs. "I was wondering when you would come out of hiding, old friend?"

"That's just a bunch of shit! You expect me to believe that you knew I was tracking you?"

"Of course, I knew; bohkors aren't exactly known for their stealth."

"Now, who's being cruel?" Commandant Knoggs held up both hands, "Don't bother answering, or we'll never get done exchanging insults. Fill me in; I hope I've arrived in time to lend a hand?"

"As always, Boz, your timing is impeccable. I believe that Rycroft and the men who freed him are holed up in that hovel." Johnathan pointed off into the distant horizon.

"I don't see anything. Are you sure it's not a mirage?"

"Well, my eyes aren't what they used to be when I was younger, but I'm pretty sure it's real."

Boz smirked, "Okay then, old man, what's your plan?"

***

After a short discussion, Commandant Knoggs started first since he would take a more hidden circuitous route over rougher terrain. Believing sufficient time had passed, Alcott rode Tess directly toward the faraway structure. In due course, the small building came clearly into view, the only building around for many miles. A sign above the front entrance read "Last Chance."

Prophetic, Alcott thought to himself as he tied Tess and the mule to the broken fence post and entered the tavern made of straw and hardened mud.

There were no structured doors or windows, just holes cut into the mud walls to allow one access and some light and air to enter. He stood silhouetted in the threshold long enough for his eyes to adjust to the diminished light and scanned the room. As Alcott had surmised from a distance, the tavern was no more than a hovel, but it did provide some refuge from the outside elements. Rats darted about, grabbing scraps of food that fell to the dirt floor, while birds hid amongst the rafters, waiting their turn to pounce upon the unexpecting rodents. Alcott counted five people in all:

four patrons and the bartender. No one spoke, but all eyes were upon him as he meandered over to the bar.

"What can I get you?" mumbled the bartender.

"A cup of cool water would be greatly appreciated."

"Mister, you're in a bar; we serve warm ale. If you want water, there's a trough just outside the door. I'm sure the other animals won't object." The room burst into laughter.

Alcott leaned down, placing both elbows on the makeshift bar, several boards nailed across the top of two empty barrels, never looking back over his shoulder. "All right, warm ale it is."

"That will be six sovereigns."

"That's pretty steep; at best, it shouldn't cost more than a sovereign."

"Exactly, but you're also buying me and my buddies a drink." Again, the room burst into laughter.

"You might as well rob me in the open then concoct that sleight of hand. I guess for the time being, I will have to stay thirsty. However, what I can pay fair money for is some information. I'm searching for somebody; perhaps one of you can help. He's an abhorrent man that reeks of mule shit, and believe me, that's an insult to my mule tied out front. However, what makes this coward so easy to recognize is a crooked index finger on his right hand. It must have gotten broken when someone punched him in that bulbous growth he calls a nose." It was Alcott's time to chuckle, but he was the only one in the tavern laughing.

Alcott turned as he heard a chair fall over. A burly man rose from the table, holding a Xagada dagger with a crooked index finger. The man closed the divide on Alcott with remarkable speed.

"So, you must be Tobias Rycroft, killer of defenseless men, women, and children," proclaimed Alcott.

Rycroft waived his blade in front of Alcott's face. "Who are you, some kin seeking revenge? Because if you're looking for trouble, mister, you've come to the right place."

"No, I can't say I know any of the poor people you've tormented. As for who I am, I'm the High Marshal for Lord Bembridge, sent to bring you to Blackpool Penitentiary.

Rycroft's blade never stopped waving back and forth. Instead, he grinned a condescending smile. "Bembridge made a big mistake; he should have sent his army if he wanted to take me."

"Lord Bembridge isn't the one who made a mistake; that was you when you thought you could commit such blatant atrocities without reprisal. As for sending an army, there's no need to send so many men after a worthless tub-of-lard like you."

"Mister, you're getting on my last nerve," warned Rycroft.

"The name's Johnathon Alcott, and are you planning to use that knife or just fan me with it?"

Rycroft could no longer tolerate Alcott's insults; he struck out in fury, the dagger heading directly for Alcott's throat. Alcott easily deflected the thrust, simultaneously kicking Rycroft's groin. Rycroft howled in pain, dropping to his knees, while in one fluid motion, Alcott grabbed a handful of Rycroft's hair and drove his face into the edge of the bar. Everyone could hear Rycroft's face break as he was knocked unconscious. Immediately, the other three men jumped up from the table, drawing their weapons; two held crossbows already loaded, and the other drew his sword, quickly moving to the front entrance to block Alcott's exit.

"You're not taking Tobias nowhere, stranger," his sword pointed at Alcott's chest for emphasis.

"Three against one, that doesn't seem fair," Alcott said.

"Count again," said the bartender from behind the counter, armed with a club. "I guess it's getting less and less fair by the second, mister," he laughed.

"You miss my meaning," Alcott calmly replied. "Whether you're three or four in number, it isn't fair for **YOU**."

"Really? I guess we'll have to take our chances. Kill him!" yelled the bartender, but he had no sooner raised his club when a battle axe sliced off his arm. As the bartender dropped to the ground screaming, Commandant Knoggs came into full view, his jaw clenched, and wide black eyes fixed upon the remaining culprits.

"Did you see that, John? I disarmed the bartender. Disarmed – do you get it? Now that's funny." Boz snickered as he glanced in Johnathan's direction.

Without warning, the miscreant blocking the doorway was suddenly and violently knocked across the room, slamming into the far wall; the onslaught didn't stop there. Adak flashed through the doorway, pinning the man face-first on the ground. The kolgarr's massive jaws clamped around the man's neck and effortlessly lifted him high, shaking him like a rag. Blood splattered against the walls as the head separated from its body. Letting loose of the limp corpse, Adak turned his attention to the remaining two; exposing bloody fangs, his violet eyes held the men in an almost hypnotic state.

The hesitation was all the time needed for Alcott to draw his long knife and throw it into the belly of the nearest attacker; it would take a few painful minutes for this one to pass.

"And then, there was only one," Alcott calmly proclaimed.

The remaining man let go of his crossbow and dropped to his knees. "Have mercy!" he pleaded for his life.

In a rage, Knoggs rushed forth, "Mercy? Did you show the BPS mercy when you ambushed and slaughtered my men without warning? Did the farmer and his family beg for mercy as you tortured them simply for fun? What gives you the right to plead for your life? There is no mercy for scum the likes of you." Knoggs looked to Alcott for confirmation; Alcott nodded slightly before Knoggs' battle-axe came down, splitting the man's head in two.

"You worried me, Boz; I was beginning to think I didn't give you enough time to get here."

"As you said earlier, John, my timing is impeccable, albeit I was momentarily delayed by a stable boy out back. Thought I should take a second to knock him out so he couldn't warn anyone." Just then, they heard hoofbeats riding away from the tavern.

"Well, it sounds like he woke up."

"Want me to go after him?"

Alcott scanned the room, four dead and Rycroft lying unconscious. "No, we got the one we wanted. I have leg irons and wrist cuffs in my saddlebags. Help me strip-search this dumb ass for weapons, and we'll get him in shackles before he wakes. The sun will be going down soon. We might as well rest here for the night; I don't think any of these scoundrels will mind."

The following morning, Rycroft finally woke up, lying cold and naked on the tavern's dirt floor. His ruddy face was swollen, and his eyes were black and blue slits. He barely made out the bodies of his friends lying where they dropped. "You'll pay for this Longshanks if it's the last thing I do!" he growled.

"I've already told you the name is Alcott, but you haven't met my friend yet. Allow me to introduce Commandant Knoggs of the BPS. I'm sure the two of you will become very close over the coming years at Blackpool Penitentiary." Rycroft looked over his shoulder to find Knoggs smiling that sardonic smile; it sent shivers down his spine.

"The boy left the gate open when he fled, but lucky for you, one horse remained behind. Otherwise, you would be walking to Blackpool," Commandant Knoggs informed his prisoner.

Alcott temporarily removed the irons and pointed to the horse outside, "Get dressed and mount up."

"And, if I refuse to cooperate?" Rycroft challenged.

Knoggs stepped in close, "Then I'll drag your naked ass behind my horse all the way to Blackpool Penitentiary. It makes no difference to me. What's your preference?"

Rycroft had to bite back his words as he got dressed, then he was cuffed again and reluctantly climbed aboard the waiting horse. Once mounted, Alcott reattached the leg irons under the horse's belly. "Try not to fall off; being trampled to death is a hard way to die."

Wary of another ambush, Marshal Alcott and Commandant Knoggs, with their prisoner in tow, took an indirect route south, avoiding the open terrain as much as possible.

"You know we were being followed earlier," Knoggs commented casually.

"I do. It was your friend, the stable boy. He broke off when he was sure we were heading for Asquith."

"No doubt he's going for help."

"No doubt."

"How about the other one who picked us up midway? Do you think he's part of Rycroft's gang?"

"I don't have a clue; at least he's keeping a healthy distance."

***

It was late afternoon when they entered the port village of Asquith. People on the street stopped in their tracks when they saw the rangy lawman and the Commandant of the BPS leading Rycroft in shackles. It was a sight to behold. The riders pulled up just in front of the Fighting Cock Public House, and Alcott released Rycroft's leg irons.

"Dismount!" Alcott abruptly pulled Rycroft down from the horse and began pulling him over to a large elm tree. "I'm going to chain you in the shade. Commandant Knoggs and I are going into the Fighting Cock for supper. If you behave, we'll bring you some food and drink."

Then, Alcott raised his voice to address the gathering crowd. "This is our prisoner. Approach him at your peril, for if he doesn't get you, my colleague and I surely will. In other words, stay the hell away from him!" Having given sufficient warning, Alcott and Knoggs disappeared into the tavern as the growing crowd encircled Rycroft but at a safe distance.

Alcott and Knoggs watched Rycroft from a table near the window as the Innkeeper brought meat, bread, and ale. As they finished their meal, Knoggs noticed the stranger they had seen earlier merging into the crowd. "He's here."

Alcott peered out the window, turning his head, he addressed the Innkeeper, "Do you have a backdoor to this place?" The Innkeeper pointed in a general direction.

"Time to check on our prisoner, Boz." As Commandant Knoggs went out the front, Alcott left via the back door.

"All right, get back!" yelled Knoggs. You were warned. Get the hell out of here!" The crowd began to disperse, but the tall lawman impeded the stranger.

"**NOT** you." Alcott grabbed the stranger by the back of his collar and forced him forward. "Are you a friend of this man," Alcott pointed toward the shackled prisoner.

"He has no friends in these parts," responded the stranger.

"Then, what's your business, and why have you been following us?" asked Knoggs.

"For now, I'm just curious."

"Curious about what?"

"I'm curious whether this is the one that killed my family." Alcott and Knoggs were taken aback. "I was returning home from getting provisions when I saw you and your men from a distant hilltop. You were burying my brother, my wife, and my boys. For that kindness, I thank you and will forever be in your debt." My name is Brian Stinson.

"Why didn't you come forward?"

"All I could think of was revenge. I needed someone like the two of you to flush out the culprit. Now, I'm here to settle the score." Stinson pulled out a hidden knife and lunged forward toward the prisoner, but Alcott and Knoggs were too fast and overpowered him. "Please," Stinson wept. "This scum killed my family. I must have revenge."

"A heinous act indeed, but at least your daughter is safe and sound at Bembridge Castle," replied Knoggs.

The man stared from Knoggs to Alcott, "I don't have a daughter; no one in my family is left."

Realizing getting the girl inside Bembridge Castle was a ruse, Alcott exclaimed, "Crux – Boz, Lord and Lady Bembridge are in danger! There's no time to waste. I'll have to travel fast to warn them. Can you manage Rycroft on your own?"

"Don't worry about me, John, I can handle that asshole, but you shouldn't risk a fast ride in the black of night. Too many things to go wrong."

"Adak can see on the darkest of nights. I'll let him lead the way." Without any further words, Alcott untied the mule and mounted Tess; away he rode at full gallop for Bembridge Castle.

Rycroft sat calmly beneath the elm where he had been chained and laughed aloud. "Say hello to MY daughter!" he yelled.

CHAPTER 7

TRUST BETRAYED

Twelve years prior, the union of Lady Amanda Winslow to Lord Walter Bembridge helped secure peace and prosperity through a matrimonial alliance between two of the great houses of Calvendar. Politics aside, Amanda and Walter
couldn't have been happier with the arrangement, for they had loved each other since childhood. The wedding ceremony was ostentatious, full of pomp and circumstance, and the citizens of Bembridge and Winslow Provinces celebrated for days.

(So writes Conrad Nightingale)

Within a few months of exchanging their wedding vows, it was announced that Lady Bembridge was with a child, and once again, the people rejoiced, for this was indeed a blessed year. Regretfully, what began as a blessing soon turned into a curse. The pregnancy did not go without difficulty.

In the first trimester, Lady Bembridge suffered from bouts of morning sickness, which did not subside but grew worse with each day's passing. Two months into the second trimester, weakened and wracked with pain, she was confined to bed rest for the remainder of her pregnancy. Lord Bembridge, ordinarily a decisive man in most situations, felt helpless.

The best doctors in Calvendar were summoned to treat the Lady of Bembridge, but to no avail. The doctors tried to console Lord Bembridge, explaining that matters such as these were entirely up to the mother and unborn child.

"Be patient," they implored. "It will work out for the best." However, it did not work out for the best; it couldn't have been worse. In the seventh month of pregnancy, a daughter was prematurely stillborn; her struggle to enter this world was too much for the tiny one to endure.

Alas, the baby was not the only casualty; Lady Bembridge had also significantly suffered, nearly losing her own life trying to give birth, the resulting miscarriage rendering it impossible for her to bear children in the future. Having lost so much blood during the birthing process, Lady Bembridge fell in and out of consciousness over the next several days. Lord Bembridge never left her side during this ordeal, praying to the deities for her recovery. When Lady

Bembridge finally awoke, she saw her love standing at the window, deep in contemplation.

"Walter," she tried calling out, but it was barely a whisper. "Walter," this time, he heard. Spinning around, he rushed to her bedside.

"My darling, Amanda, I thought you were lost to me. Don't speak now." He poured a cup of water from the bedside table. "Here, try to drink some water."

Lady Bembridge raised her hand in protest. "I will speak first. I must tell you…," her words broke off midsentence.

"Tell me what?"

"How truly sorry I am that our daughter is dead, yet I still live. Please forgive me and know I would gladly have given my life in exchange for her."

Lord Bembridge leaned in close, looking deeply into her eyes, and began to weep. "No, my darling," he said, shaking his head back and forth. "No, Amanda, you must never hold yourself responsible. Only the gods know why such tragedies befall us. When you have fully recovered, and then, only if you should choose, we can try to have another child."

"I know my own body, Walter, and I suspect the doctors have already informed you that I will never bear your children. It's not right; you deserve an heir, and the Bembridge lineage must continue. Please go and find another wife, one more befitting the station. I truly understand, and so will the people."

Lord Bembridge would have been within his legal right to preserve his title and properties by annulling the marriage, but he refused to turn his back on his beloved wife. "Lineage be damn! There is no woman worthier to be Lady Bembridge.

I would be lost without you by my side. Amanda, promise me that we will never speak of this again."

A SECOND CHANCE

Over the following years, Lady Bembridge kept her promise not to speak of the matter, although she never fully recovered from the loss of their daughter. There was an emptiness within her; she was a mother without a child. Perhaps that was why Amanda instinctively took to the young orphan, Eleanor, when brought before her husband late that fateful evening. At just twelve years old, the same age her child would have been, Eleanor's eyes had witnessed more death and destruction than anyone should endure in several lifetimes. Left alone and in shock, Eleanor now needed Lady Bembridge's comfort as much as Lady Bembridge needed to nurture this unfortunate child. The girl would not be subjected to any further trauma; Lady Bembridge would see to it...

(So writes Conrad Nightingale)

Until more suitable quarters could be arranged, Eleanor shared the same bed with Lady Bembridge while Lord Bembridge was relegated to the sofa in his study. It was a fitful first night, as Eleanor awakened in a panic several times, but Lady Bembridge was there to soothe her fears. Unfortunately, the following day wasn't much better. Eleanor hung so tightly to Lady Bembridge that they might as well have been moving in lockstep.

Finally, the third day showed some signs of progress, and by the fourth morning, Eleanor's demeanor had changed for the better. Feeling less vulnerable, she started to acknowledge others rather than fear them. She began to explore the castle, although she never wandered far from Lady Bembridge. Eleanor was astounded by the enormity of the castle.

"I couldn't have imagined such a great house even in my dreams. Why are there so many rooms? Do you ever get lost?"

"When I first came to live in the castle, I too got lost," Lady Bembridge confided. "When that happened, I asked someone for help. As for why there are so many rooms, I can only say that every room has a purpose. For example, take the room at the end of the hallway." The two strolled hand-in-hand to the doorway.

"This, my dear, is your room." Lady Bembridge pushed open the door to expose the most irresistible girl's bedroom imaginable, decorated in brightly colored fabrics, with dolls and toys strewn about the room. The two wandered about, ending up at the window.

"Look here, Eleanor, you even have a view of the Royal Garden."

"It's all so wonderful. Does this mean I can stay with you?" Eleanor asked hesitantly.

"It would make Walter and me very happy if you agree to stay."

"Oh, yes!" Eleanor rushed into Lady Bembridge's open arms. "Can we go see the garden, Mother?"

Lady Bembridge's heart leaped when she heard Eleanor refer to her as Mother; it was the second chance for which she longed. "Of course, we can."

***

They were only briefly in the garden when Lord Bembridge and Chancellor Oswalt approached them.

"Amanda . . . Ellie." Lord Bembridge greeted them each directly. "I trust that this beautiful afternoon finds you both well. Amanda, may I speak with you privately for just a moment?" Lord Bembridge looked toward Chancellor Oswalt, then shifted his head slightly toward Eleanor.

The Chancellor took his cue, bowing and extending his hand to the girl. "Lady Eleanor, I would be honored if you would accompany me on a walk through the garden. I'm quite the horticulturist if I do say so myself."

"You're a what?"

"Horticulturist. It's a fancy word for a gardener."

"Well, why don't you just say gardener? You talk funny," she said while accepting his hand. The adults smiled, amused by her response. As she and Chancellor Oswalt walked away, she looked over her shoulder, smiling and waving at her new mother and father.

As they walked, Chancellor Oswalt pointed out the various species of flora, droning on and on as if such things would impress a young girl when they came upon an arbor cut into the side of a tall hedge.

"Where's this go?" asked Eleanor.

"Here, and there, and back again. It's called a labyrinth, more commonly referred to as a maze. Have you ever been through a maze?" Chancellor Oswalt questioned. "A maze can hold incredible wonders, but it is scary if you don't know which way to turn and end up getting lost. Do you want to go in?" Oswalt didn't wait for an answer before proceeding through the portal.

"The object of any maze is to go in one way and find your way out another; easier said than done unless you know the trick."

"What's the trick?"

"This is a very special maze because the trick is to get lost deliberately.

Eleanor shook her head. "I'm already lost, and we haven't even started."

"Patience, child, and soon all will be revealed. Listen carefully and remember everything I say as though your life depended on it. Can you do that for me?"

"I'll try."

"**TRYING** isn't good enough. You must pay attention and remember what I say. Do you understand?"

"Yes, I understand." Eleanor was becoming annoyed.

"All right then, as we enter the maze, immediately turn left. Continue down the hedge row, ignoring the first two openings, the one on the right and the one on the left. Enter the very next opening on the right. Walk forward, ignoring all openings to the left, and take the second opening on the right. You're almost there. This time, take your second left and then your immediate right. That's it; you've beaten the labyrinth. Do you want me to repeat the directions?"

"That won't be necessary."

"Really? Okay then, let's see how fast you can run it. You lead, and I'll follow." Before Eleanor could compose herself, Oswalt signaled, "Go!"

Eleanor took off running with Oswalt close behind. "*Turn left, second right, second right, second left, first right,*" she thought. But instead of exiting the labyrinth, she stared at a stone wall. "I don't understand; I must have taken a wrong turn."

"On the contrary, you're right where you should be."

Eleanor stomped her foot, "I'm tired of all your riddles."

"Don't be such an impatient child; this is important. Do you see the family crest carved upon the wall? It's called a hextar, a mythical double-headed bird of prey; it's the same symbol as on the pendants flying over the castle's ramparts. On each corner of the crest is a four-pointed star, a compass of a sort, signifying that the hextar watches over the four corners of Calvendar. If you turn the upper right star clockwise, one-quarter turn, and the lower left star counter-clockwise one-quarter turn, it will reveal a secret door that leads outside the castle where you can move unseen directly into the woodlands beyond. **NOW**, do you understand?"

Eleanor nodded her head yes.

"More importantly, do you fully understand what is required of you?"

Again, Eleanor nodded her head yes.

"Good, then take this dagger and hide it on your person. The deed must happen this evening." Eleanor took the knife with a jeweled hilt, a Xagada dagger approximately six inches long, with razor-sharp edges on both sides of the blade.

Eleanor passed the blade before her eyes, "This will serve the purpose quite nicely." She quickly brought the knife just under Oswalt's chin. "Deception comes in many forms, Chancellor. Don't misconstrue your place because of my youthful appearance; I'm not as young and inexperienced as you may think. If you ever speak to me again in that condescending tone, I'll cut out your tongue. Now, do **YOU** fully understand?"

Chancellor Oswalt shook his head rapidly in the affirmative.

As the two came back into view, Lady Bembridge saw Eleanor skipping, and she smiled; Amanda was experiencing a different feeling of happiness. "Look at her, Walter; it's a miracle how quickly she has reclaimed her innocence." At that moment, Walter saw Amanda not only as his beloved wife but also as the mother she was always meant to be. He, too, was overjoyed.

"Children can be very resilient." Walter hugged Amanda closely. "One last thing, my love, Lord Driscoll arrives this afternoon to discuss the pending coalition. He is, shall I say, reluctant to commit. I'll need your feminine powers of persuasion by my side. Have your Lady-in-Waiting feed and dress Ellie for bed tonight."

After kissing her cheek, he beckoned Chancellor Oswalt over, and they left the Royal Garden in deep conversation on their way to the High Council Chamber. At that moment, Lord Walter Bembridge could never have imagined the events to come.

CHAPTER 8

TIME IS OF THE ESSENCE

The high desert of Jadhar was subject to extreme swings in temperature between day and night. The days are always oppressively hot, while the nights tend to be cool, even cold if the winds pick up out of the northern Sawtooth Mountains. Since a fire could be seen for miles over this barren terrain, thus giving away their position, Commandant Knoggs and his prisoner would have only their blankets to ward off the chill. Under the circumstances, catching any sleep proved difficult, and it was a blessing to see the sunrise…

(So writes Conrad Nightingale)

There was but a soft glow of the sun cresting the distant horizon when Commandant Knoggs rose from his broken slumber. Mumbling obscenities under his breath, he stretched and rubbed himself briskly, trying his best to get the blood moving to his cold extremities. After relieving himself, he turned his attention to his prisoner.

"Get up!" roared Boz as he tossed Rycroft some scraps from the previous night's dinner. "Eat quickly; we leave in five minutes."

"What's your hurry, kory?"

Boz jerked Rycroft to his feet by his shirt collar and held him before his face.

"I promised Marshall Alcott to get you to Blackpool Penitentiary; it's a promise I would like to keep. However, I'm growing restless. – And, when I'm restless, I get angry. – And, when I'm angry, I just might lose control and kill you." He looked into his prisoner's eyes with deep intent.

"I don't want to break my promise, so I suggest you help us both by not vexing me further. Oh, and one last thing – If I ever hear you say the word kory again, I will break every tooth in your foul mouth. Do you understand?"

"Just unchain me; I need to take a shit."

"You'll figure out a way or shit in your pants; I couldn't care less. Now, you've got four minutes."

"Are you planning to unchain me so I get on the horse, or am I supposed to figure that out too? Of course, Rycroft was right, and it didn't please Knoggs to relent.

Boz unchained Rycroft long enough to finish his personal business and mount the horse. Once aboard, Boz reattached the bracelets and cuffed the leg irons under the horse's belly. Then he tied Rycroft's horse and the pack mule together.

"Just in case you get any ideas about running away, that horse won't get far trying to drag two asses. Ha! Drag two asses. Do you get it? That's funny. I wish John could have heard that one."

Southeast, they traveled. Wary of another cowardly ambush, Boz kept in the open, away from the scattered boulders and out of an arrow's range. As it turned out, the precaution wasn't necessary, for it wouldn't be an ambush but rather a full-on assault.

Shortly after setting out, four riders advanced directly toward them. They were making no effort to remain concealed as they closed the gap. Boz could see that one of the four riders was smaller than the rest, no doubt the stable boy.

"Looks like we have company!" Boz spurred his horse toward a large lone boulder; the hastened pace made for a somewhat precarious ride for his prisoner, who yelled obscenities and tightly gripped the horse's mane to keep from falling off. Upon arriving, the two dismounted, and Knoggs reattached Rycroft's leg irons.

"Sit down with your back against this rock, and remember, if you try anything, I'll kill you without hesitation!"

"What about your promise, kory?" Boz didn't answer; he just kicked Rycroft in the mouth, laying him unconscious and most certainly knocking out several teeth. Afterward, he casually walked over to the pack mule and untied the leather saddlebag, exposing several weapons. He selected a long sword and turned to face the approaching riders.

The assassins charged while three fired crossbows. Two arrows harmlessly missed their target. The third bolt whizzed past Boz's head and hit the pack mule just behind its foreleg, piercing the heart and instantly bringing the animal to the ground. Still charging, all three dropped their crossbows and drew swords. Boz deftly dodged to the side of the first horse, swinging his sword on a low path, cleaving the horse's leg; down went the horse, throwing the rider a good twenty feet. The other two reined in their horses, attempting to swing around.

Again, Boz's sword found purchase, not on the man, but rather on his animal's exposed neck. Blood sprayed, and the horse dropped, pinning the rider's leg below its dead weight. Like a turtle on its back, the rider lay immobile, staring up into the sky; it was the last thing he saw.

The third rider was quick to dismount; while Boz was dispatching his partner, he attacked from behind. The sword sliced the back of Boz's shoulder, barely penetrating his leather mantle. Boz swung about and stabbed in the direction of the assailant. The sword buried itself deep into the attacker's chest and out his backside. Three up and three down in only a minute; then something unexpected happened.

The stable boy dismounted and recovered his partner's sword. "Put down the sword, boy, or I'll have to kill you too." No sooner were the words spoken than there was a chain around Boz's neck with the total weight of Rycroft pulling him to the ground.

Rycroft continued to apply pressure to his hold. "Your days of killing are done, kory." There was an audible sound as Boz's neck snapped. "Did you hear that boy? Pop! Now, that's what I call funny, kory. Find the keys to these shackles, boy; I've got urgent business to attend."

The boy rummaged through Commandant Knogg's clothes until he found the keys and released Rycroft. "What business can be so urgent? We've got to ride for Elsdon Forrest and find the others before we're captured or worse."

Rycroft pushed the bohkor's body clear, and he rose to his feet. "Grow a set of balls, boy.

Elsdon Forrest is precisely where we're heading because that's where the lawman went, and I've got a score to settle with Longshanks."

EVERY SECOND COUNTS

It was a moonless, starless night, far too dark to cut through the dense woods safely. Luckily for Alcott, he had Ada. The kolgarr's heightened senses were keenly adapted to these conditions and this environment. Even so, it was slow going because Adak would have to continually stop to stay within Alcott's limited sight as the two pushed on through Elsdon Forrest. It was a difficult and slow journey, and Alcott hoped he wouldn't arrive too late...

(So writes Conrad Nightingale)

When dawn finally broke, Alcott was still within a long day's ride of Bembridge Castle. He and his horse, Tess, were spent and at a heightened risk of having an accident due to sheer exhaustion; a few hours of rest were needed. Alcott laid out his bedroll, keeping his back close to the cliff's edge; one less direction to guard.

Adak sensed that trouble was nearby, and when he left his napping companion to investigate, he was surrounded by Rycroft's men. Desperate, he rushed toward a small opening in the gauntlet only to find himself immobilized by hidden netting and staked to the ground. The men should have used this opportunity to kill the beast, but they thought the animal was secure until Rycroft arrived; he alone would determine the kolgarr's fate. However, few people know much about the intelligence and physical prowess of the elusive kolgarr. Leaving Adak unattended to go and help capture Alcott was a mistake. When the men were out of sight, the kolgarr's extremely sharp teeth and claws went to work on the thick net.

Alcott must have been more tired than he realized, for he fell asleep and rested longer than intended. He was startled awake by the sound of brush being trampled under many footsteps. When his eyes adjusted, Alcott found himself surrounded on three sides. "Stay back; this one is dangerous. We'll keep him cornered until Tobias arrives."

Half the day passed away.

"Hello, Longshanks; I had to travel hard and fast to catch up with you. I hope you appreciate the effort."

Alcott recognized the voice and immediately knew he was in dire straits. There were too many to fend off alone. *How could this have happened? Where is Adak,* he wondered.

"Looking for your kolgarr? Don't bother; my men netted him a couple of miles back. Oh, and as for your friend, Commandant Knoggs, he won't be coming to anybody's rescue anymore." This time, Tobias Rycroft had the upper hand.

"You know, Longshanks, you caused me to miss a critical meeting with my daughter at Bembridge Castle; fortunately, I made other arrangements." Rycroft took a dramatic pause before speaking again.

"Normally, I would toy with you and kill you slowly, but I've learned my lesson where you're concerned. It will be a quick death for you." Rycroft drew his sword and stepped forward.

It simply came down to a matter of life or death when Alcott decided to make good his escape by turning and leaping off a fifty-foot cliff into the raging rapids below.

He hit the river with such force as to knock the wind out of him; nevertheless, he resisted the urge to breathe. The undertow wrapped around him like a squid's tentacles, pulling Alcott ever deeper, when he noticed shafts of sunlight skipping on the water's surface. His lungs felt like they would burst as he frantically battled the undertow, swimming toward the guiding light. Every fiber of his body begged him to breathe, and he was just about to pass out when his head broke the surface.

As waves crashed around him, Alcott gasped for precious air. Like his companion, Adak, Alcott was caught in his own net, a watery net, and the river was relentlessly trying to claim its prize. Even against seemingly insurmountable odds, Alcott would not surrender. The current swept Alcott along, slamming him into rocks and rolling his limp body over natural weirs, and the river still wasn't through with him yet. When Alcott was struck from behind by a tree limb, he could take no more abuse. With one final burst of effort, he managed to pull himself on top of the passing log.

The last words he heard before losing consciousness were those of Rycroft echoing through the canyon, "This isn't over, Longshanks! I promise you a long and painful death!"

AN UNAVOIDABLE TIMEOUT

The Harrington brothers were walking along the riverbank on their way to their favorite fishing hole when they noticed a man lying face down on the edge of the water...

(So writes Conrad Nightingale)

"Do ya think he's dead?" asked Elliot, the youngest.

"Don't know," replied James, his older brother. "Why don't ya grab a stick and give him a poke."

"I'm not pokin' him."

"Yer a chicken."

"I'm not a chicken, yer the chicken."

As the two threw challenges at one another, Alcott softly moaned, "Help me."

"Did you hear that, Elliot? He's alive. I'll go get dad; ya stay here and watch him."

"Crux it. I'm not staying here by myself. The guy might be a thief or, worse, a murderer."

"Okay, chicken, come on, but I'm tellin' mom and dad yer swearin' again."

"Go ahead, see if I care, ya chicken shit."

"That's it, yer in trouble, little brother," and off the two ran.

About a half hour later, the boys arrived with their father. "There he is," said Elliott, pointing to the unconscious man.

"Okay, ya boys, stay put and let me check things out." Their father cautiously approached Alcott and rolled him onto his back. "Mister? Can ya hear me, mister?"

Alcott strained to open his eyes. "Help me, please."

"Don't ya worry, mister, I'm gonna help ya. My name is William Harrington; these are my boys, Elliott and James. Yer gonna be all right, mister, but first, we gotta get ya back to the house. You're too big for me to carry on my own. Do ya think you can walk with some help? My wagon is up on the road just above the riverbank."

Alcott nodded, and together, they managed to get him into the back of the wagon.

"Gotta get him home, boys; your mother will know what to do. Hold on to him so he doesn't fall out."

When they arrived at the house, Martha, William's wife, directed them to lay Alcott on the boy's bed, and she went to work cleaning and bandaging his wounds. She placed a cooling salve on his cuts and bruises where the rapids had smashed him against the rocks; fortunately, there were no broken bones. When she finished treating him, she spoon-fed him some soup she had been preparing for the evening meal, and he washed it down with cool, fresh spring water. After a short nap, Alcott woke, sore to his very core but glad to be alive.

"Ah, I see yer back with the living. How do ya feel?" asked William.

"Much better, thanks to you."

"Not me, friend; the thanks go to my wife, Martha; she's the healer in this family."

Alcott tried to stand. "Slowly, cautioned Martha, yer hurt pretty bad." Alcott rose the rest of the way to his feet.

"My gratitude, Mrs. Harrington."

"Call me Martha, please. And what might be yer name, stranger?"

"Oh, forgive me. My name is Alcott – Johnathan Alcott. Please call me John."

"John, do ya mind tellin' us how ya came to be out here in the middle of nowhere, beaten to within an inch of yer life, no less?"

"Exactly where is the middle of nowhere?" asked Alcott.

"We're in Elsdon Forrest, about twenty miles from Roderick," chimed in James.

Only twenty miles, thought Alcott; the river carried me much further than I would have guessed. "William, how I ended up here in this condition is a long story that I hope I can share with you over an ale someday, but I must be going. After all your kindness, I hesitate to ask, but do you have a horse I can borrow? It's truly a matter of life or death."

"I only have the one mule tied to the wagon, and I'm sorry, but I can't let ya borrow her." That animal is worth her weight in gold to our family." Of course, it was only an expression, but even as a novice farmer, Alcott understood a mule's value when scratching out an existence.

"I understand, and it gives me no pleasure, but I'm taking the mule. I swear on my life that I will bring back the animal once I have completed my task. Please, I'm begging you, don't try to stop me."

"Yer gonna take our damn mule after all we've done for ya?" shouted Elliott. I told ya he was a damn thief when we first saw him. Elliott stomped forward, "Mister, ya take our mule, and I swear when I grow up, I'll hunt ya down and cut off yer balls!" Elliott's parents were more shocked at his language than the possibility of Alcott taking their mule.

"I believe you, Elliott, so I hope you'll find a way to forgive me before that happens."

Even in Alcott's present state, William knew better than to press the challenge. "All right, John, ya can take the mule. Better I give it freely than think ya robbed me.

I hope yer a man of yer word, Johnathan Alcott."

CHAPTER 9
MATTERS OF STATE

In the High Council Chamber, Lord Bembridge and Chancellor Oswalt spent the afternoon laying out arguments in front of Lord Driscoll for a united coalition. By dinner time, it seemed Lord Driscoll was leaning in their favor, but one last push wouldn't hurt. That's where Lady Bembridge would use her extraordinary talent for persuasion; she had a way about her…

(So writes Conrad Nightingale)

"Why do you have to go, Mother?" Eleanor made it sound more like a plea to stay than a question.

"In matters of State, it is expected to show proper decorum. Lord Driscoll is an important man and, hopefully, an equally important ally." Eleanor frowned, appearing to care nothing about matters of State. "You'll be all right, little one. Adeline will watch over you just as she watched over me when I was younger. Promise me you will be good for her."

"I promise," Eleanor pouted.

"Don't worry, my Lady, we'll get by just fine. Hurry along; keeping your husband and Lord Driscoll waiting wouldn't do. And you, Eleanor, why don't you show me around your lovely room."

Little more than an hour passed when there was a knock on the door. Dinner was brought in for Adeline and Eleanor. Since this was Eleanor's room, she acted as hostess, presenting the plates of food and serving tea.

"Do you think it would be nice to ask Charlotte to join us? She's over on the window seat. Would you be so kind as to get her?"

As Adeline walked over to get the doll, Eleanor removed the hidden knife and twisted the jeweled hilt, exposing a tiny compartment filled with a white powder. She adroitly poured the mixture into one of the two cups and then served her guest, ensuring Adeline received the cup with the poison. Eleanor held forth her cup.

"A toast to the House of Bembridge." As they sipped their tea, Eleanor asked, "Have you had a full life, Adeline?" Before she could respond, Adeline's mouth began to foam profusely, her body began to convulse uncontrollably, and her face turned purple as she clutched at her throat, falling face-first onto the dinner plate.

"I'll take that as a yes," mused Eleanor. Grabbing her doll, she slipped out of the room and headed straight for Lord and Lady Bembridge's private chambers.

As she approached, the Impregnable Guard standing outside Lord and Lady Bembridge's private chambers stepped forward.

"Where are you off to so quickly, little miss?"

She showed her doll and explained, "I left Charlotte's friend in my parent's room."

"I'm sorry to hear that, but I can't let you in without the Lord's or Lady's permission."

Eleanor stuck out her lower lip, showing disappointment.

"My mother told me that you're all here to serve me. Please, I'll only be a minute, and you can come in with me." The girl was attempting to intimidate the guard.

The guard looked about to see if anyone was watching. "Well, if we're quick, I suppose it will be okay." He opened the door, and the two stepped inside. "Where's your doll's friend hiding?" he asked.

"Right here!" Eleanor pulled forth the dagger and, reaching up, raked it across his throat. The guard tried vainly to yell a warning, but the sharp knife had severed his vocal cords. He dropped to the floor, choking on blood, and quickly bled out.

Eleanor rushed into Lord Bembridge's study, searching the room for any information that might expose what Lord Bembridge was planning.

TO CLOSE FOR COMFORT

While at the dinner reception for Lord Driscoll, Lady Bembridge did her best to be the consummate hostess, but truth be told, her mind was elsewhere. This was her first time away from Eleanor since she came to stay. Of course, Adeline would take good care of her, yet a mother can't help but worry about her child…

(So writes Conrad Nightingale)

"Amanda . . . Amanda, my dear," Lord Bembridge broke her trance. "Bernard and I were commenting upon how vital the Preservation Coalition will be to us all. Wouldn't you agree?" Lord Bembridge was setting the stage for Amanda to play her part.

"Um . . . yes, of course. I wouldn't dream of challenging you men at matters of State." She placated them, but did nothing to help close the deal, which confused her husband.

"Gentlemen, I pray you excuse me; I am not feeling well."

"Shall I call for the doctor?" asked Lord Bembridge.

"No, thank you, Walter. It's just... feminine matters." In truth, Lady Bembridge was off to see Eleanor.

"I hope Lady Bembridge isn't too ill," said Lord Driscoll.

Then Lord Bembridge realized precisely what was happening and couldn't help but smile.

"She will be all right, I'm sure."

***

As Lady Bembridge ascended the stairs to her quarters and Eleanor's room, she noticed no guard standing before her door.

Hmm, that is highly unusual, she thought. It warranted further investigation. She slowly opened the door to the private chambers and froze in place. Before her, lying in a pool of blood, was the guard. Thinking immediately of Eleanor, Lady Bembridge panicked.

"Ellie!" she called out. Amanda turned to run for Eleanor's room when she heard a commotion in Lord Bembridge's study. Picking up the guard's pike, she tipped-toed into the study.

"Eleanor!" Relieved to see her child unhurt, Lady Bembridge dropped the pike and swung her arms wide. Eleanor came running.

"Are you okay?" she asked.

"Better than you," came the curt reply. Eleanor slipped the knife between Lady Bembridge's ribs directly into the heart. It was a highly skilled kill stroke, where the victim hardly feels a thing, and death comes quickly.

Eleanor left the dagger in Lady Bembridge's body. She wanted it to be found. This was a clear message from the Xagada: **WE ARE COMING; NOBODY IS SAFE.**

Turning her attention back to the matter at hand, Eleanor pulled the stuffing from her doll and replaced it with the papers she had found in Lord Bembridge's desk; then, with the doll tightly in hand, she bolted down the hall to make good her escape.

***

As Eleanor made it to the Royal Gardens, she was confronted by Crofton, the Master Gardener.

"Lady Eleanor, what are you doing outside at this hour?" Before she could answer, there came shouting from within the castle. One or all the victims must have been discovered. The castle would be going into lockdown; they would be hunting for the girl if for no other reason than to ensure her safety, but the truth would be ferreted out soon enough if she was found.

"There, in the bushes!" Eleanor pointed behind Crofton.

"Where? What do you see?" Crofton could not make anything out, and while he concentrated on the spot where Eleanor pointed, she picked up a nearby shovel and hit him with such force that his body immediately went limp.

There had been too many unforeseen encounters, and her escape was taking too long. Eleanor could hear voices getting closer. Soon, she would be discovered. She was scared, perhaps for the first time in her life.

Run! she thought. *Run for your life!* She managed to arrive unseen at the entrance to the labyrinth, and in she went.

***

Within minutes, the Impregnable Guards were in the Royal Gardens, where they discovered Eleanor's latest victim, Crofton. She was leaving a trail of bodies in her wake. "Spread out and find the child!" Captain Fleming ordered. "Let no harm come to her; we need answers."

"She must have gone into the maze!" yelled one of the guards.

"You five men go around the pond and block the exit. You five are with me. Everyone converges when I signal; we'll flank her inside. Eleanor! You're trapped! There's no way out! Give yourself up!" There was no answer, for Eleanor was running the maze as instructed earlier.

"Move in, men, and yell out if you see her!" ordered the captain.

I can't locate the secret passage, thought Eleanor, then she realized she had gone too far; she was lost, and time was running out. She had to double back, which meant the possibility of running straight into the guards, but it was a chance she had to take. She remembered the last turn was to the right, not the left.

At last, Eleanor saw the family crest on the garden wall. She ran to it and began to turn the corner stars as Chancellor Oswalt had instructed.

A crack appeared in the wall, and Eleanor threw herself against the opening, but it was too heavy; the wall would not move. Damn!

TWIST OF FATE

When it was built more than a hundred years ago, the intent of having a secret passageway within the Royal Garden's labyrinth was to provide Lord Roderick Bembridge with a backdoor should the castle ever be breached. Simply a means for a quick retreat, this heavy block door was designed to slide open, assisted by the gentle slope of the terrain. The architect never considered concealing one's movement by closing the garden wall once open. However, to avoid being followed, Eleanor needed to escape undetected, and so far, things weren't going as planned...

(So writes Conrad Nightingale)

The guards were nearly upon her, and Eleanor began panicking as the wall slowly slid open, as intended. She wasted no time squeezing through the opening as soon as her slim body could fit. She expected to see her father, but a wicked-looking orc stood waiting for her on the other side of the wall.

Like all orcs, his skin had a green tinge, his face was accented with beady yellow eyes, and tusks protruded from his jowls. Then, there was the matter of his teeth; as part of the orc ritual, when reaching maturity, orcs file their teeth into sharp points to make themselves look more frightening, and it worked.

Eleanor disliked orcs even more than bohkors. Orcs constantly grunt when they speak, first by sucking in air through their tiny nostrils, then after having their say, heavily exhaling through their sloppy jowls. It gave the impression they are little more than dumb pigs, but nothing could be further from the truth. Orcs were cunning and manipulative, and when they couldn't cheat you outright, they were often brutal when taking what they wanted.

Once on the other side of the labyrinth, ignoring her surprise, she spun around and pressed against the wall, trying to stop its momentum.

"The guards are close behind me; help me push the wall back into place, or we're as good as dead."

Images of what could be flashed through her mind. She instinctively knew that death would be the least of her worries if she were taken alive. The orc pushed Eleanor aside, lowered his shoulder, and threw his weight forward.

Olav Tyan grunted and furiously pumped his thick legs, trying to gain purchase on the ground beneath his feet. It took all the orc's considerable strength, but it was working; the wall reversed direction and slowly moved back into place just as the guards rounded the corner inside the maze.

Olav Tyan and Eleanor held their collective breaths, trying to stay quiet while wondering if anyone had detected anything unusual. Eleanor could feel her heart pounding in her ears, and she was sure others could also hear her frantic heartbeat. Then came a mutual sigh of relief when one of the guards announced it was a dead-end, and they went about exploring the rest of the garden labyrinth.

While the guards continued to search in vain, Eleanor and her rescuer hugged against the outer wall and made their way unseen into the woods, where several other orcs waited to escort her back to her people.

Although safe now, Eleanor couldn't stop shaking from the ordeal. It was the first time she came face-to-face with her mortality. The sensation devastated her, and she did not want to experience it again.

CHAPTER 10

CONDOLENCES ALL AROUND

When Alcott finally made it to the city of Roderick, there were no signs of people going about their business; in fact, there was no activity at all, for a curfew had been initiated. Alcott pressed on toward Bembridge Castle's main gate, not allowing himself to think the worst. Once there, he was immediately placed under arrest and brought before Captain Spencer Fleming...

(So writes Conrad Nightingale)

"Please take a seat, John." Captain Fleming and Alcott were old friends.

"I would rather stand Spence; I don't intend to be here long. I have urgent business with Lord Bembridge."

"I'd rather you sit," came a voice from the room's shadows. "Because you will be here as long as I have questions, longer if I don't like the answers." It was Chancellor Oswalt. "I suggest you cooperate."

"What I have to say is for Lord Bembridge's ears alone."

Then, I guess we're done for now. We'll continue our conversation tomorrow. Take him away."

"Wait!"

"I'm in no mood for games, Alcott, so here's how it will play out; I ask the questions, and you provide the answers. If I think you're lying or being evasive in any way, you'll be locked up. Understand?" Alcott shook his head in the affirmative.

"Not good enough – speak the words." The order was given not only to ensure compliance but also to demean Alcott.

"Yes, I understand," Alcott spoke the words softly but loud enough to be heard.

"Good, then let's start with an easy question. Where were you for the past several days?" asked Oswalt curtly.

Trying to restrain himself, Alcott took a deep breath before answering. "I was doing my best to get to the castle to warn Lord Bembridge that he and Lady Bembridge are in danger."

"That doesn't answer my question as to where you were. However, first, I would like to know what makes you think the Lord and Lady are in danger?"

"I tracked and captured Tobias Rycroft in the high desert of Jadhar. While taking him to Blackpool Penitentiary, I discovered there was no girl living with the Stinson Family when Rycroft and his gang slaughtered them. This means the girl, Eleanor, is a plant."

"Am I to believe that you were miles away in an effort to capture Tobias Rycroft all on your own?" Of course, Oswalt was aware of Alcott's abilities and continued to demean him. "Under whose authority?"

"Under Lord Bembridge's authority!" Alcott was getting angry, arguing with this idiot. Then, he reached inside his tunic and produced the warrant. Unfortunately, the document was destroyed while Alcott fought for his life in the river.

"And what am I supposed to make of this, a torn parchment with no legible writing?"

"Lord Bembridge's seal is still intact. If not my authority to serve the warrant for Rycroft's capture, what type of document would I be carrying?"

"I'm sure I don't know, but let's not forget who is asking the questions here. Tell me, did you successfully deliver Rycroft to Blackpool? If so, it should be quite easy to corroborate your story with Commandant Knoggs."

"Knoggs was with me when Rycroft was captured. When we heard about the girl, we knew I needed to get here as quickly as possible. So, I left Rycroft in the capable hands of Commandant Knoggs." Alcott intentionally omitted the part of his story regarding the subsequent encounter with Rycroft at the cliff.

"Apparently, not as capable as you might believe. We received a message from Blackpool by carrier pigeon. Commandant Knoggs was found by a BPS search party with his neck broken. The confirmation of Boz's death hit Alcott particularly hard, but he showed no sign to Oswalt. "As for Tobias Rycroft, he's nowhere to be found, but maybe this isn't news to you?"

Alcott held Oswalt in his steely gaze, "What are you trying to say?"

"I'm not saying anything; you're doing all the talking. However, you must admit that if you were in my boots, you probably would have your suspicions. You claim that Lord Bembridge authorized you to bring this notoriously violent criminal single-handedly to justice, but you can't produce a legible warrant. You say you left Rycroft in Commandant Knoggs' custody, but your alibi is murdered. The only thing I can say for sure is that you are here in Roderick after curfew. I've heard enough for now. Captain Fleming take Mr. Alcott to jail for violation of curfew."

"Violation of curfew? That's dog shit! I need to see Lord Bembridge at once. Lord and Lady Bembridge are closer to peril every minute I answer your ridiculous questions."

"You're too late, Alcott! Lady Bembridge was murdered yesterday by the little girl, along with several others, I might add. Now, what is so important that you must intrude on Lord Bembridge's time of mourning? Tell me!" For the second time since starting this endeavor, the news of the death of a close friend hit home for Alcott; he was without words.

"Captain Fleming, if I must give the order again, I will relieve you of command."

***

Fleming reluctantly escorted Alcott out of the office, heading for the jail cells. Once out of sight, Fleming stopped. "John, whether you have proof of a warrant or not, I believe you. Your story has merit. Go home."

"Oswalt will have a fit when he discovers you let me go."

"Perhaps, but something tells me he won't want to make his case before Lord Bembridge when the time comes.

So, hurry up and leave here before I change my mind."

NOBODY LEFT BEHIND

Barely rested, the following day, found Johnathan ready to set out again. Tess had found her way home, one less thing for Johnathan to worry about. He secured Harrington's mule behind and mounted up. Ingrid brought forth a saddlebag holding enough fresh bread, cheese, and dried meat to last for several meals should it be necessary. She also had an animal skin of fresh spring water for his journey…

(So writes Conrad Nightingale)

Ingrid never let on how upset she was when Tess showed up alone, and now she didn't want to let Johnathan out of her sight. "I'd be happy to go along and keep you company. It would allow me to meet and personally thank the people who saved your life."

"If that were my only reason for the trip, I would gladly welcome your company. However, as soon as I drop off their mule, I'll be off in search of Adak. I must find him; he might be injured and need help. If he didn't make it, at least I can give him a decent burial."

"I'm sure Adak is okay. Go find your friend, and the two of you come home quickly." Ingrid climbed the porch steps before turning back, "One last thing, John, swing through Roderick and get the Harringtons some supplies to thank them for their kindness."

Alcott smiled, "You're always thinking of others."

***

After a brief stop in the city for provisions, Alcott rode into the Harrington's farm shortly after noon. "Hello, in the house!" he called. Seconds later, William and the boys appeared.

"Well, John, I see ya brought back my mule; ya restored my faith in humanity."

"No choice if I didn't want to spend the rest of my life looking over my shoulder for Elliott. I'm too fond of my balls not to keep my word," Alcott chuckled.

Just then, Martha joined William and the boys. "John, welcome back. Are yer injuries healing?"

"I'm much better thanks to you, Martha. My wife, Ingrid, sends her thanks and would like to meet you and the family soon."

"It would be our pleasure. Please come in out of the sun and rest awhile."

"Thanks, but I still have pressing business; as soon as I turn over your mule and some supplies, I'll have to be on my way."

"Yer kind, John," said William, "but we can't accept any charity."

"None given. You helped Lord Bembridge's High Marshal in a time of need; the supplies will be expensed accordingly."

"Well, in that case, we accept with gratitude. Please be sure to thank Lord Bembridge for us. Alcott nodded and began to unload the supplies, mainly food staples, a small barrel of ale, a sharp new axe, colored cloth for Martha, and a couple of toys for Elliott and James; they all were elated.

"John, at least rest long enough to share a cup of this fine ale with Martha and me." William poured three cups. "Can ya tell us of yer business, or is it of a confidential matter?"

"When I was ambushed a couple of days ago, I was separated from a close companion. I'm going to try to find him. Hopefully, I won't be too late this time."

"Ya said, too late this time. Does that mean ya didn't make it to Bembridge Castle in time to warn Lord Bembridge?"

"I did not, and Lady Bembridge ended up paying the ultimate price for my failure." Alcott went slightly flush.

It was shocking news that their Queen had been murdered, and Martha could see the burden that Alcott was shouldering. "Ya mustn't fault yerself, John. In yer condition, it was a miracle that ya got out of bed, let alone rode to Bembridge Castle. I'm sure ya did everything possible."

William interjected, trying to change the subject, "What's the name of yer friend, and what does he look like? We can keep an eye out for him, and if he shows up, we'll let him know yer looking for him."

"His name is Adak, and he is easily recognizable. Usually, his fur is silver-gray, although he can easily blend in with the surroundings should he choose; a thick bone plate guards his skull, and he has violet eyes and long white fangs. In my opinion, he's the best-looking kolgarr that ever roamed Calvendar.

"A kolgarr? I thought they were just a myth."

"Extinct and elusive, yes, but they're no myth."

"Well, if that don't beat all. Come to think of it; an animal was howling just before sunrise. Got me out of my warm bed. I thought it might be a wolf trying to get to my livestock. I can't say, though, because I never saw him. Do ya think that might be Adak?"

"It's worth a look." Alcott walked out of the house and mounted Tess; the Harringtons followed close behind. "Thanks again for everything, folks. Boys, you behave yourselves, especially you, Master Elliott." Alcott gave him a quick wink. Elliott just grinned.

***

Alcott decided to backtrack over land to the campsite, where he was ambushed. From that spot, he would search for where Adak had been captured. The thought of finding his friend netted and killed with no chance to defend himself made Alcott nauseous.

On the other hand, if Adak was lucky enough to escape, Alcott was confident he could pick up his tracks before sundown. Barely out of sight of the Harrington's Farm, he saw the footprints.

He dismounted and examined the prints closer; they were of an extremely large kolgarr and still fresh. Adak was alive, and he was nearby. Alcott brought his fingers to the corners of his mouth and let loose a long whistle followed by two shorter whistles. He waited – nothing happened.

Again, one long whistle followed by two short blasts. Adak pounced, knocking Alcott to the ground. Alcott tried to get up, but the kolgarr wasn't having it. There was plenty of affectionate play; it was a joyful moment.

That night, the two friends slept closely, waking at the slightest sound and keeping a watchful eye on one another.

***

The following day, Alcott and Adak headed for home. Maintaining a quick but comfortable pace meant they should arrive before supper.

Within a mile of Albem, Adak yelped and ran ahead. When Alcott finally arrived, he found the front door wide open. Adak darted in and out of the house, frantically barking.

Suddenly, a dark feeling engulfed Alcott, and he jumped from his horse, yelling for Ingrid. When he entered the house, he went rigid in place. Ingrid was naked, nailed face down on the table; her throat had been slit. He knew immediately what happened to his beloved and who was responsible. Alcott fell to the floor and screamed,

"**NO**! Please, no!"; he lay there crying for the rest of the night.

When morning dawned, Alcott was cried out, and his throat was raw from wailing. He raised himself off the floor and moved closer to where Ingrid lay. It was a gruesome sight; there were no words to describe it. He retched as he began to remove the nails from her hands; he couldn't leave her that way, no matter how difficult the task.

Recomposing himself, he went back to work. After freeing Ingrid from the table, he bathed and wrapped her body in clean linen before starting to dig a grave.

RESPECTING THE CHAIN OF COMMAND

Captain Fleming glanced up from behind his desk as Chancellor Oswalt swaggered into his office; he didn't look happy, but then again, he never did . . .

(So writes Conrad Nightingale)

"When I enter a room, I expect you to stand to attention."

Fleming rose slowly and assumed the appropriate position.

"How may I be of assistance today, Chancellor?"

"I hoped a day in jail would loosen Alcott's tongue, but when I stopped by the jail this morning to continue my discussion, you can imagine my surprise to learn that he had never been booked as I had ordered."

"I didn't think you were serious. You really wanted me to lock up the former Commander of the Ranger Regiment on a charge of curfew violation?"

"Captain Fleming, soldiers aren't expected to think; they are, however, required to obey orders. Go and bring Alcott back for further questioning." Oswalt began to walk toward the door, then turned back.

"And, once you have Alcott safely in a cell, lock yourself in one as well. I intend to deal personally with your insubordination. Captain, you may not respect me, but you will respect the chain of command before I'm through with you."

Oswalt was trying to prove something to Alcott, and though he wanted no part of it, Fleming had no choice but to follow orders.

***

Captain Fleming rode alone to Alcott's farm; taking others was unnecessary. Alcott would either return with him willingly or stand and fight. He hoped it wouldn't come to that.

It was eerily quiet as Captain Fleming approached Alcott's house; he dismounted and walked toward the open door. Peaking inside, he saw the walls and floor smeared with blood; he drew his sword and readied himself for a fight when he noticed Alcott sitting in the corner, cradling his wife's dead body. He called out, but Alcott didn't respond. It was as if he was in a catatonic state.

"I'll go get help," Fleming was off at full gallop for Bembridge Castle. This time, Lord Bembridge would receive the message directly and woe be to anyone who dared to stand in the way, especially Chancellor Oswalt.

Upon hearing the morbid news, Lord Bembridge snapped out of his own mourning and swiftly rode to Alcott's aid.

NO TIME TO MOURN

Alcott stepped into the empty hole and again began to weep as he gently lowered Ingrid's body into the grave. It was just then that Lord Bembridge and his Impregnable Guard arrived. With one passing glance through the open door, there was no need for an explanation. Lord Bembridge signaled his men to stay back, and then he took the shovel from Alcott's shaking hands and helped his friend finish burying Ingrid...

(So writes Conrad Nightingale)

While Lord Bembridge was consoling Alcott, his guards inspected the surrounding area. It was near the stables where they came upon the three bodies of the family who stayed to help Johnathan manage the fields. The family had been cut down while trying to flee.

Lord Bembridge placed a comforting hand upon Alcott's shoulder, "John, we have both lost someone we loved in a most heinous manner, and we are not the first. But, perhaps by working together, we can be the last. It is time to hold all the Xagada accountable."

"You once told me that for the sake of justice, Rycroft must serve his sentence in Blackpool Penitentiary, and I promised to bring the fugitive back. However, circumstances have changed. I can no longer keep that promise. Rycroft will not be brought to Blackpool Penitentiary as I previously agreed; he will die by my hand."

"Kill him with my blessing, but let's also send a message – the days of Xagada terror are in the past. Allow me to reinstate your commission; your former team of Rangers await your return."

"I shall place myself again in your service under two conditions: First, I answer only to you, and this time, everyone, citizens and government officials alike, will know it, especially Chancellor Oswalt."

"I understand Nigel has been a nuisance of late."

"He is always a nuisance where I'm concerned."

"Agreed, and your second condition?"

"I want to be informed about how my missions fit into the bigger picture. I will no longer unknowingly follow life and death commands. If I have your complete trust, this should not present a problem."

"Also agreed, too, Commander."

"Let's stick with the title of High Marshal. It gives me sufficient authority while remaining vague about my exact responsibilities."

"Then, High Marshal Alcott, it shall be."

Alcott extended his hand. "Lord Bembridge, I am, once again, at your service. Let's get to work."

"We shall get to work once you have had enough time to grieve the loss of Ingrid and your friends. Johnathan suddenly realized that he had never thought of the Kershaws; he was ashamed.

"What did you find?" Lord Bembridge simply shook his head. "We will need to dig more graves," said Johnathan.

"It's been taken care of, John. Now it's time to grieve."

"There will be time enough for grieving. As the saying goes — He who procrastinates is lost."

Lord Bembridge called to Captain Fleming, "Captain, we bivouac here tonight. Post the guard accordingly."

Walter and Johnathan began reconstructing the past week to the most minute detail of their combined recollection. They spoke until late into the evening before retiring to rest. Lord Bembridge moved off into the center of camp, encircled by the Impregnables. Marshal Alcott chose to remain separate. Wrapped in a blanket, he lay next to Ingrid's grave. He had thought himself cried out, but there were still more tears to shed.

***

The troops broke camp and left for Bembridge Castle at daybreak. The Impregnable Guard surrounded Lord Bembridge and Marshal Alcott as they rode. It allowed the two men to concentrate on their previous discussion, although they spoke in hushed tones so nobody else could hear. Interestingly, they had come to the same conclusions:

First, Eleanor's main objective was to obtain intelligence on Lord Bembridge's plans to form the coalition and eliminate the Xagada.

Second, gaining unfettered access inside Bembridge Castle was necessary to accomplish this task.

Third, the inflicted atrocities were met to demoralize Lord Bembridge from taking any further action. Yet, what remained a mystery was how Eleanor managed to escape undetected.

There could only be one reasonable answer – the Xagada must have an inside accomplice, and he would need to be someone of high stature with access to matters of State. That could only mean it was someone within Lord Bembridge's High Council.

Now, Bembridge and Alcott needed a plan for ferreting out this traitor before more damage could be inflicted or, worse, before the traitor could escape unpunished.

"Any ideas where to start?" asked Lord Bembridge.

"When playing a game of cards that your opponent can't seem to lose, you need to take control of the game.

"And how do we accomplish that?"

"You examine the cards, reshuffle the deck, and start a new game, but this time with different rules."

CHAPTER 11

BREACH OF CONTRACT

Once safely outside the castle walls, Eleanor, Olav Tyan and a escort detail of orcs took a circuitous route through the small woodlands. There was no talking, and after several hours of walking at a brisk pace, they entered the orc campsite...

(So writes Conrad Nightingale)

Second, in command, Garth Hegel, spent no time pulling Olav Tyan aside where they could speak privately. As the two removed themselves, Olav Tyan ordered the other orcs, perhaps two dozen in all, to provide Eleanor with comfortable quarters and plenty of food and drink.

However, when he returned from his discussion with Garth Hegel, his demeanor had changed, and not for the better.

The orc took the typical audible breath as he began the conversation: SNORT… "I join you?" HARRUMPH… Before receiving an answer, Olav Tyan sat down directly across from Eleanor but said nothing more. Instead, he stared at her, contemplating what to say. The pause was only a few seconds but seemed much longer when Olav Tyan finally broke the awkward silence.

Again, Olav Tyan grunted while trying to speak, SNORT… "Enough to eat and drink?" he asked halfheartedly. HARRUMPH…

"Enough, thank you," responded Eleanor. "But that's not really what's on your mind, is it?"

SNORT…" Tobias Rycroft captured. Tobias Rycroft paid me fifty gold pieces to bring you from Bembridge Castle. You here safe. Me did job. Where my money?" HARRUMPH…

"It is not the first time he has been taken," she answered. "Until he is free, you deal directly with me. I am Eleanor Rycroft, daughter of Tobias Rycroft and granddaughter of Kayla Rycroft, Xantara of the Xagada Nation. Your debt will be honored; you have my word."

SNORT… "Agreement no more good. Bembridge wants you. Xagada wants you. I ransom to highest bidder." HARRUMPH…

Eleanor jumped to her feet, and while clinging to her doll, she grabbed the knife from her dinner plate with her free hand. "You'll be a dead fool-of-an-orc if you break your agreement with the Xagada."

Olav Tyan laughed. SNORT…" You feisty. Work off debt in brothel. Orcs like young and feisty. Make much money. When done, I throw away." HARRUMPH…

Eleanor lunged forth with the knife, but Olav Tyan stopped her advance by grabbing her wrist with a vice-like force. He slapped her face hard, knocking her unconscious. She went limp, dropping the knife and doll to the ground. Then, calling out to one of the guards, he ordered Eleanor to be taken to a location more befitting her present status as a hostage rather than a guest.

While she was being carried out of the tent, Olav Tyan turned his gaze to the knife and ragdoll lying on the ground; something was out of place. Although she appeared to be only twelve, Eleanor was unusually mature for her age and more comfortable wielding a weapon than playing with toys, yet she constantly clung to the doll. Olav Tyan picked up the toy and slowly turned it in his big hands. Upon closer examination, he discovered that the doll was stuffed with paper rather than old rags. When he read the papers, the doll's importance became apparent; the documents regarded the formation of a secret coalition bent on exterminating the Xagada Nation.

Olav Tyan became ecstatic; he could hardly believe his good luck to have stumbled across Lord Bembridge's plans to form a coalition of provinces against the Xagada. This information was worth a fortune, and he had every intention of exploiting the opportunity.

The following day found Garth Hegel fidgeting and darting back and forth, getting into everyone's business;

patience was never his virtue. When he saw Olav Tyan emerge from his tent, he made a beeline over to him.

Without so much as a greeting, he began to ask questions. SNORT… "Me tell you Tobias Rycroft captured. What we do with little shit girl?" HARRUMPH…

SNORT… "Do as I order, or you regret." HARRUMPH…

SNORT… "Me obey, others restless. Want coin. HARRUMPH…

SNORT… "You earn coin. Make sure clan obeys. How I get message to Bembridge, with no capture?" HARRUMPH… The two sat around the morning campfire ruminating when an idea came to Olav Tyan, SNORT… "I need emissary!" HARRUMPH…

SNORT… "What emissary?" HARRUMPH…

SNORT… "Fuckin' knucklehead. Emissary is diplomatic messenger." HARRUMPH…

SNORT… "Not me, you think?" HARRUMPH…

SNORT… "Coward. Nothing happens to emissary. Treat you like fuckin royalty. Tell them this…" Olav Tyan shared his discovery with Garth Hegel, whose eyes grew wide with daydreams of riches. SNORT… "You set meeting. Me do rest." HARRUMPH…

Garth Hegel was beginning to like the plan. SNORT… "Easy. When me start?" HARRUMPH…

SNORT… "Now! Move fat ass. Take Frin Ivers as lieutenant. Tell him nothing." HARRUMPH…

SNORT … "No babysitter. Go alone." HARRUMPH…

SNORT … "You play part. You have lieutenant. Heed me: talk only to Bembridge." HARRUMPH…

When their minds are set on a task, orcs can be tenacious in achieving their objectives. Garth Hegel and Frin Ivers quickly set out and never once stopped to rest. Shortly after midday, they arrived at the outer gate to Bembridge Castle, just before the drawbridge. This is as far as they would get without an invitation to enter the castle's grounds, so Garth Hegel set about pleading his case before the guards on duty.

SNORT… "You, shit-for-brains, no understand. Me emissary. Have message for Bembridge. Take me or cost you big." HARRUMPH…

Ignoring his plea, the guards began to taunt Garth Hegel by exchanging disparaging remarks. "Emissary or not, orcs are butt ugly," said one of the guards.

"I don't know, he kind of looks like your wife," said the other.

"He looks nothing like my wife; perhaps my mother-in-law but not my wife." The two let out a big belly laugh when the Sergeant of the Guards came into view. From the look on his face, he was not amused.

"This is hardly the time for joking and laughter. If Lord Bembridge heard the two of you carrying on while the province is in mourning, he would have your tongues. Someone better explain what is happening here and be quick about it." The guards relayed the story to Sergeant Wickham. The Sergeant walked over to the gate and peered through the iron lattice, quietly sizing up the matter.

Sergeant Wickham finally broke his silence. "I understand you are Garth Hegel, Emissary to Lord Olav Tyan? And this, I presume, is your lieutenant?" Garth Hegel nodded.

"I've been told you have a message of grave importance for Lord Bembridge?" Garth Hegel nodded again.

"Wait here until I return." Garth Hegel nodded one last time.

When Sergeant Wickham returned, he was being led by another soldier; it was Captain Bolick, Chancellor Oswalt's personal bodyguard.

"Let him in," commanded Bolick. But, as Garth Hegel stepped through the gate, Bolick prevented him from going further. "Leave your lieutenant and your weapons behind with the guards," it was an order.

SNORT… "Lieutenant stays, orc never without weapon," Garth Hegel objected. HARRUMPH…

"Then turn around and be on your way." Bolick would not be dissuaded and started back over the drawbridge.

Garth Hegel knew that Olav Tyan would take his failure to obtain an audience with Lord Bembridge seriously.

SNORT… "Yes!" he shouted. Bolick stopped. Garth Hegel reluctantly gave up his sword. "No good way to treat emissary." HARRUMPH…

***

Garth Hegel was taken to the castle's Great Hall, a large open room decorated with victorious depictions on colorful tapestries; however, under dimly lit torches, the room had a sobering atmosphere. Before him stood a sullen-looking man; around his neck, he wore a gold medallion. At last, this must be Lord Bembridge, thought Garth Hegel. He was mistaken. Captain Bolick presented Chancellor Nigel Oswalt.

Another fuckin' roadblock. Garth Hegel was perturbed.

SNORT... "Tired of games. Me have message for Bembridge. Demand to see!" HARRUMPH...

Bolick didn't like Garth Hegel's tone and began to draw his sword, but Oswalt signaled him to stop.

"Of course, as a fellow Emissary, I know how frustrating it can be to get through all the official channels. However, these are special times. Are you aware that Lord Bembridge's wife was murdered just yesterday, and to make matters worse, the perpetrator escaped?" Unbeknownst to Garth Hegel, Oswalt was playing him.

SNORT..." Why me here." HARRUMPH... This response got Oswalt's immediate attention, but he remained calm, wanting to know what the orc had to say.

"Please forgive me. Where are my manners? You must be thirsty after your journey. Wine?" Oswalt pointed to a small table in the corner of the room, where he poured two goblets.

"To our respective masters' health." They clanked goblets, and Garth Hegel drained his cup, getting nearly as much on himself as down his throat.

"Under the circumstances, I am sure you will understand how important it is to verify your information before disturbing Lord Bembridge's mourning period. You would no doubt take the same precautions for Lord Olav Tyan." Oswalt treated Garth Hegel as an equal, trying to build a rapport.

Garth Hegel was beginning to feel comfortable in his new role of Emissary; this is how he should be treated – with respect.

SNORT… "Yes, me understand. Share with Lord Bembridge's confidant." HARRUMPH…

Oswalt bowed slightly, "You honor me. Pray, tell me this important news that you bear." The flattered Garth Hegel forgot Olav Tyan's warning to speak only to Lord Bembridge. He spilled forth the entire story, from helping Eleanor escape Bembridge Castle to finding the hidden documents within the ragdoll.

"Do you still have the child and the documents in your possession?" Garth Hegel nodded.

"Does anyone else know?"

SNORT… "Olav Tyan and me; not even my second. Lord Bembridge can have for price." HARRUMPH… Garth Hegel was clearly overstepping his authority.

"You were correct in coming," Oswalt said in soothing tones. "Let me go implore Lord Bembridge to see you at once." While Oswalt was gone, Garth Hegel helped himself to more wine. About fifteen minutes passed when Chancellor Oswalt stepped back into the Great Hall but stopped short to speak with Captain Bolick.

"Put the orc's head in a bag with this note and leave it with his lieutenant. The note read:

Olav Tyan,

Stick your offer, along with the emissary's head, up your ass. Effective immediately, all orcs found south of the Sawtooth Mountains shall be killed on sight.

Lord Bembridge

Of course, this note was nothing more than a forgery, for Chancellor Oswalt never delivered Garth Hegel's message to Lord Bembridge. However, Olav Tyan had no way of knowing this when Frin Ivers delivered the head of his lifelong friend to the campsite.

SNORT… "You pay dearly for this, you human swine!" HARRUMPH… Olav Tyan just sat there staring into Garth Hegel's blank eyes; then his next move came to him.

Even dead, you can still help me, although I may have to twist the truth a bit. Olav Tyan gathered everyone together.

SNORT… "I have news to share. You question why girl still here? You wonder about payment? Garth Hegel also asked many questions." HARRUMPH…

Olav Tyan jumped upon a log to stand prominently above the crowd. Taking Garth Hegel's rotting head from the bag, he held it high in the air.

SNORT… "I said, you greedy bastard. Stay out of my business. He did not. You also ask, you end up like my friend. Shut fuck up. You do as told." HARRUMPH…

No one dared to respond. Olav Tyan replaced Garth Hegel's head in the bag and continue.

SNORT… "Tobias Rycroft agreement no good." HARRUMPH… No faster way to get an orc perturbed than to cheat him out of what he thinks is his due, and now the disquieted group began to show signs of aggravation.

SNORT… "Hold tongues!" HARRUMPH…

Olav Tyan yelled above the ruckus.

SNORT… "No one cheats Olav Tyan Clan. I talk to Xantara of Xagada Nation, grandmother to little shit girl. While gone, you take prisoner to Berwo slave markets.

Xantara pay more, or brat sold as slave. You get paid." HARRUMPH…

The small band of orcs cheered and banged their weapons against shields as Olav Tyan stomped away to his tent for a somewhat restless night's sleep.

CHAPTER 12

RUNNING TRAPLINES

The trip from Albem Farm to Bembridge Castle is about a thirty- minute horseback ride over gently rolling hills. When viewed from the crest of the highest hill, Bembridge Castle is both inspiring and ominous. The citizens of Bembridge Province are known throughout Calvendar as specialists in masonry, and Bembridge Castle stands predominately as a testament to those skills...

(So writes Conrad Nightingale)

Built upon a collapsed volcano, high on a bluff overlooking the South Cove inlet to the Baracosa Sea,

Bembridge Castle was every bit a fortress, as a home to the Bembridge family for five generations. More than a hundred years ago, when battles between futile states were commonplace, Roderick Bembridge built this stronghold with material from the granite quarries of Movig. Each weighing more than a ton, large granite blocks were painstakingly moved and interlocked to form the forty-foot-high ramparts. The castle itself was a massive multi-room citadel with numerous areas from which to mount a defense.

However, before one could reach the castle, one must first maneuver the streets of Roderick, which were no wider than two oxcarts. Built like a maze, the roads had tight ninety-degree turns, some feeding back upon themselves, others leading to dead ends, making it nearly impossible to advance any war machines. Four towers were strategically placed within the city, giving skilled archers a protected and advantageous shooting platform. Even if a hostile force managed to breach the city's first line of defense (no small feat in and of itself) they would still need to march uphill, break through a massive iron gate, and make it across the drawbridge without falling to the castle's defenses.

Needless to say, the only way to gain access was by invitation or subterfuge.

***

Barely a week had passed since Eleanor's despicable acts of espionage and murder, and the morale throughout Bembridge Province was bleak. Nevertheless, Lord Bembridge wasted no time gathering his cabinet of ministers responsible for administrative policies throughout his domain. Although many thought he hadn't mourned the passing of Lady Bembridge long enough before getting back to business, they held their tongues, not wishing to give offense. A wise choice for Lord Bembridge was in no mood for his actions to be called into question.

Usually, the last to enter the High Council Chambers, Lord Bembridge was already seated when the ministers began to arrive. As a matter of formality, the chair to his immediate right was held for Chancellor Oswalt while the other ministers selected their seats randomly, each vying to get as close to the head of the table as possible as if their location somehow signified their worthiness.

However, today, there was a chair reserved to Lord Bembridge's immediate left, a symbol that didn't go unnoticed and would soon be revealed to those in attendance. Bembridge did not speak to the ministers as they found their seats, not so much as to acknowledge their condolences for his loss; the silence filled the chamber with a chilly atmosphere. Once fully assembled, the doors to the High Council Chamber were closed and audibly locked from outside.

Every member of the High Council was taken aback. Still, without uttering a word, Bembridge scanned the room, locking his gaze upon each council member in turn, looking for any sign that might give them away. Nothing out of the ordinary was apparent. His staff was either ignorantly unaware of any treason or well-trained in the art of deception. Finally, Lord Bembridge spoke.

"I want to announce the formation of a new ministry; it is the Ministry of Justice headed by High Marshal Johnathan Alcott."

Alcott stepped forward from an alcove where he was observing the council members and sat in the chair to the left of Lord Bembridge. Some of the High Council were notably unhappy with this sudden appointment, not only because they had no input in the decision but also because Alcott's role and responsibility were undefined, matters that Lord Bembridge intended to put to rest immediately. Never having any trouble mincing words, he cut right to the point.

"I can see from some of your expressions that you have concerns regarding this appointment, so allow me to alleviate those concerns. Foremost, I apologize if my past actions led you to believe you serve in a democracy. It was my Great Grandfather, four times removed, Roderick 'The Righteous.' who founded Bembridge Province, and it is mine **ALONE** to rule through the right of succession. If this is not abundantly clear, or there is any dissent, speak now."

Lord Bembridge only gave them a few seconds should they choose to object before continuing.

"Excellent."

Although meant for the entire group, the animosity between Nigel and Johnathan was well known, so Bembridge directed his following edict toward Chancellor Oswalt.

"As for Minister Alcott's role, none of you need to concern yourselves since he reports directly to me. As for his responsibilities, he is charged with bringing anyone who flaunts the law to justice. In performing his duties, it suffices to say he speaks for me on all civil matters, so challenge him at your peril."

That last sentence immediately ended any second-guessing or argument on the matter. Alcott looked toward Chancellor Oswalt, who was clearly irate but held his tongue for the time being.

"One more thing, I've asked Minister Alcott to learn how each of you conducts business on behalf of the House of Bembridge. I demand your complete cooperation. That is all for today. We shall reconvene the High Council tomorrow at noon."

Lord Bembridge called to the guard to unlock the door. All rose silently as Lord Bembridge, followed by Johnathan, exited the room. Once he was gone, they began to cackle like chickens.

Lord Bembridge's rebuke cut the High Council like a knife, and the mood was somber as the members filed out of the High Council Chamber. Edgar Addison, the Minister of Finance, was anxious to speak with Chancellor Oswalt, and as he rose from the table, he made a surreptitious gesture which Oswalt furtively acknowledged. As established in previous clandestine meetings, the two met at midnight at the abandoned ruins of Kinsley Tower.

In a bygone era when feudal wars were commonplace, Lord Kinsley was one of the first warlords to build his house, which was more of a single tower out of granite. Albeit strong, the tower stood isolated on a gentle slope in the piedmont. Although this site offered a commanding view, the countryside failed to provide any geographical barriers to adversaries. Consequently, Kinsley was one of the first houses to fall to machines of war. Catapults relentlessly bombarded the tower, causing the structure to collapse, thus relegating Lord Kinsley to little more than a historical footnote. Still, the tower's rubble provided a good hiding place to conduct covert meetings while ensuring no uninvited guest approached unseen.

"Addison, you're jumping around like a cat walking on hot coals. You wanted to talk, so stop pacing, sit, and speak to me, or I'm going home to my warm bed."

"Just because you have ice water running through your veins doesn't mean we can all behave so calmly in the face of this pending disaster."

"Disaster. That's a bit melodramatic, don't you think?"

"You heard what Lord Bembridge said; it couldn't have been clearer. Our new Minister of Justice speaks with the Lord's authority, so challenge his investigations at your own risk. With all the skeletons in your closet, I think you would be more nervous than most. It's no secret how Alcott feels about you."

"I've been sparring with Alcott since my early days as Chancellor. He is like a splinter — more of an irritation than an injury. His recent appointment as Minister of Justice is nothing more than a minor inconvenience."

"If he discovers that we've been embezzling money from Lord Bembridge's coffers, it will be significantly more than an inconvenience." As the Minister of Finance, Addison had used his position to unfairly tax the masses and then skim monies from the collection before totaling the accounts. As yearly accounts fell short, he raised the tax base with Lord Bembridge's consent only to skim more off the top. Over the years, he had become one of the wealthiest people in Bembridge Province, intending to retire in the level of luxury to which he had grown accustomed. Nigel Oswalt had discovered Addison's scheme early in its inception and promised to keep this transgression quiet for a percentage of the take.

"And just how will he come by this information? Neither you nor I will tell him, and no documentation can be traced back to us." Even in this dark hideaway, Oswalt saw the blood drain from Addison's face and knew at once the dumb son-of-bitch had been keeping a secret ledger of their inappropriate dealings.

"What do you propose we do?" asked the befuddled Minister.

"I propose you take your beautiful wife and child for a respite at your countryside estate in Edgewater. While there, take charge of your concerns and recompose yourself before returning to Roderick."

"And what of tomorrow's Council Meeting? Won't such an action draw unnecessary attention?"

"I will explain to His Lordship that we spoke, and considering the recent death of Lady Bembridge, followed shortly after that by unforeseen administrative changes, is causing you distress. I'll tell him I suggested a brief furlough to compose yourself.

"Won't that make me look weak and unable to perform my duties?"

"You are weak, Addison. Now, do as I tell you. I'm going home to bed."

Shortly before the High Council met again, Chancellor Oswalt mentioned Minister Addison's absence to Lord Bembridge, taking responsibility for his leave. Under the circumstance, he thought Lord Bembridge would acquiesce, but he was wrong."

"Perhaps you missed the part of yesterday's discussion where I reaffirmed my sole right to govern over Bembridge Province?" Oswalt stood mute. "Because of your service to date, I will allow this one indiscretion, but if it happens again, you will not like the outcome. Am I perfectly clear his time?" Oswalt shook his head, yes. "Then repeat to me what I am saying to you. I want to be sure you understand."

" As Chancellor, my duty is only to advise. I do not speak for Your Excellency."

"Exactly. Go, convene the Council. I will be there presently." Once Oswalt departed, Lord Bembridge called Alcott to his chambers and conveyed his conversation with the Chancellor.

"I don't like it," responded Marshal Alcott. "It's a flimsy excuse to be absent, considering everything that has happened. I believe Addison is taking advantage of your grief, having lost Lady Bembridge so recently."

"I agree. Let's play this hand and see where it takes us."

***

The High Council met as scheduled, and the Minister of Finance's absence was conspicuous to the other Council Members. Of course, Lord Bembridge had previously been advised by Chancellor Oswalt, but this was a teaching moment.

"Does anyone know the whereabouts of Minister Addison? Anyone?" Bembridge looked over to Alcott.

"Minister Alcott, find Minister Addison, arrest him, and bring him to Bembridge Castle for questioning." Alcott nodded his acknowledgment and left the room.

Everyone, except Chancellor Oswalt, was stunned. Addison was about to become Oswalt's sacrificial lamb and perfect decoy. Lord Bembridge continued.

"On to a more pressing matter – the Xagada. We have spoken about this blight on humanity for several years, and while we talked and talked, the Xagada have grown bolder with each passing day. The time when a loosely banded group of nomads committed petty misdemeanors against the weakest of us has been replaced by well-executed acts of organized crime, resulting in the loss of life and property.

"However, even these sporadic acts of violence don't seem to appease the Xagada's insatiable appetite for power. They are intent on destroying me. I'm speaking, of course, of the murder of Lady Bembridge.

"With all due respect, my Lord," interjected Chancellor Oswalt. "I fail to see the connection between the loss of our Lady and the Xagada. Was this not simply the act of a deranged child?"

"There was nothing simple about this egregious act, Chancellor. Do you seriously believe that a deranged child went on a killing spree within the castle with no intended purpose? If so, how did she come by the Xagada dagger, and why did she leave it behind in Amanda's body to be found?

"Lastly, how do you explain her ransacking my office and absconding with confidential documents regarding the pending Preservation Coalition? No, I contend that none of these acts were the actions of a deranged twelve-year-old. The child is not deranged at all. The meticulous manner in which she murdered all her victims, all dying before they could react, indicates a highly skilled assassin, albeit a young one.

"As for the Xagada dagger left behind — it is a clear message that no one is safe, not even in the inner sanctuary of Bembridge House."

The Council Room was quiet. The argument presented by Lord Bembridge was compelling, even though its conclusion was hard to speak — "The Xagada have already struck the first blows of war."

"What shall we do, my Lord?" asked Oswalt.

"We reach out to the other provinces; we compare our losses and concerns and then make plans to eliminate the Xagada together."

"I will assemble the Heads of State at once!"

"No, Chancellor Oswalt, I will take charge of the invitations personally. You are to ensure that the meeting comes off without any impediments."

***

Lord Bembridge wrote the invitations to each Head of State based on his knowledge of their characters and cultural protocols. While remaining as cordial as possible, he wanted no misunderstanding regarding the critical nature of this meeting and how their failure to attend would be perceived. Regarding the subject at hand, there would be no dialogue through emissaries.

Once the invitations were dispatched, he could only hope he had not inadvertently offended anyone.

CHAPTER 13

LATE NIGHT VISITORS

Minister Alcott accompanied by several deputies, arrived at Edgar Addison's countryside estate shortly before the dinner hour. A servant led them into the parlor, wherein Lady Addison and young Master Colton Addison entertained themselves…

(So writes Conrad Nightingale)

"Lady Addison, allow me to introduce myself; I am the Minister of Justice, Johnathan Alcott. Please forgive me for this intrusion, but I must speak to Minister Addison immediately."

"It is a pleasure to make your acquaintance, Minister Alcott. My husband has told me about your recent appointment to the High Council. Please accept my congratulations." Alcott smiled and bowed slightly.

"I thank you, but again, I must see your husband on a grave matter. Can you advise him that I await an audience?"

"Of course, he has been in his study upstairs all day. As a matter of practice, Colton and I do not disturb him when the door is closed, but I'm certain he will happily receive you. Please follow me." Lady Addison led Minister Alcott and his men upstairs to a door at the end of the hallway; she tapped lightly, calling his name,

"Edgar, my dear, you have a guest." There was no response. Alcott gently moved Lady Addison to one side as he signaled his deputies to enter the room. With swords drawn, they opened the door but were met with no resistance. From an overhead rafter hung the body of Minister Edgar Addison. Lady Addison swooned.

Once downstairs, Lady Addison and Master Colton were left with a deputy to watch over them. Alcott and the other deputies returned upstairs to investigate. Inside the study, they discovered a ledger book showing the misappropriation of funds over the past several years. It was incriminating evidence on its face, but little did they know then that it was not in Addison's writing. It was more what they did not find that was curious; there was no written admission of guilt – no suicide note – and no parting word left to his wife and child.

All too convenient, Alcott thought.

After securing the ledger, Alcott had Addison's body lowered to the floor. Upon closer examination, Alcott noted skin and hair under Addison's fingernails, which he undoubtedly obtained while defending himself.

When Lady Addison regained her composure, Alcott set about gently questioning her.

"Lady Addison, has your husband received any other guest in the past day?"

"Only you and your men," she responded under her tears.

"I saw…" The boy's words were broken off mid-sentence.

"You saw what, boy?" asked Alcott.

"I saw a man visiting my father late last night. They were arguing and woke me up when they entered my father's study."

"Do you know who this man was?"

Colton shook his head no.

"Have you ever seen the man before?"

Again, Colton shook his head no.

"Can you describe the man?"

"I've said too much already. Please stop asking me questions."

Lady Addison hugged her child close. "It's all right, Colton. You're not in any trouble; tell me what you remember."

"He was tall and mean-looking, dressed all in black. He wore a white scarf held by a golden broach with a large green stone."

That was all the description Alcott needed.

HATCHING A PLAN

The news of Minister Addison's suicide shocked every member serving on the High Council, except of course, for the traitor himself. Minister Alcott previously informed Lord Bembridge that his investigation of Addison's study concluded that the suicide was a staged murder; this information they kept to themselves, hoping the traitor would drop his guard after the announcement. Any person who advances their goals by betraying those who have misplaced their trust is genuinely loathsome, and it was time to bring this despicable degenerate into the light…

(So writes Conrad Nightingale)

Despite their separate stations in life, Johnathan and Walter had been close since childhood, yet over the past week, they became inseparable. Nearly every minute from early morning until late evening, they could be seen strolling throughout the castle and its grounds in deep deliberation, heads held close, their conversations but a whisper. Considering that within days of one another, each had lost their wife in a most heinous manner, it seemed only natural that two old friends would be drawn together to commiserate and mourn. However, one member of the High

Council, Chancellor Nigel Oswalt, was growing evermore suspicious that there may be an ulterior motive.

"John, the other day, as we rode back to Bembridge Castle, we agreed that Eleanor could not have managed to carry out her egregious acts and vanished without the help of someone on the High Council. Are you still of this belief?" asked Lord Bembridge.

"I am," came the short reply.

"Have you come up with any ideas?"

"Initially, I thought that magic might be involved. However, a druid friend assures me that the act of invisibility is an incredible feat of power even for the most learned scholar of the magical arts."

"Then it goes without saying that the traitor has some special knowledge of the castle and its grounds that no one else possesses.

"How can that be?"

"Perhaps our scholar, Hayden Radcliff, can shed some light on the matter. I think a visit to the Hall of Records is overdue. Care to join me?"

***

Lord Bembridge and Minister Alcott, accompanied by two guards, went directly to the Hall of Records in the tower adjacent to the High Council Room. The tower served as a repository of official records and a library nearly equal to that at the Druid Keep of Thorsten. Upon entering, a young scribe rose and bowed, "Lord Bembridge, how may I be of assistance?"

"I wish to speak with Minister Radcliff. Where may I find him?"

"I will retrieve him at once, my Lord." The scribe darted back into the vaults, returning shortly with Minister Radcliff, huffing and puffing.

"My Lord, to what do I owe this unexpected pleasure?" gasped Radcliff, trying to catch his breath.

"Johnathan and I would like to speak with you." Then, he turned to the scribe. "You are to remain at your desk, young man; we may also need to speak to you. Sergeant Womack and Corporal Hawkins stand guard outside the door. Short of an emergency, we are not to be disturbed. Understood?"

Sergeant Womack affirmed the order and closed the door behind them. Lord Bembridge turned back toward Minister Radcliff.

"I presume we four are alone; no one else working back in the vaults?" Radcliff confirmed the assumption with a rapid headshake.

"Good. Perhaps we will be more comfortable speaking in your office?"

"Of course, please follow me, gentlemen." Radcliff led the two to his office and offered Lord Bembridge the oversized down-stuffed leather chair behind his desk while he and Alcott sat on wooden stools. Minister Radcliff looked perplexed but said nothing. No one spoke, and Lord Bembridge stared blankly for what seemed an eternity. Finally, the silence was broken.

"Most people would find your job tedious, but I disagree. You are in a unique, somewhat enviable position, Minister Radcliff. You are entrusted with chronicling and maintaining all we are as a civilization. It is a great responsibility."

"One that I do not take lightly, my Lord, this I assure you."

"No assurance necessary, Hayden. You have served my father and me with the greatest integrity, and you have my complete trust, which is why I know you will keep this conversation strictly confidential."

Radcliff nodded, "Yes, of course, you can rely upon my discretion."

"Unfortunately, some serve the House of Bembridge for their own interest. We have at least one traitor amongst our inner circle." Upon hearing the words, the expression on Radcliff's face was one of genuine shock, exactly the expression Bembridge and Alcott hoped to see, for it confirmed his innocence.

"Can you share with me who it is?"

"I'm afraid we don't know, which is why we have come to you for help."

"I will do anything for Bembridge House; you need only to ask."

"Then, tell us, Hayden, does the Hall of Records contain any documents regarding the design and construction of Bembridge Castle? If they exist, the documents would be over 100 years old. Perhaps you could do some research?"

"No research is necessary, my Lord; such documents do exist and, of late, are the subject of great interest to Chancellor Oswalt. Young Gilmore has been assisting the Chancellor."

"Is Gilmore the scribe sitting outside?" asked Alcott. Radcliff responded with a head nod. "Please ask him to join us." Minister Radcliff shuffled to the door and motioned Gilmore to come in.

When he entered, Alcott gave up his stool and stood towering over the young man, who was now more nervous than ever.

Lord Bembridge immediately started the interrogation.

"Gilmore, Minister Radcliff tells us that you have been assisting Chancellor Oswalt with some research regarding the design and construction of Bembridge Castle. Is this true?"

"Yes, my Lord."

"When did his interest in Bembridge Castle start?"

"Perhaps a couple of months ago."

"Did you and Chancellor Oswalt find anything interesting?"

"I only pulled the documents for Chancellor Oswalt's review. I never looked closely at the documents."

"Did Chancellor Oswalt ever have any questions?" interrogated Alcott. Gilmore rolled his eyes back, trying to recall any discussion with Oswalt.

"Yes, once he asked if I could read a note on a drawing of the Royal Gardens; however, I was unfamiliar with the language, so I suggested he ask Minister Radcliff."

"Is this true, Hayden?" asked Lord Bembridge. He seemed excited about the prospect.

"Yes, it is coming back to me now, my Lord. I'm sorry for not recalling earlier; my mind is not what it was when I was younger."

"That's okay. Remember anything you can, for it can be of great help."

"I remember the language was an ancient dialect. I had to use several books to decipher the note." Minister Radcliff jumped up and came around his desk.

"Excuse me, my Lord." Bembridge pushed back from the desk as Radcliff rifled through the drawer. As he was doing so, Minister Alcott asked Gilmore to retrieve the drawing in question.

"Oh, I also remember that Chancellor Oswalt was interested in the wing of the castle where he resides. Shall I bring those drawings as well?"

"Most definitely," replied Alcott. "Thank you, Gilmore. The boy smiled and ran off to the archives.

"Here is the translation, my Lord. It reads – North, East, South, West, the hextar watches for that which cannot be seen."

"It's simply the Bembridge House coat of arms and motto?" injected Alcott.

"Not quite, John, the Bembridge family motto reads – North, East, South, West, the hextar watches."

Marshal Alcott expresses skepticism, "The hextar watches, or the hextar watches for that which cannot be seen, could simply come down to a translation error."

"I don't make translation errors, Minister Alcott," proclaimed Minister Radcliff.

"I didn't intend to impugn your capabilities; however, is it possible the translation could have more than one meaning?"

"I suppose anything is possible, although highly unlikely."

"Gentlemen, let there be no squabbles amongst us, for we all seek the truth. Let's see if the drawings can shed light on the matter."

Gilmore entered the room with the documents in question; he spread them out on the desk. The four huddled over the two drawings and immediately noticed the Family Crest with the same note in an ancient dialect on both drawings: one within the maze located on the garden wall, one located on the mantel of the bookcase in Lord Bembridge's study; and one on the bookcase of Chancellor Oswalt's private quarters.

"These locations are very specific and warrant further investigation. Minister Radcliff, the Hall of Records is temporarily closed, let's say, for cataloging purposes. You and Gilmore shall remain inside, searching for similar notes on other drawings.

I cannot post guards without inviting undue suspicion; therefore, keep the doors locked for your safety.

CHAPTER 14

STRIKING A BARGAIN

Olav Tyan was up and on his way to Thammarat while the other orcs in his small clan were still hunkered down in their bedrolls. Before long, a marmalade sunrise cracked open the black night, forcing even the laziest orc to get up and begin his day. After breakfast, the group started for the slave market in Berwo, just as Olav Tyan had ordered. Whether they were compelled by fear of Olav Tyan or driven by insatiable greed, they were doing exactly as told...

(So writes Conrad Nightingale)

Eleanor had been given a few scraps to eat and water to wash down the meager meal, but that's where the courtesy stopped, after all, she was nothing more than a slave in transport. The beloved granddaughter of Kayla Rycroft was being led around like a dog on a leash to keep her from running free. The rough fibers of the rope rubbed her neck raw; it was a humiliating act, and almost more than Eleanor could bear.

The orcs slogged along on open ground for hours, finally stopping at noon for a short respite and lunch. While Eleanor patiently waited for leftovers, a strange thing happened: an old man calmly walked into the camp. The orcs had been caught entirely off guard and, grabbing their weapons, jumped to their feet.

How had this senior citizen managed to approach the group unseen?

"Hello, in the camp!" were the only words he managed to get out before being surrounded by hostiles.

SNORT… "Don't kill!" yelled Finn Morin. "Bind him; me have questions." HARRUMPH… Once bound, the interrogation began, but the old man didn't appear distressed by the ordeal and remained composed.

An overly excited Finn Morin let forth a barrage of questions. SNORT… "Who you? HARRUMPH… SNORT… Where come from? HARRUMPH… SNORT… You alone? HARRUMPH…

"Slow down and catch your breath. I'll happily answer all your questions. As for who I am, my name is Vennick. I come from the Isle of Sask across the Baracosa Sea. I travel alone to speak to this young girl, and most importantly, I mean you no harm if you cooperate." Finn Morin lashed out and slapped Vennick hard across the face. Eleanor immediately winced, recalling the smack Olav Tyan gave her, but it appeared to have no effect on Vennick.

"Was that necessary?" Vennick stared directly into Finn Morin's beady yellow eyes, who was completely taken aback but didn't want to appear weak in front of the others.

SNORT… "Dumb-ass old man. Stumbled into camp." HARRUMPH…

SNORT… "You bring two sovereigns at the slave market. Don't die on way there." HARRUMPH… Finn Morin let out a belly laugh as he returned to the others.

Vennick and Eleanor sat staring at one another for at least a minute before Vennick finally spoke.

"Two sovereigns - that's only the cost of two tankards of ale. I'm insulted. What do you think?"

"I agree with Finn Morin; you're a dumb-ass," responded Eleanor.

"Not the politest of responses, but I suppose it could appear that way under these circumstances. Nevertheless, I've come to save you from a miserable life of slavery in exchange for a future of unlimited possibilities as my apprentice."

"That sounds wonderful except for one small thing…" Eleanor stared toward Vennick's restraints and snickered.

"No need for sarcasm or skepticism." Instantly, both Vennick's and Eleanor's bonds vanished. "Are you ready to go?"

"Wait!" Eleanor didn't act the least bit astounded, as though she had witnessed such magic daily. Nevertheless, she was hesitating, and Vennick knew she wanted something more.

"Say the words."

Eleanor raised her voice so all the orcs could hear, "Kill one another!"

Immediately, a fight to the death broke out between the orcs. It was over in minutes until one lone wounded orc stood before Vennick.

"Well, finish the job," Vennick ordered. Finn Morin fell upon his sword. Turning back toward Eleanor, Vennick acted as though nothing out of the ordinary had happened. "I knew you were the one. Are you ready now?" Eleanor smiled and nodded her head.

The two vanished instantly, without a trace.

A LESSON IN OBEDIENCE

Eleanor awoke from a deep slumber and was immediately assailed by the unusual sights, sounds, and smells of her new home. She pushed aside the silk sheet and rose to her feet. Donning the robe at the foot of her bed, she strolled over to the open window and inhaled deeply. Looking down and out across the jungle canopy, she could barely distinguish the Baracosa Sea on the distant horizon. So beautiful, so peaceful, she thought to herself, and then she remembered Vennick's warning . . .

(So writes Conrad Nightingale)

"You're not in Calvendar anymore; this is the Isle of Sask. In Sask, there are many creatures, both big and small, that fly in the sky, roam on land, and swim in the waters that would love to make a meal of you; others will harm you simply because they can. So, don't go outside the house unless I am with you."

"I thought I was to be your apprentice, not your prisoner."

"Be patient. The time will come when you go where you want, when you want, and all will fear you. However, for the time being, **HEED** my warning," Vennick said.

Bullshit! she thought. *Fear-mongering is just another means of manipulation. Besides, how bad would it be if I stayed close to the house?* Eleanor slipped out through the window to avoid any contact with Vennick.

The grass was soft and lush against her bare feet like a pillow. At first, it felt refreshing, but then came the stinging. Fire ants were quickly making their way up her legs. She brushed them from her skin and ran into the jungle to escape. When she looked back, it appeared as if the ground itself was moving toward her. Deeper and deeper into the jungle, she ran, not stopping until she had placed enough distance between her and the pursuing insects.

"*Crux*!" The numerous bites burned her skin like hot coals. But Eleanor knew she had a bigger problem. How would she get back into the house undetected when those little biting bastards were guarding it?

There was little time to formulate a plan when Eleanor heard crashing brush, and the sound was getting closer. Something big was approaching her quickly, and she was directly in its path. Lost and scared, she had no choice, "Vennick! Help, Vennick!"

"Vennick! Help, Vennick!" came a mocking reply. "Do you think he can hear you this far from the house? Even if he can, do you think he can get here in time to save you?"

Eleanor turned in the direction of the voice. The beast loomed over her, and it was horrifying. Before her stood Lyndrick the Annihilator, the legendary red dragon, in all her magnificent glory. Fifteen feet in length, nine feet high at the shoulders, her spiked muscular body covered in thick scales the envy of any manmade armor. Her leather wings remained folded, making the span impossible to estimate.

Then there was the matter of her personal arsenal: ten-inch claws on both her front and hind legs, strong enough to tear stone asunder; multiple rows of sharp teeth capable of crushing bone into dust; and a fire that stoked deep within her maw hot enough to melt the air. For all that, the most terrifying aspect of this creature was its eyes. Eyes that could hold you in their gaze while staring into your very soul.

"Dragons are real?" asked the bewildered girl out loud.

"Unfortunately for you," responded Lyndrick.

"How are we communicating? Are you reading my mind? Curiosity was getting the best of Eleanor, even in this precarious moment.

"You have a knack for stating the obvious. Besides, it is much more refined than listening to that hideous screeching you humans call a voice.

"So, what do you normally sound like, may I ask?"

Suddenly, Lyndrick let out a growl that sounded like thunder bursting directly overhead. The hot wind from her roar blew back Eleanor's hair, and her body was drenched in dragon drool.

"Oh, crux! I suppose you're going to eat me now."

"Covered in all that slobber? No way." Lyndrick began to snicker, and Eleanor couldn't help but to join in. Soon, the two were laughing like old friends, sharing a joke.

***

"What did I miss?" It was Vennick.

"Not much. I was just deciding whether to eat the girl."

"I wouldn't like that."

"Maybe I don't care what you like."

"Maybe you better start caring."

"Or what?"

Vennick was tired of sparring with Lyndrick. "I see I'm going to have to discipline you. Harshly." The sky quickly took on an ominous green glow.

"Settle down, old man. I was just kidding." Looking toward Eleanor, she said, "The old fart can't take a joke." The two began to laugh again.

"This is no laughing matter," Vennick scolded Eleanor. "I demand complete obedience if you are to be my apprentice. Is that PERFECTLY clear?"

"Yes."

"Not good enough. Get on your knees and swear your fidelity to me, or I shall leave you here to your demise."

Eleanor lowered herself to the ground. "I swear."

But that still wasn't good enough for Vennick. With a wave of his hand, Eleanor's brain began to swell. The pain was excruciating.

"Stop!" yelled Lyndrick. You're killing her." The dragon wrapped its wings like a shield around the girl.

Vennick regained his composure. Nevertheless, Lyndrick gave him an icy glare. The two just stood there staring at one another.

Eleanor needed to break the tension quickly before it was too late. "Does anyone mind if we head back to the house? I need to get cleaned up." Eleanor did look quite the sight.

"Excellent idea. Vennick turned away and headed down the path while Eleanor stayed a moment longer with Lyndrick.

"Thanks for sticking up for me," Eleanor whispered to Lyndrick.

"Well, you're beginning to grow on me."

"I like you too. You remind me of my grandmother."

"Oh, crux! Lyndrick launched herself into the air, spreading her wings, and flew off without another word.

Catching up to Vennick, *that was an interesting first day,* she thought.

"You can say that again," responded Vennick.

"Don't tell me that you also read minds?"

"Who do you think taught the dragons?"

***

Once home, safe and sound, Eleanor proclaimed that she liked Lyndrick. "Do you think she likes me? she asked Vennick.

"I can say with certainty she does."

"How do you know?"

"Because if she didn't, even under threat by me, she would have killed you.

IFYOU WANT THINGS DONE RIGHT

Olav was already a sweltering day as people went about their affairs. Nomads by nature, Thammarat is the Xagada's only permanent settlement. Although not an everyday occurrence, it was not unusual to occasionally see small bands of orcs within the town, for the transient Xagada and orcs have had a tenuous but mutually beneficial business relationship for many years. However, with the recent assassination of Lady Amanda Bembridge and the disappearance of their own Eleanor Rycroft, these were worrisome times, and everyone was on edge. The heightened sense of nervousness was only exasperated when Olav Tyan started questioning people on the street as to how he could gain an audience with the tribe's Xantara. People would mutter something indistinguishable and turn away, but it wasn't long before a large, rough-looking character blocked Olav Tyan's way...

(So writes Conrad Nightingale)

"I understand that you're looking for Kayla Rycroft."

SNORT... "Yes. Where me find her?" grunted Olav Tyan. HARRUMPH...

Two other hard-looking thugs joined the man; one of them spoke. "What do you mean by find? She's not lost, but you are by the look of things. What's your business with the Xantara?"

SNORT…" Granddaughter. Tell her if you want to keep your balls." Olav Tyan dissolved into laughter, imagining these three thugs as eunuchs. HARRUMPH…

SNORT… "I leave tomorrow." HARRUMPH…

Olav Tyan was finished talking and proceeded into the Boar's Head Tavern. Sitting at the bar, he threw back a long drink of ale, no longer paying attention to the thugs standing confounded outside on the street.

***

The three returned to the tavern early the following day, their faces badly bruised from an apparent beating and their demeanors much more contrite. They found Olav Tyan just where they had left him, slumped over the bar, sleeping off a hangover; they nudged him awake. "The Xantara extends an invitation to meet at your earliest convenience; we will escort you when you're ready."

Olav Tyan slowly lifted his head as drool ran down his chin. He coughed a couple of times, then spoke.

SNORT… "Ready now. We go!" HARRUMPH…

Olav Tyan was led to a sizeable timbered house in the town center. Besides its size, there was nothing to distinguish this building from the other surrounding wooden structures, but once inside, it was a different story. Paintings adorned the walls, cut flowers in silver vases sat atop intricately carved tables, and the furniture was padded with thick cushions; even the plank floors were polished and covered with colorful rugs.

As an additional comfort, oil-burning lamps were strategically placed throughout the dark wooden house to chase away shadows.

This was the home of a rich and powerful person. In a room adjacent to the long hallway came a feeble voice.

"Please come join me, Olav Tyan." Olav Tyan followed the voice and turned into a large room to find Kayla Rycroft, Xantara of the Xagada Nation, sitting on an ornate wooden throne. She was old and hunched over; her weathered face had the look of tanned leather, but bright blue eyes beneath a shock of white hair bellied any frailty.

Olav Tyan was taken aback when he noticed Blox Nye, the Supreme Commander of the Orc Clans, sitting at the Xantara's right hand on a smaller but equally ornate chair. Seeing the two sitting together had a profound effect on him.

"Welcome to my home, Olav Tyan. I believe you are already acquainted with the Supreme Commander?" Over the past decade, Olav Tyan has had several encounters with the notorious Blox Nye, none of them pleasant, for Blox Nye is ruthless when he wants something, and those who oppose him do so at their peril.

"I've asked Blox Nye to join us in our conversation since he has a stake in the matter. I trust you don't mind?" Kayla Rycroft said. Blox Nye gave Olav Tyan an icy stare.

SNORT… Olav Tyan, ya sneaky, cock suckin', worthless piece of pig shit," declared Blox Nye.

Olav Tyan felt himself go flush, and it wasn't from the previous night's binge. Then Olav Tyan returned Blox Nye's insult with a sheepish grin and turned to the Xantara, attempting to take charge of the conversation.

SNORT… "We speak alone, private matter that concerns granddaughter." HARRUMPH…

"You speak my language well enough for an orc, Olav Tyan, but I think you have a slippery tongue. My friendship with Blox Nye goes back many years, so I value his council when it comes to matters with orcs. Besides, if you truly have information regarding my granddaughter, you may have inadvertently stumbled into one of Blox Nye's and my latest endeavors."

Olav Tyan was taking a chance speaking back boldly, but insatiable greed got the best of him.

SNORT… "Mean no disrespect, Xantara. Tobias Rycroft and I have agreement. HARRUMPH… SNORT… "Get girl out of Bembridge Castle and bring her to him." HARRUMPH…

SNORT… "You want granddaughter no harm; you cover Rycroft's debt, with interest." HARRUMPH…

"I see," Kayla said. "What is the amount that shithole agreed to pay, and what exactly will it take to bring this matter to its conclusion? Pray, speak the truth, for I have ways of discovering those who wish to deceive me?"

Olav Tyan caught the fish but didn't want it to shake free of the hook before landing it.

SNORT… "Hundred gold pieces—you pay one hundred fifty for trouble. All is good." HARRUMPH…

"One hundred and fifty pieces of gold. That's three times our bargained price," came a voice from behind Olav Tyan.

Olav Tyan turned just in time to see Tobias Rycroft lumber into the room. Caught in a lie, it was all Olav Tyan could do not to wet himself.

"Well, Blox Nye, you can add 'cheat' to your list of characteristics describing Olav Tyan. You disappoint me, Olav Tyan. I warned you to choose your words wisely."

SNORT… "Let me rid you of this shit-for-brains." HARRUMPH… interjected Blox Nye.

Kayla Rycroft held up her hand, signaling for silence. "Where is my granddaughter now?"

Olav Tyan hesitated but thought better of lying any further. SNORT… "On way to Berow slave market." HARRUMPH…

The Xantara's body reacted involuntarily as she dug her nails into the arms of her throne at the thought of her granddaughter being sold into slavery; it didn't go unnoticed by any of the attendees.

"Tell me, Olav Tyan, what is your life worth?" she asked through a clenched jaw.

Olav Tyan understood that if he answered anywhere near the fifty pieces of gold that he originally bargained with Tobias Rycroft, the Xantara would take it as an affront to the worth of her granddaughter. SNORT… "Ten gold pieces," he responded timidly. HARRUMPH…

"Fair enough, you shall return my granddaughter, unharmed, plus forty gold pieces, and I will let you live. However, should you fail to do as I order, I shall turn you over to Blox Nye for his pleasure." Then, turning her gaze upon Tobias, she continued.

"Go with this pig that walks on its hind legs and see that Ellie comes home safely." Olav Tyan's future had been sealed; the discussion was over.

***

Two horses were saddled and waiting outside the grand house as Olav Tyan approached.

"Mount up and ride like your life depends on it, for it does," said Rycroft.

Off they galloped, and within a few hours, they came upon the sight of a recent skirmish. They both dismounted and looked around in disbelief. Olav Tyan's small clan of orcs lay bloodied and strewed about the ground; Finn Morin was leaning forward on his blade, but there was no sign of the child and no footprints leading away in any direction. It was as though Eleanor had vanished. Rycroft couldn't contain himself any longer and drew forth his sword.

SNORT… "Wait! yelled Olav Tyan. Something else – important!" HARRUMPH…

"No more of your lies, orc."

SNORT… "Papers! – Important papers!" HARRUMPH…

Rycroft immediately realized Olav Tyan had the documents Eleanor smuggled out of Bembridge Castle.

"Where are these important papers?" he asked.

SNORT… "Set free, I will tell you." HARRUMPH…

Rycroft couldn't take the chance. "Lie to me again, and there's nowhere in Calvendar you will be safe." Olav Tyan knew that Rycroft would make good on his threat, so a new bargain was struck; Rycroft would get the documents, and Olav Tyan would go free.

***

That afternoon, Tobias Rycroft returned to Thammarat without Eleanor but nonetheless with something of value—Lord Bembridge's plans to form a secret coalition to eliminate the Xagada Nation. Although the Xantara understood Rycroft's motive, she could not be consoled, for her granddaughter appeared lost.

Scared for his life, Rycroft swore to the Xantara to never stop looking for Ellie until she was home with her people.

CHAPTER 15

DAY TERRORS AND NIGHTMARES

Dusk was waning when Oswalt noticed through the heavy paned glass of his chamber window that Lord Bembridge was sitting alone in the Royal Garden. Alone at last, he thought to himself. The time is right to see if you can figure out what Bembridge and Alcott are up to. Oswalt burst through his chamber door and scurried down the staircase; he didn't want to miss his chance at getting Lord Bembridge alone, but just as he approached the doors to the Royal Garden, Captain Fleming showed up from another direction. In their haste, they nearly knocked one another down…

(So writes Conrad Nightingale)

"Hold fast, Captain!" ordered Chancellor Oswalt. "I must speak with Lord Bembridge – alone."

"You can talk to him all you want once I deliver my message," came the curt reply. Captain Fleming was still angry about the way he had been treated by Oswalt earlier in the week.

"I know these are troubling times, Captain, but how dare you use that tone with me. You'll be lucky if I don't have your commission. Just give me the message and be on your way before you regret this meeting."

"To tell you the truth, Chancellor, I always regret our meetings. However, this time, my orders come straight from Lord Bembridge, and regarding this matter, I speak only to him or Minister Alcott. Now, allow me to pass, or I will remove you by force."

Captain Fleming fingered the hilt of his saber to emphasize the point; Chancellor Oswalt was perturbed but prudently responded with a slight bow and gestured Fleming toward the garden.

As Captain Fleming approached, Lord Bembridge rose to greet him. Both intentionally turned their backs to Oswalt, and he could not hear them speak from this distance. Nevertheless, it was evident from their respective gestures that something important was happening. Lord Bembridge clasped his hands on Fleming's shoulders; it was nearly an embrace. Then, as he departed, he turned back and ordered Captain Fleming to find Minister Alcott and bring him immediately to his private chambers.

When he reached the garden doors, Chancellor Oswalt spoke up. "Lord Bembridge, you appear flustered. Is there anything I can do to help?"

"Everything is fine, Nigel, in fact, better than fine. We are about to get answers to all our questions – Eleanor Rycroft's hiding place has been found. I expect Minister Alcott shortly; see to it that we are not disturbed." Lord Bembridge never broke stride as he rushed past Oswalt and headed directly for his chambers.

Oswalt's heart pounded as he returned to his room. *I must get to the girl before all is lost, but where do I look?*

When he heard footsteps echoing down the hallway, he poked his head through the door and saw Minister Alcott and Captain Fleming in lock stride. Lord Bembridge's guards stood at attention, allowing the two to pass unchallenged. Once they had reached the door, Captain Fleming gave orders that nobody was to enter, and as the two disappeared inside, the clang of a deadbolt locking in place was heard.

It was now or never. Chancellor Oswalt bolted his door and rushed across the room to the carving of a hextar on the bookcase. After a few furtive movements, his bookcase slid open, revealing a secret passageway between his room and Lord Bembridge's private study. Hopefully, he would find Bembridge, Alcott, and Fleming discussing their plans to capture Eleanor Rycroft. Through strategically placed hidden holes in the wall, Oswalt could see and hear the discussions without anyone being the wiser.

"Do your men understand their orders, Captain?" asked Lord Bembridge.

"They will not fail you, my Lord."

"*Fail you at what?*" wondered Oswalt. Then, the answer came – Oswalt heard a battering ram break his chamber door loose from its hinges. He rushed back down the passage only to find the bookcase pushed back into place. A secret no more, he was trapped within the passageway.

Preoccupied with this dire turn of events, Oswalt never heard the secret door slide open in Lord Bembridge's private study, but he did sense he was no longer alone.

Turning just in time to see a dark figure lunge toward him, a heavy fist knocked him senseless to the floor.

THIS IS NO HANGOVER

Oswald's eyes fluttered open; he was slowly regaining consciousness and could already sense something was amiss. His stomach felt queasy, and his head throbbed with each beat of his pulse. It was as though he was suffering from a massive hangover, but that couldn't be the case. Oswalt learned early in his climb to the top to never over-indulge and always be ready to take advantage of every opportunity. Better sober than sorry is one of many mottos by which he lives. Why do I feel so out of sorts? he thought to himself. Almost intuitively, Oswalt touched the side of his face and immediately winced. His left eye was completely swollen shut, and his tongue found an empty space where a molar once resided. Then the reason came rushing back to him — A hard fist landing alongside his face, knocking him senseless. Alcott, you insolent dog, you've gone too far this time and will pay dearly…

(So writes Conrad Nightingale)

Having deduced why he felt so bad, there were still the matters of discovering his location and getting back home without further mishaps. Oswalt concentrated. He was lying on his backside, the ground beneath him hard and uneven. Slowly turning his head from side to side, he attempted to scan the adjacent area with his one good eye, but try as he might, nothing came into view. It was simply black, the deepest, darkest black imaginable.

Could it be that Alcott's blow rendered me sightless?

Incensed at the thought he might be blind, Oswalt bolted upright, immediately smacking his forehead against something hard and immovable. A litany of obscenities burst forth into the dark abyss.

As Oswalt lay there rubbing his forehead, a primal fear came to mind, overcoming any chance for reasonable thought.

I've been buried alive!

Instantly panicked, he thrashed about when the back of his hand hit iron bars. He reached through the bars into the darkness; he hadn't been buried alive but was locked in a space no bigger than a coffin.

Get yourself under control, Oswalt, and take long deep breaths. Where there is life, there is hope, another one of his many mottos. Once settled down, Oswalt used all his faculties to try and figure out the present situation; at times like this, logic must trump emotion.

Remaining motionless, he sucked in a long deep breath, this time noting the dank, musty smell so strong he could taste it. He held his breath and lay perfectly still. The air was stagnant yet cool against his skin. He listened closely but could only hear a repetitive dripping in the distance. He slowly stroked the walls of his cell; they were ruff as though they had been gouged into the rock.

Where am I being held? Oswalt pondered. *It's a dark, cool place with minimum airflow and near a water source. My cell is hewn out of the rock instead of being built of manmade blocks.*

The Paupers' Catacombs came to mind. It was the only place that made any sense. Yet, Roderick Bembridge had intentionally collapsed the catacombs when the castle was constructed over a hundred years ago and since, all but forgotten, or so it was believed. Trapped below Roderick Square, only yards from freedom.

You must think yourself a clever bastard, Alcott, but too smart for your good, I'll wager. You couldn't arrange this all alone, which means you have co-conspirators. It makes no difference, for I will get free and find everyone responsible for this indignity; you shall all hang together.

Oswalt called out, "I know someone is out there and that you can hear me! This is your only chance for mercy! I am Chancellor Nigel Oswalt, and I demand my immediate release on penalty of death!" He waited, but there was only silence. For the next several hours, Oswalt vainly screamed the same message; the only response was the sound of dripping water.

Lying alone in the darkness for what seemed days, Oswalt eventually lost all sense of time. He had grown weak from a lack of food and water and was forced to lie in his bodily waste.

Then, when he had all but given up hope, Oswalt caught a faint glimmer of light. A torch descended slowly into the pit. As the torch bearer came closer and the light filled the cavern, he could make out the chamber.

Oswalt's deductions were correct. His holding cell was cut horizontally into the rock wall; it was just large enough to hold a body, obviously once a tomb before the iron bars were added. The hooded figure approached and drew a large key that he used to unlock the cell door.

"Come out!" demanded the guard. Oswalt was moving too slowly when a strong hand grabbed his hair, jerking him out onto the floor. "Stand up!"

Oswalt rose to stand face-to-face with the cloaked figure; he then noticed the distinctive features of the bohkor. Attempting to put on a brave face, Oswalt asked, "Who are you? I demand to know."

"You shall address me as Sir. "

"Do you know who I am?"

"I don't care," came the response.

"I am Nigel Oswalt, Chancellor to Lord Bembridge."

"I don't care."

"I am innocent of any wrongdoing."

"I don't care." The bohkor shoved Oswalt forward. "Move or die."

As they climbed, Oswalt counted twenty-two steps in all. Such information could prove helpful if an opportunity for escape presents itself. A heavy wooden door at the top of the stairway opened onto Roderick Square, a market where farmers, fishermen, and other merchants sell their wares.

Even under these circumstances, Oswalt had to grin to himself, for he had figured out where he was being held, and he loved being right. The two crossed the square and proceeded to Bembridge Castle unchallenged. Once inside, they went directly to the High Council Chambers, where Lord Bembridge waited. The bohkor sentry led Oswalt through the doorway and, once inside, pushed him down onto his knees.

"My Lord, is this necessary? Why am I, your Chancellor, being treated in such a manner?"

"Because you are no longer Chancellor; a Chancellor must be above reproach."

"I don't understand what is happening, but I assure you I am trustworthy and loyal."

"**ENOUGH**! I have only granted this audience for one reason— to hear your confession."

"And what am I being charged with that requires a confession?"

"Treason and murder."

"With all due respect, my Lord, such allegations are preposterous.

Lord Bembridge shook his head in disgust. "You are the fifth generation of Oswalts to serve as Chancellors to the Bembridge family. Why would you throw that honored history away like garbage?"

"Perhaps it is time to step out from under the shadow of the House of Bembridge."

"Then you admit your treasonous acts?"

"I admit nothing; I am merely speculating."

"Take the prisoner back to his cell, order Lord Bembridge. "We will speak again tomorrow, though I assure you, it won't be as civil a conversation."

CHAPTER 16

CONVENIENT AMNESIA

The vendor stalls had been moved to the outer perimeter, and now a raised platform stood at the center. On the platform sat Lord Bembridge; at his right hand stood Minister Alcott. For the first time in days, Oswalt was optimistic. This is my chance. Once I determine what drives Lord Bembridge to take these measures, I will turn the table on that traitor, Alcott. There is no way that oaf can successfully debate me; soon, he will find himself in chains. The entourage stopped before Lord Bembridge, and Oswalt was forced to his knees. All the time, the citizens of Roderick moved in closer to witness first-hand what was about to occur...

(So writes Conrad Nightingale)

Breaking protocol, Oswalt was the first to speak before Lord Bembridge acknowledged him.

"You're Excellency, I don't understand what is happening to me. No doubt, Alcott has been filling your head with stories. I demand to be heard."

"You're in no position to make demands of me, and you shall not speak unless I first grant you permission."

"Lord Bembridge, as your Chancellor, I must strongly object."

Lord Bembridge signaled one of the cloaked sentries, who brought forth an iron mask resembling a pig's face. The bohkor closed the mask around Oswalt's head, shoving the built-in bit under his tongue, thus rendering him speechless.

"First, as a point of clarification, you are no longer Chancellor. I have stripped you of all titles, properties, and other assets. Your present status is lower than that of a feral alley cat, which at least provides Roderick the service of keeping down the rodent population." The spectators laughed at hearing the comparison.

"Second, I am not here to listen to you, but you shall hear me clearly while you still possess ears. Shake your head if you understand." Oswalt was too slow in responding and received a sharp blow with a club to the back of his mask to entice him to answer. Oswalt frantically shook his head up and down, acknowledging he understood Lord Bembridge.

"Do you think there is any defense you can propose on your behalf? Do you expect me to believe you don't remember how you found yourself in this predicament?" Of course, gagged as he was, Oswalt couldn't answer and just sat on his knees looking bewildered, but maybe he should have tried. He was about to receive another crack to his skull when Lord Bembridge held up his hand.

"Perhaps when you came upon him in the secret passageway, you hit him too hard, Minister Alcott?"

"I suppose it could be possible. Maybe another sock to the jaw will jog his memory?" Oswalt started to visibly shake in anticipation of what may come.

"Are you ready to listen and speak only when permitted?" Oswalt shook his head in the affirmative, and Lord Bembridge signaled for the mask to be removed.

"Allow me to refresh your memory – Minister Alcott trapped you within a secret passageway between our respective chambers. So, just how long had you been spying on me?"

"I know nothing of secret passageways and spying. I have always been loyal to you."

"I wonder just when it was that you stopped serving me and started to be concerned only with your welfare? I think you must have charted your course long before coming to Roderick. How naïve you must have found me and the other High Council members as you scheme your way to the top. It seems our trust and admiration were merely building blocks to be manipulated for your gain." Oswalt began to fumble for words.

"**SILENCE**! Whether you can or can't recall your deeds, the evidence against you is irrefutable. In your study, we found copies of building plans showing secret passageways within Bembridge Castle. We also found disturbing communications between you and the Xagada. There is no doubt that it was you who helped the child gain access to the most private areas of the castle. There is no doubt it was you who twisted Lady Bembridge's dream for motherhood against her. And there is no doubt that you helped the Xagada child abscond with State secrets while on a murderous rampage."

The crowd began to madden and close ranks around Oswalt; Minister Alcott signaled the guards to keep them at bay. Oswalt began to protest but was interrupted by Lord Bembridge.

"I won't abide any more lies! I expect a full, unequivocal confession if you want any mercy from me. I suggest you sit here in the square among the people you have betrayed and carefully think about everything you have done."

From the corner of his eye, Oswalt could see two of the bohkor sentries roll a large keg into the center of the square. As the top of the barrel was removed, the entire crowd was repelled from the smell; it was filled halfway with the most putrid contents that could be gathered: blood, entrails, rotting fish, meat, and even feces.

Oswalt tried to hold his ground, but the bohkor easily dragged him to the barrow and lowered him inside. Once submerged up to his neck in the vial concoction, the lid was tightly replaced, and a single small hole was drilled to allow minimal airflow. Oswalt's muffled screams for mercy fell upon deaf ears. "Listen closely should he wish to confess. I will reconvene court after dinner. Until then, the lid stays shut."

Left in the sun, the temperature within the keg slowly rose, and the stagnant air grew more difficult to breathe. Oswalt was stewing in waste. He could only imagine the litany of diseases he could catch as maggots crawled over his face and found refuge inside his mouth, nose, and ears.

Never had Oswalt experienced time passing so slowly. Will this agony ever end? he wondered when he finally heard Lord Bembridge order the lid to be opened.

"Take him out, and let's get this over before I lose my dinner from the stench." Dripping with slime, Oswalt was presented before Lord Bembridge and Minister Alcott.

"Are you thirsty?" Oswalt nodded, yes. "Bring him water." Oswalt drank in the cool liquid until he could hold no more.

"I trust now you are ready to speak?" Again, Oswalt nodded yes. "Well then, what say you?"

In a hushed tone, almost a whisper, Oswalt declared, "I am innocent."

"Return to your cell and reconsider your declaration, for tomorrow brings new tribulations." Bembridge and Alcott turned their backs and walked away. The bohkor sentries smiled.

***

After a thorough scrubbing with coarse bristle brushes and salt water, Oswalt was finally locked within his cell for some needed rest, but it didn't come. Oswalt's sleep was fitful and broken. He dreamed he was dead, and the deities cast him into the underworld to be eternally tormented by all sorts of demons, not far from the truth he realized when he woke from the sound of his cage opening.

Before him stood one of the bohkor sentries with a broad grin across his ugly face. "Good morning! Are you ready to face a new day of challenges? Minutes later, Oswalt stood again before Lord Bembridge, Minister Alcott, and an ever-hostile crowd.

"Before we begin today's activities, is there any burden from which you wish to relieve yourself?" asked Lord Bembridge. With little more than a second to respond, Lord Bembridge continued. "You had plenty of time to think about your answer yesterday, so I'll take your silence as a no. Most unfortunate for you." Lord Bembridge motioned toward the nearby guards; they brought forward a sizeable wooden armchair, its entire surface covered with blunt metal studs.

"Strip him naked!" he ordered the sentries. "Oswalt, take your seat."

The bohkor sentries grabbed Oswalt and slammed him down onto the chair; his chest, wrist, and legs were bound tightly with thick leather straps that could be periodically tightened if required. He sat alone all day in the sun; his skin burned to a bright cherry red. The pain was excruciating; even the slightest twitch pressed the studs harder against his skin and muscles. Shockwaves ran through every fiber of his body. Nevertheless, all Oswalt could think about was revenge against Alcott.

After dinner, the court was reconvened. Lord Bembridge and Minister Alcott took their places directly across from Oswalt.

"Well. You've had two days to ponder your circumstances. Any change of heart? Confess your crimes, and I promise you a quick death." Lord Bembridge's questions were met with silence.

"Nothing? I must admit, I find it fascinating that after being caught in the act of treason, you continue to endure such pain rather than confess. Have you been driven insane by the deities, or are you simply a pathological liar who believes in his innocence?"

"I am innocent."

"Of course you are," came Lord Bembridge's sarcastic response. "Take the prisoner back to his cell. I shall see you again tomorrow morning."

***

The bohkor removed Oswalt's restraints and still had to peel his limp body away from the chair. Although no skin was broken, the studs left deep imprints. It was nearly impossible for Oswalt to walk under his own power, but somehow, he managed.

***

The following morning, the bohkor sentry shoved a cold bowl of gruel and a cup of water in front of Oswalt.

"Eat up; it's best to start on the right foot," and the bohkor laugh deep and hard. "Sorry, it's an inside joke, but you'll find out soon enough."

Oswalt couldn't remember the last time he had eaten, and although he felt sick from the previous days' activities, he devoured the meal.

"Hurry up. You have an appointment with Lord Bembridge, and we need to get you ready. Sit!" Oswalt sat on a nearby stool.

"We're going to fit you with a nice pair of custom boots." Oswalt felt a spiked yoke pole slip over his head and around his neck. It was the same device the BPS used to transfer prisoners; any attempt to move would cause the spikes to bite deeply into the soft flesh. Oswalt did not attempt to move.

"Extend your right foot for me." Oswalt complied immediately – he was learning obedience, if nothing else. The sentry placed a heavy metal boot on his foot. The sole of the boot was covered in studs like those on the chair, and once closed about his ankle, it was tightened with a bolt strategically placed against the tendon. The weight of the boot, in combination with its placement, meant that with each step, the studs would push into Oswalt's soft foot.

Then, Oswalt's left foot was fitted with the same contraption. On the toe of each boot was a joker's bell to shamefully announce his coming.

"Let's go! The sentry pushed the yoke pole forward, bringing Oswalt into a standing position. Oswalt let out a cry, but one couldn't tell if it was from the yoke pole or the boot – perhaps it was both.

As on the previous days, Oswalt and his escort climbed the twenty-two steps, albeit much more slowly, and walked out into the courtyard where Lord Bembridge and Minister Alcott waited. The crowd was bigger today, curious to see what next was in store for the traitor, Nigel Oswalt.

***

"I see the BPS has you out for a morning walk. Before I let you go, do you have anything you wish to say to me?" asked Lord Bembridge.

"You're Excellency, why are you doing this to me?

"No, nothing more to say? Well, enjoy your stroll. We'll speak again this afternoon. Lord Bembridge and Minister Alcott turned their backs and walked away. Like a dog on a short leash, Oswalt was led over the city's cobblestone streets – each step was excruciating. Typically, the entire town of Roderick can be walked within a half hour, but constrained by these specially made boots, it took Oswalt nearly two hours to complete the circuit.

***

After the agonizing march, Oswalt found himself back in the square facing Lord Bembridge and Minister Alcott. This time, Lord Bembridge made a new accusation, "Tell me, did you have anything to do with Minister Addison's death?"

Finally, Oswalt thought. Even that buffoon Alcott can't ignore the ledger. This will shift the blame from me. I need to hang on a little longer. "I don't know what you're talking about; it seems you believe I am responsible for every misfortune. I am innocent of all charges."

"You're a stubborn bastard; I'll give you that much. We'll talk again tomorrow."

Once back at his cell, the bohkor removed Oswalt's boots much to his relief. He was fed and allowed to rest the remainder of the day and night. Still, he was far from comfortable, and his nightmares came for him.

The next morning found Lord Bembridge curt and to the point. "It is time to pay the piper," he said. With that declaration, the bohkor brought forth a new device that resembled a flute; it was strapped about his neck on a spiked collar, and his fingers were attached with screws tightened just over his cuticles. The pain was excruciating, but if Oswalt attempted to adjust his position, the spiked collar dug deep into his neck. As passersby jeered at him, he was left standing in the square, holding up the flute for the better part of the day. By now, every part of Oswalt's body was wracked with pain. He knew in his heart that he might break and give a full confession in return for a swift death.

***

Late that afternoon, the parties reconvened. "I hoped the past days' indignities would have shamed a confession out of you, but clearly, I was wrong. Your position of innocence remains intransigent. Can you at least accede to the fact that you were trapped and captured by Minister Alcott in a secret passageway leading from your room to my chamber?"

Now, he wants less than a full confession. I'm winning the battle of wills; I need to hold firm, and this will be all over soon. "I have no knowledge of secret passageways, nor do I have any recollection of ever having been in such a place," responded Oswalt.

"I saw you lying unconscious on the floor myself. Do you dare challenge my integrity?"

"Of course not, my Lord. However, as you have said, I was unconscious. I contend that first Minister Alcott knocked me out and then dragged me into this secret passageway, of which I know nothing, for an all too convenient discovery."

"That is preposterous. I planned to lure you into the passageway, and Alcott went inside for you under my order. You are delirious if you genuinely believe you were set up as a scapegoat. I'll hear no more of your ridiculous allegations. Since you refuse to confirm the truth regarding the irrefutable evidence, I must help you understand simple reality. The BPS has many ways to loosen your tongue; none are as pleasant as the past week's activities. Take him back to his cell; we shall reconvene tomorrow.

The BPS has many ways to loosen your tongue; none are as pleasant as the past week's activities. Oswalt didn't like the sound of that; it certainly gave him something to ponder.

***

This fifth morning's routine was the same as the previous four days, but the judicial stage was set up differently when he arrived in the courtyard. Today, the entire High Council sat in chairs flanking Lord Bembridge.

"I have only two questions: First, how do you plead to the charge of treason?"

"Not guilty."

"I'm not surprised. Second question: are there any members of the High Council before you that should be standing in your place, or at least, alongside you?" The Ministers were shocked and prayed that they wouldn't be falsely accused.

"Minister of Justice, Johnathan Alcott."

"Again, I am not surprised. I promised you yesterday that we would make things increasingly uncomfortable for you, so let's get right to it. Do you remember your lounge chair? We've made a slight modification by sharpening the studs into short spikes."

Oswalt's legs stiffened, and he attempted to backpedal away, but the bohkor sentries dragged him over and slammed his body upon the chair. The experience was like sitting on a nest of angry hornets, stinging repeatedly. Oswalt wailed in pain, and several of the Ministers cringed, glad they hadn't been named as a co-conspirator. The BPS tightened the leather arm and leg straps, pressing Oswalt down on the spikes. As they did, Oswalt's natural reflex was to stand up, impaling him deeper on the chair. It was a cycle of agony.

"Sit there and think about your future, Nigel Oswalt. The High Council and I will be back before sunset, and we'll speak some more. Then, hopefully, you will accept your inevitable fate and cooperate."

That evening, they reconvened. "For the sake of justice, I feel obligated to ask, have you reconsidered?"

"No."

Lord Bembridge shook his head in frustration. "Very well. I promise you will not like what tomorrow holds for you. Take him away," he commanded in disgust.

As a broken Oswalt rolled into his cell, something unexpected happened – the bohkor leaned in close and whispered, "I have a message from Tobias Rycroft. Don't give up; you are not alone. Try to rest and wait for my coming tonight." Oswalt didn't understand, but at least there was a glimmer of hope.

***

"Wake up; it's time."

Oswalt woke quickly, and although his eyes needed a few seconds to adjust, he could hear the key turning in the lock. The cage door fell open with a loud clang, but nobody else was around to hear other than Oswalt. Is it possible? Is my freedom close at hand? Oswalt's heart was pounding with excitement and perhaps some trepidation that he could be caught any minute. If so, he could only imagine the punishment that would be inflicted.

Put it out of your mind, he thought. *Remember, where there is life, there is hope.*

Out of the shadows came the familiar voice of one of his sentries, "Shall I lock you back in, or are you coming with me? Others are at risk, and they won't be waiting long."

Oswalt swung his legs over the side and slid into a standing position. His feet were badly cut and bruised, and he winced immediately from the pain.

"I can't walk. Can you help me?"

"There is a limit to my assistance. If you can't walk, I suggest you try crawling. Time is running out, so what will it be – back to the cell or forward to freedom? Make your choice and be quick about it."

It was a rhetorical question because the bohkor had already turned and was leading the way. Oswalt began to crawl on his hands and knees. The light from a single torch was all the two had to brighten the path. Often, the tunnels would fork, but the bohkor didn't hesitate in his choice of direction.

"Stay close; you wouldn't want to get lost. I doubt anyone would find you in these catacombs."

It wasn't easy crawling on uneven ground, but Oswalt endured the pain following the bohkor for nearly fifteen minutes. Eventually, Oswalt noticed a distinct change in the air; a breeze was blowing, carrying the salty, pungent scent of the sea. Finally, about twenty feet ahead, the bohkor came to a stop. Oswalt moved forward, stopping short of the opening to his freedom.

He looked out to the horizon. A full moon lit the night sky, and moonbeams danced upon the water below. The sea was calm, and Oswalt could make out the silhouette of a small boat containing two rowers and a steersman.

"I assume those are the others at risk, which you spoke of earlier? Who are they? Is one of them Tobias Rycroft?"

"There will be plenty of time for introductions once you're aboard the boat."

"But how do I get down; it must be at least thirty feet to the water. I don't have the strength to climb down the cliffside; you'll have to lower me."

"Do you see a rope anywhere? You need to jump."

One would have thought that by now, Oswalt would have learned that when a bohkor gives you an order, you don't hesitate, but his fear of heights got the best of him. The bohkor grabbed hold of Oswalt and tossed him into the open air. Down he fell, screaming all the way; he barely had enough time to take a breath of air before hitting the water with a thunderous crash. Under he went.

*What a cruel stroke of fate to have endured so much and been so close to freedom only to drown during my escap*e, he thought.

When he rose to the water's surface, he began to panic, knowing he was too weak to swim under his own volition. As he began to sink back down to a watery grave, his only regret was that he hadn't been able to exact revenge on his archenemy, Johnathan Alcott.

Suddenly, Oswalt could feel himself being pulled to the surface and dragged into the boat like a gaffed fish. He was being shaken like a ragdoll as sharp blows were administered to his back. Water spurted from his lungs, leaving a salty brine aftertaste, as he tried to catch his breath. When he could finally speak, he expressed his heartfelt gratitude to his rescuers.

"Thank you. You saved my life," he said repeatedly. "No thanks necessary, came the reply. As you're fond of saying, "Where there is life, there is hope." The speaker removed his hood, and Oswalt recognized him immediately – Alcott!

Then he looked at the others: Sergeant Rivka and Corporal Hirth.

"We thought you might enjoy a little stay at Blackpool Penitentiary; we have something extraordinary planned for you there."

As they began to row the boat, Oswalt glanced up at the cliffside, where he saw Rawl Knoggs standing and waving goodbye. He had the same sarcastic grin as his late father. Oswalt began to cry uncontrollably.

CHAPTER 17

A CHANGE OF HEART

Dawn was starting to break as the warship Stratagem raised anchor. In addition to the crew on board were Oswalt, Alcott, three Blackpool Penitentiary Sentries, and a half dozen Rangers led by Captain Fleming. With fair winds ahead, the swift ship should reach the port village of Asquith by tomorrow afternoon. There would be no delay in confining Oswalt in a prison transport wagon and reaching the prison later that night. The transport was uneventful, as no one dared to challenge the escort party on sea or over land. Warden Ogdon was busy making preparations when Oswalt arrived at the outer gates of Blackpool. The sentries had orders to bring the prisoner straight to his office…

(So writes Conrad Nightingale)

Oswalt stood at attention before the newly appointed Warden, Cil Ogdon, as he slowly looked up from his papers. "I understand you were told to expect some special treatment during your stay with us. Do you know what that means?"

"I assume it is a euphemism for more torture, each day more devastating than the previous," responded Oswalt.

"Bohkors have suffered directly and indirectly from your treasonous ways, and as delightful as that sounds, I regret that such is not the case. While you are here in Blackpool Penitentiary, you will be our guest. Well, not exactly a guest, as you cannot leave the confines of the prison, but you will not be treated as a prisoner. Doctors will tend to your injuries, and you'll be bathed, fed, and rested."

"Why the sudden change of heart?"

"Because Lord Bembridge wants you to be of sound mind and body when you face the Executioner's axe twenty-four days from tonight." It was the proverbial last straw; Oswalt fainted on the spot.

***

Mentally and physically exhausted, Oswalt awoke two days later on a down-filled mattress. As promised by Warden Ogdon, he had been bathed and fitted with a clean nightshirt. His wounds had been cleaned and bandaged, especially the soles of his feet. A salve had been spread over his body, its healing powers searching out the bruises, sprains, and muscle aches that ran deep.

Oswalt slowly scanned the room; it was clean and bright, and a cool breeze gently parted the curtains as it wafted into the room. Then, he saw *him*, rocking in the corner of the room – Alcott. At that very moment, Oswalt was snapped back into reality.

"By the gods, what must I do to rid myself of you?"

"Now, don't be like that, Nigel. You know we're more alike than you might think. Under different circumstances, we may have been friends."

"I have no idea what you're talking about; we are nothing alike."

"Are you sure? We both want the same thing – to be out from under Lord Bembridge's thumb. After serving the House of Bembridge since I was a child, I tried to retire and spend the remainder of my days farming, but Bembridge wouldn't have it, calling me back into service. So now, my beloved Ingrid is dead, and I have nothing."

"It's too late to confide in me. Haven't you heard I'm to be executed in twenty-four days?"

"More like twenty-two days; you've been sleeping for a while."

"Crux!" yelled Oswalt as he stared at the ceiling. "Sorry.

Still, there is one way you could turn things around for the better."

Oswalt snapped his gaze toward Alcott. "What are you saying?"

"You challenge Lord Bembridge to combat, under the Right of Accession."

"Brilliant! I should challenge a seasoned veteran to mortal combat.

"I've seen you in fencing competitions; you know your way around a sword."

"Even a half-witted peasant knows that there is a distinct difference between fencing for sport and mortal combat. How have you made it this far in life?"

"I've made it this far because I know my adversaries. I've been personally training with Lord Bembridge since we were both children, and I've sparred with him more times than I can count. I know his swordplay and combat tactics better than any man living, perhaps better than he understands himself. You can beat him if you know what to expect and when to expect it."

"And you're willing to share this information with me; why, and in exchange for what?"

"As for why, it's simply a matter of self-preservation. As for what, I'm thinking the new Lord of Bembridge Province will need his own Chancellor."

"Finally, you say something I can understand – greed and lust for power. When do we get started?"

"Rest the remainder of the day and get your energy back; there will be enough time to perfect the necessary killing moves."

***

Once he felt himself again, Oswalt and Alcott spent from sunrise to sundown practicing combat tactics with wooden swords. Alcott kept emphasizing one main move.

"Lord Bembridge has used this decoy maneuver in every encounter he has ever fought. You need to keep alert, for it means the end is near. First, he draws his opponent in close.

Then, after exchanging several parries, he will appear slightly off balance, getting the challenger to lunge forward. It is a fatal mistake, for he is not actually off balance and will easily sidestep the advance. Once the opponent has overstepped the range with his back facing him, he will bring his sword down. Cut the spinal cord deep enough, and you are paralyzed, defenseless against further attack, which most certainly will come."

"How can I stop him?"

"When fighting him, there will be no time to think. Therefore, you must practice this countermove until it is a reflex. As you lunge, Bembridge will use his sword to fend you off and continue your forward motion, thus drawing you off balance. Although you will be looking straight ahead, you must immediately throw your sword over your shoulder, protecting your spine. You won't need to see his next move; believe me, it's coming.

"Do not fear; both swords will collide, but there will be no resulting damage. This next step is critical; it cannot be stopped if executed properly: You must resume your attack quickly before he can regain his composure. Immediately after fending the blow, grab your sword with both hands and spin around, keeping your blade low across his ankle. He won't be able to drop his sword in time to block the strike. You'll cleave his foot from his leg with one fluid swing, leaving him immobile and at your mercy."

The two practiced this move repeatedly for the remaining days until it became a habit.

With the help of his new friend, Oswalt healed both physically and mentally. His skill with a sword had greatly improved, and he felt ready for anything that might come.

***

When the time came, Oswalt climbed into the prison transport wagon; he thought how fickle fate could be. It took three days over land to reach Bembridge Castle, and when he arrived, Lord Bembridge, the High Council, and the Executioner were waiting for him. When the cage was opened, Oswalt practically hopped out and swaggered over to confront his destiny.

"You look no worse for the wear. The BPS must have treated you well?"

"Warden Ogdon complied with your orders, albeit he wasn't pleased."

"As long as he did what he was told, a lesson you never learned. Let's get on with it; I'm a busy man, and I've wasted enough time on you. You have been found guilty of treason, espionage, and murder. The sentence is death. Have you anything to say before the sentence is carried out?"

Oswalt straightened himself to full height, puffed out his chest, and loudly demanded mortal combat per his Right of Accession.

"The Right of Accession has not been invoked since the time of Roderick the Righteous. How is it that you know of this custom?"

"Does it matter how I came by this knowledge?"

"Not really, since it does not apply to you. The Right of Accession is reserved for disputing nobles to determine who shall rule. As I previously told you, you have been stripped of all titles and property, and therefore, you have no such standing." Checkmate, the game was over for Oswalt; he went pale.

"Nevertheless, I shall grant you a special dispensation. I shall rest easier knowing that I gave you more of a chance than you gave my beloved, Lady Bembridge. As the person challenged, the place, time, and weapon of choice are mine to make. I choose here, now, and swords." Lord Bembridge turned to one of his bodyguards, "Give him your sword."

"If it's all the same, I prefer to use my friend's sword. Johnathan, may I have your sword, please?"

All in attendance looked bewildered as Minister Alcott presented his sword to Oswalt; he didn't look happy about being outed. Then, lowering his voice to just above a whisper, Oswalt spoke.

"Just in case something goes wrong, I wanted Lord Bembridge to have a reason to hold you. I'm sure you understand," Oswalt's smile was scornful.

Lord Bembridge stepped down from the podium and drew forth his sword. "Prepare to die." The two touched blades, and the fight began.

Nigel Oswalt, who never had to fight for his life, found himself in mortal combat with Lord Bembridge, a renowned champion on the battlefield. However, he remained remarkably calm under the circumstances, recalling all that Alcott had taught him over the past several weeks.

The advantage of the sword is its reach. It allows one to stand back while still being able to inflict injury on his opponent. Therefore, the job is to close the distance, thus limiting Lord Bembridge's full range of motion.

Oswalt immediately advanced, keeping the parries tight. Whenever Lord Bembridge tried to back up, Oswalt advanced. Oswalt could see the frustration on Lord Bembridge's face, and he began enjoying his advantage.

Then, Oswalt recalled another critical lesson: *Don't just concentrate on your opponent's body; attack his mind at every opportunity.*

When they crashed close enough to be face-to-face, Oswalt began to jibe Lord Bembridge quietly.

"When you awoke this morning, could you imagine such a turn of events? The condemned prisoner becomes your executioner."

With an explosive burst of energy, Lord Bembridge shoved Oswalt back. He was agitated and began to swing erratically. Oswalt moved back in closer.

"It must vex you something terrible to realize the man who deceived you will soon be sitting on your throne."

Lord Bembridge sidestepped and slipped away. Oswalt was pleased with his swordplay. A few more parries and the two found themselves together again. Being ever so quiet that just the two of them could hear the conversation, Oswalt continued.

"All you wanted was a confession. Well, it's the least I can give to a dying man. Yes, I betrayed you with the Xagada. I helped the child kill your beloved Amanda and escape justice. And lastly, it is I who, through the Right of Accession, will be sitting on your throne by nightfall."

"I waited a long time to hear those words," Lord Bembridge proclaimed. "Thank you for the confession; however, I am growing bored with our dance."

Oswalt felt a burning pain under his arm as Lord Bembridge's dagger slid from the armpit to the hand, cutting muscle and vital arteries. He could no longer hold his sword, so he dropped it to the ground and followed.

"That's not fair." he began to protest.

"What's not fair?" responded Lord Bembridge. "Didn't your new friend explain that mortal combat has no rules? The only goal is to stay alive. Or do you mean it's not fair because you didn't get to perform the lunge of death move? When Alcott told me that he talked you into throwing yourself off balance, I couldn't believe my ears; that would have been amusing to see."

Oswalt searched the crowd for Alcott's face; when he saw him, Alcott was grinning a big smile.

"Yes, I lied. It seems the self-proclaimed master of logic and deception has been duped. How does betrayal taste, you smug, narcissistic asshole?"

Lord Bembridge ordered the guards to drag Oswalt over to the block. "Lay him out face up. I want the traitor to see what is coming."

Then, motioning the Executioner aside, Lord Bembridge stood above Oswalt, who laid before him like a turtle on its back.

"One final comment: there is no such thing as the Right of Accession. You are truly a buffoon." Those words cut

Oswalt's ego as sharply as Lord Bembridge's sword would across his throat, but the death blow never came.

"Bind his wound. I don't want him passing away too quickly from lack of blood." Lord Bembridge glared down on Oswalt, "A beheading is too merciful for the likes of a Xagada spy. Oh yes, I know who you are; your lover and personal bodyguard, Captain Bolick, couldn't hold his tongue nearly as well as you. Assuming you were dead, he was happy to sing your accolades."

Lord Bembridge motioned for the guards to bring a small iron cage into which Oswalt was jammed. "Hoist this traitor, or spy if you prefer, above the square for all to witness what I hope will be an agonizing death."

As the cage swung into place, it slowly rotated into view of another cage. The crows had picked at the neighboring corpse to the point that it was unrecognizable, except for the bloody white scarf held in place by a gold broach with a green gemstone — Captain Bolick.

MAKING ONE'S CASE

The time it took to ferret out the traitor, Nigel Oswalt, obtain his confession and serve as judge and executioner had taken a toll on Lord Bembridge. He was sure that once he had rid Bembridge Province of this scum, he could focus on the more pressing matter of dealing with the Xagada Nation. Yet, there was still the issue of the missing child, Eleanor Rycroft, gnawing at his soul. After all, it was the girl who deceived him, committed espionage, and ultimately murdered four innocent people, including his beloved wife. No matter what, Lord Bembridge vowed to himself to never give up the hunt; Eleanor Rycroft would pay dearly...

(So writes Conrad Nightingale)

Nearly three months had passed since Lord Bembridge requested a meeting between the respective Heads of State; long enough time for the message to reach even the most distant corners of Calvendar and enough time for all invitees to digest the gravity of the invitation.

The sweltering summer days were now just a memory, and autumn brought cooler temperatures and pounding thunderstorms that wreaked havoc on the few major roads connecting the various provinces of Calvendar.

Lord Bembridge could only hope that the dignitaries wouldn't treat the weather as an excuse not to attend. Thankfully, the skies cleared a week before the meeting, and everyone invited showed up as requested.

During their stay, the guests, as well as their entourage, were provided with accommodations befitting their stations. However, only the dignitaries were allowed admittance into the Great Hall for the meeting.

Oversized wooden chairs with thick cushions, seven in all, were placed along the perimeter of the Great Hall; above the chairs hung the coat of arms from each of the houses in attendance:

At the far end of the room sat the host, Walter Bembridge, Lord of Bembridge Province. On the flag above him was the family crest - a white, two-headed hextar on a sky-blue field, a four-pointed star in each corner.

In no order of prestige, at the wall to his left sat Bartok Livingstone, crowned head of the dwarf Kingdom of Remmelic, located in the Staghorn Mountains in Eastern Calvendar. A golden flag embroidered with crossed black pickaxes swung freely above his head.

Immediately across from King Livingstone along the wall to Lord Bembridge's right was seated Lilliana Hollyfield, elfin Queen of Gwaii, located deep in the ancient woodlands of Garwood, in southeast Calvendar. The elfin flag of forest green bore a giant silver tree bracketed between two rearing stags.

Equally spaced along both walls came: Kivik Runskar, the Grand Aduel of the Bohkor Territory, which is sandwiched between Bembridge Province and the high desert of Jadhar. The Bohkor flew a red flag bearing a black scorpion.

Lord Bernard Driscoll competently represented the province of Edgewater. The House of Driscoll flew a white ship on a dark blue background.

Lady Kenzie Winslow represented the House of Winslow on the Kenosha Plain. Three ponies pranced on a field of light green on her flag.

Lord Wyatt Marston, elected Governor representing the freeborn people of the Kermatic Territories, located on Calvendar's southwestern corner, flew a red, white, and blue striped banner.

Once everyone had taken their seats, Lord Bembridge rose to address the assembly; he waited until the last murmur faded and had everyone's undivided attention.

"As mentioned in my invitation letter, I've requested your specific attendance here today to discuss a matter of profound importance, a matter that I had hoped to keep confidential among those of us in attendance. But unfortunately, I can no longer guarantee secrecy. As some of you may have heard, my Chancellor, Nigel Oswalt, turned out to be a traitor. Through his treachery, any preemptive plan to form an alliance to rid Western Calvendar of the Xagada scourge has been disseminated to the enemy. Under the best circumstances, such a task would have proven difficult; now, I fear it may be impossible.

"Nevertheless, with Xagada raids on the rise, it is a challenge I must accept. I hope you will find merit in my concern and fight alongside me to preserve our way of life. What say you?"

Lord Driscoll of the House of Driscoll in Edgewater Province was the first to respond. "I am considerably older than the rest of the distinguished Lords and Ladies at this assembly," he began.

"Perhaps it's the fresh sea air in Edgewater that keeps you looking so young and virile," interrupted Queen Hollyfield as she flashed him a quick wink and smile; the others chuckled.

"Careful, my Lady, this old man has only so many heartbeats left; pray do not take them with your beguiling ways." Once the laughter died, he continued.

"My point is that although my body is frail, my mind is as sharp as a razor's edge. I remember my childhood days when the Xagada nomads would journey through our lands in brightly colored caravans. They would sell trinkets and potions; some would entertain through song and story, while others would take on seasonal work, rarely completed as promised.

"Nevertheless, they all shared a talent for getting something of value in exchange for very little. They were also experts at evaluating the climate, and I'm not talking about the weather. When the community's demeanor worsened, the caravans would slip away in the still of the night.

"The following year, when their previous escapades were but a fading memory, the scenario would repeat itself.

"Then, a generation ago, the Xagada changed their tactics as they began to settle amongst us. Never changing the goal of getting something for nothing, the Xagada wove their nefarious thread into the cultural tapestry of our society. We all knew something was amiss but chose to turn a blind eye to their deceptive activities, and now this malady consumes us."

Governor Marston, representing the freeborn of the Kermatic Territories, stood to speak next.

"Lord Driscoll speaks with the wisdom of many years of personal experience. We would all do well to heed his words. I have witnessed such atrocities as far removed from civilization as the territories. I am not alone in saying the Xagada's minor acts of deception and guile have recently been replaced by whole-hearted criminal coordination."

"Accurately stated Governor Marston," injected Lady Winslow, "but not harshly enough. Mayhem and murder are all too common occurrences, as evidenced by the assassination of my daughter. The Xagada might as well have taken my heart, and I wish to follow her through the veil, but I cannot, for I still hold a duty to my people. I believe it is past time for us to join forces and take a stance."

King Livingstone stood and held up an open hand, gesturing a need to be recognized; as all heads turned in his direction, the room quieted. Although under five feet tall, yet broad and stalky of build, the dwarf King cut an imposing figure. On his head sat a golden crown, and his robe was tailored from the finest cloth in Calvendar. Precious gems from the mines of Staghorn were interwoven in his thick, well-groomed hair and beard. Yet, despite his apparent wealth, the exposed parts of his body showed an accumulation of calluses and scars of someone not afraid to do hard work.

"Judging from the similar attestations I have heard thus far," King Livingstone said, "it appears the Xagadas are a criminal blight here in Western Calvendar. However, east of the Eskridge Range, especially within my beloved Staghorn Mountains, the Xagadas are merely an occasional nuisance. Certainly, these nomads have committed no acts within my Kingdom that warrant we dwarfs join into such a coordinated and prodigious response."

"Your good fortune may be attributed to nothing more than the physical differences between humans and dwarfs," Governor Marston said. "The Xagada would be readily identified in Remmelic and captured for any egregious acts committed against the dwarf kingdom, so they tread cautiously. However, not all of us can afford such a cavalier view."

Raw emotions ignited at even the inference of a dissenting opinion, and soon, everyone was shouting over one another. Lord Bembridge needed to act swiftly, or the alliance would be over before a coalition could be formed. He took a pike from one of the guards and banged the staff on the wooden plank floor. The sounds were like cracks of thunder, and the commotion quieted. Noticeably perturbed, Lord Bembridge admonished everyone.

"You are guests in my home, and while under this roof, all will be treated with respect. This Great Hall is a sanctuary where every opinion is welcomed in the friendship which it is given."

"Well said, Lord Bembridge, and it is in that spirit of respect and friendship that I wish to make a statement," Queen Hollyfield said.

"This assembly recognizes Queen Hollyfield of the Kingdom of Gwaii." The Elfin Queen's appearance was not nearly as ostentatious as the other Lords and Ladies present, yet every bit as elegant. She had a sense of purity, wearing a simple white dress that caressed her long, slim figure. The Queen wore no traditional crown but rather a wreath of wildflowers that held her long golden hair back behind the tips of her distinctive elfin ears.

"Like the dwarfs, we elves consider ourselves fortunate in our physical dissimilarities with humans. I mean no offense." There was a chuckle in the room as tensions began to melt.

"And also, like the dwarfs," she continued, "we elves have never had to endure the atrocities committed by the Xagada on the good citizens of the West. Although I sympathize with your dilemma, I see it as more of a civil matter to be resolved within your race.

"Unfortunately, under the present circumstances, I cannot, in good conscience, commit any resources to this endeavor. However, as Queen of the elfin race, I will pledge to all those in attendance that Gwaii will not give any aid or comfort to the Xagada."

Lord Bembridge turned his attention toward Kivik Runskar, leader of the bohkor.

"We haven't heard from our friends to the north. Do you also embrace your physical dissimilarities with humans?" he said tongue in cheek.

"That goes without saying; you humans are such an ugly bunch." The entire assembly burst into laughter. Kivik Runskar raised his voice above the chortling.

"The bohkor and human races have stood alongside one another since the time of Roderick the Righteous, first Lord of the House of Bembridge. It is more than a mutually beneficial alliance; it is an enduring friendship. I see no reason our bond would be diminished due to these Xagada interlopers. We stand united."

Lord Bembridge stood, scanning each Head of State as he spoke.

"We have all been allowed to voice our opinions and concerns, and I extend my gratitude to all participants. I believe the immediate formation of a Preservation Coalition is warranted. Tomorrow morning, all those of a like mind are invited to attend a meeting where we will discuss the details of the alliance.

"Until then, the Great Hall shall be prepared for an evening of entertainment, fine food, strong drink, merriment, and good wishes. I look forward to seeing you all tonight."

CHAPTER 18

AN OLD WOMAN'S IRE

Xantara Kayla Rycroft sat alone inside the house. Worried about her granddaughter, she had eaten very little and slept even less since sending Tobias to retrieve Eleanor. Gregor slipped up behind the Xantara; bending down close, he whispered into her ear that Tobias had been seen riding into town — he was alone. The news sent a sharp jolt through Kayla's chest as though her heart was being squeezed by the reaper's cruel hand. She gasped, then quickly recomposed herself as though nothing unusual had happened. Reaching for Gregor, she said softly, "Take me to the front porch; I will wait there..."

(So writes Conrad Nightengale)

As Tobias rode up to the house, he could sense the Xantara's displeasure. She did not speak, but the boards beneath her chair creaked out an ominous warning as she slowly rocked back and forth. Tobias stood silent before her, feeling the weight of her despotic stare. Finally, Kayla spoke.

"Gone and returned in one day without my granddaughter. Am I to assume Ellie is dead, and if so, where is her body?"

"I cannot say whether Ellie is still among the living or passed over to our ancestors, for she has vanished," Tobias said.

Kayla sprang unassisted from her rocking chair. Her face turned bright red, and the purple veins in her forehead pulsated.

"Your response is inexcusable! If such a thing is possible, you're a worse father than a son-in-law. I rue the day my daughter married you, and you took the name Rycroft as your own. If you had an ounce of compassion for your daughter, you would be scouring Calvendar and not cowering before me. Quickly then, tell me your story and pray I won't have you flayed alive."

Rycroft shook uncontrollably and could hardly get the words out, "Olav Tyan and I rode at full gallop, stopping only for short breaks to rest our horses. Within a few hours, we found the tracks of his clan. As customary with orcs, Ellie had been tied and forced to walk barefoot to prevent her from bolting. That meant they were moving slowly and had to stop frequently. Encouraged, we spurred on our horses and soon caught up to his companions in an open spot where they had stopped for a respite. As we approached the orc camp, it was clear that something was dreadfully wrong. – Everyone, that is, every orc, was dead; apparently, slain by their own hand, as there was no evidence of an outside attacker."

"Are you expecting me to believe that the orcs committed mass suicide and Ellie simply walked away? How do you know Ellie hadn't escaped captivity before the melee?"

"We found Ellie's footprints, as well as those of another human, scattered among the dead."

"Then, why didn't you follow?" the Xantara's anger began to return.

"Because no tracks were leading away from the campsite – they simply disappeared. I know my story sounds absurd, but I speak the truth. I swear on my life; I shall never give up looking for Ellie."

"Prophetic words, for every breath you take from here forward is on borrowed time. Tell me, at least, you brought me Olav Tyan's head?"

"My sword was unsheathed; the orc knelt before me begging for his life when he started to yell – 'Important papers!' I assumed these important papers were the documents Ellie stole from Lord Bembridge's private chambers. Therefore, I granted Olav Tyan a stay on his execution in exchange for the documents. Under the circumstances, he was happy to lead me to where he had hidden the papers." Tobias walked over to his saddlebag and drew forth the papers, handing them over to the Xantara.

"At least Ellie's efforts were not in vain."

"And, once the documents were in your possession, why didn't you finish the pig off."

"Because we had struck a bargain, and there was no honor in killing him."

The Xantara began to laugh. "There was no honor in breaking your word to an orc. You don't know the meaning of honor." Tobias was feeling demeaned.

Tobias Rycroft's recounting of the day's activities was more than the Xantara could bear, and she felt exhausted.

"Until my granddaughter has returned home, safe and sound, you are no longer welcome in this house. Leave me now and thank whatever deity you follow for each minute you live." The Xantara handed the documents to Gregor; he took her arm and led her back inside.

***

Kayla Rycroft spent the next couple of days carefully considering the documents Eleanor had retrieved. It was clear that Lord Bembridge intended to form a coalition of fiefdom states with the sole purpose of ridding Calvendar of the Xagada, those whom he perceived to be a blight on humanity.

You did good, little one, she thought to herself. *We will heed this warning and strike first.*

***

Wasting no further time, the Xantara called the various leaders for an emergency meeting; conspicuously absent was

Tobias Rycroft, who had lost the Xantara's favor for failing to bring her granddaughter home. After praising Eleanor's courage and cunning, she shared Lord Bembridge's papers with her minions.

"The people of Western Calvendar have finally awakened from a long slumber to discover that the Xagada have taken advantage of their hospitality over the past twenty years. Consequently, they intend to join together and, by sheer force, get rid of us down to the last man, woman, and child. Believe me when I say they'll find out; it's a task easier said than done."

"What can we do?" several council members inquired.

"We do what we do best — disrupt the norm."

A RUDE AWAKENING

Xantara Rycroft had her plan for disrupting the norm, and if successful, it would be sure to devastate Lord Bembridge and all citizens of Western Calvendar...

(So writes Conrad Nightingale)

Like a mirror, the still water of South Cove Harbor reflected the black moonless sky, a perfect night for conducting a clandestine operation. Isolated and anchored several hundred yards offshore, floated the pride of Lord Bembridge's fleet, Stratagem, the most advanced warship in all Calvendar.

Nearly two hundred feet in length and weighing in at over two hundred tons, she was fast and highly maneuverable when under full sail in the open sea. She was also a formidable weapon when crewed by her highly trained officers and sailors. Her forward and aft decks were affixed with giant crossbows capable of hurling massive harpoons nearly a quarter mile. Rock-throwing catapults lined the port and starboard sides of the deck, and each of her three masts held protected platforms for skilled archers.

However, tonight, with most of the crew on shore leave, the great ship would be protected only by a skeleton crew of a half dozen men. The fruit was ripe for picking.

***

Acting on the Xantara's orders, thirty miscreants cloaked in black made their way unseen through the back alleys of the waterfront district down to a large waterfront warehouse with a reputation for less than scrupulous activities.

Once at the dock, they silently boarded three small fishing skiffs and pushed off from the water's edge. Their objective was clear: to commandeer Stratagem on behalf of the Xagada Nation — it would make an invincible pirate ship.

Doing their best to muffle any sound that would give them away, they wrapped the oarlocks in cloth and slipped the oars quietly beneath the inky water, each silent stroke bringing them closer to their prize.

Minutes later, the raiders eased up against the behemoth hull of Stratagem and carefully began to climb the nets to the upper deck. Luck seemed to be on their side as they met no resistance when a large sling hovered above them. As the sling ripped open, ammunition for the catapults rained down on their heads.

Battered bodies and heavy rocks fell upon the skiffs below, smashing the boats into splinters. Those who did not immediately sink bobbed up and down, splashing and gasping for air as Lord Bembridge's soldiers sent volley after volley of arrows into the churning water.

When the screaming stopped, and there were no signs of struggle, the giant forward and aft crossbows swung into position, taking dead aim at the distant warehouse. Wrapped and soaked in a flammable substance, the harpoons were set afire and streaked through the black sky toward their target. The impacts were heard throughout the city of Roderick as the huge bolts crashed through the walls and set the building ablaze.

***

The ill-fated Xagada mission was over as fast as it began. When the Xantara received the news, she barely showed any emotion.

"Explain to me, Gregor, when a flawless plan is executed under ideal conditions, how can it go astray?

"I have no idea, Xantara.

"The answer is quite simple; we have been betrayed."

FIRST BLOOD

The night's festivities were in full swing when Lord Bembridge noticed Captain Fleming and Minister Alcott waiting in the hallway. Rising from the table, he motioned the minstrels to cease playing and spoke loudly over the high-spirited guests. "Honored dignitaries and good friends, today's activities, in combination with copious amounts of drink, have caught up with me, and I require rest." A chuckle ran through the Great Hall, along with protests that the night was still young. "Those who have more fortitude, please feel free to continue celebrating. Until tomorrow, I bid you all a good night...."

(So writes Conrad Nightingale)

As soon as the three were out of earshot, Lord Bembridge asked Captain Fleming for a full report.

"The Xagada raid to take possession of Stratagem was an abysmal failure. At least thirty picaroons were exterminated, and the Xagada's warehouse along with half the pier were destroyed."

"What casualties have we taken?"

"Not so much as a splinter," responded Alcott.

Lord Bembridge gleamed, for this scrimmage marked the first victory for the Preservation Coalition in what he hoped to be a long list of conquests.

"Gentlemen, a late visit to the dungeon is warranted."

***

When the three arrived, Captain Fleming ordered the guard to open the door and leave them alone. The guard's heavy iron key clanked as it found purchase and slid the deadbolt free. Ever vigilant, with a torch in hand, Minister Alcott led the way, followed by Captain Fleming and Lord Bembridge. Rats scurried about, attempting to hide amongst the flickering shadows. The small windowless cell stank from years of previous occupants' vomit, piss, and shit that permeated the very rock structure itself.

Young Jason Sinclair sat partially illuminated in the far corner, trying to adjust his eyes to the light.

"Stand up!" ordered Lord Bembridge, but Jason didn't move fast enough for Captain Fleming's liking, and he rushed the boy, grabbing Jason by the hair and jerking him to his feet. The two stood eye-to-eye, and Fleming's stare spoke volumes: Insolence will *not* be tolerated.

"It appears that your information regarding the pending raid on Stratagem proved valuable," Lord Bembridge said.

"How valuable?" Jason challenged, never taking his eyes off Fleming.

"It's bought your freedom unless you prefer your new accommodations?"

"I was free before I sought you out and betrayed my people. I would think you would be more grateful."

Fleming pulled back his hand to slap the boy.

"Hold fast, Captain."

Lord Bembridge stepped toward the boy who turned to meet him.

"You haven't thought this through, have you? By now, you must know that I plan to rid Western Calvendar of every Xagada. So, even if I paid for your information, where would you go to spend the money? Do you, a mere boy, plan to return to Thammarat with a bulging purse? No doubt that would raise many a question."

"Tobias will protect me."

"Tobias Rycroft cares for nobody but himself. I suspect that the Xantara is looking for a traitor, and Tobias will no doubt be pinning the blame on the poor Xagada bastard being tortured within the dungeons of Bembridge Castle. Of course, we will do our part to confirm his allegations."

Jason flushed white as he realized Lord Bair was correct in his assessment.

"Wha…what can I do?" Jason stuttered.

"You can close the cell door on your way out.

CHAPTER 19

A FRAGILE TRUCE

Lord Bembridge joined Queen Hollyfield and King Livingstone for an early breakfast, where he made a final plea for their representation in the Preservation Coalition. "You should be aware before departing that the Xagada attempted to commandeer my flagship, Stratagem, late last night. Fortunately, I was prepared, and the uprising was quickly contained. Nevertheless, I consider such a blatant overture an act of war. Given the circumstances, I implore you to reconsider your respective positions…"

(So writes Conrad Nightingale)

"An act of war, no doubt, but it remains a civil war for the political destiny of mankind and does not concern the dwarfs."

"Although this is disturbing news, I agree with King Livingstone. I wish you well and pray for a swift resolution."

"I understand. However, considering these latest circumstances, please allow me to provide you both with an escort to the end of the Preservation Coalition's boundaries."

"I don't believe that is necessary," replied King Livingstone. "The Xagada would be foolish to pull the dwarf and elven nations into a war against them."

"Agreed, but the Xagada aren't well known for diplomatic or strategic planning."

"Then, we graciously accept your offer of protection," smiled Queen Hollyfield."

DECISIONS – DECISIONS

Lord Bembridge mistakenly believed that after the Xagada's demoralizing defeat trying to commandeer Stratagem, the ad hoc raids would stop or at least slow down long enough for the Preservation Coalition to formulate its plan of attack. However, it turned out to have just the opposite effect. By early morning, the Xagada had framed Stratagem's defensive measures as an unprovoked attack against Xagada-held dockside facilities. The general population was both incensed and frightened, pitting neighbor against neighbor. With everyone on edge, the slightest infraction escalated into an unruly riot. It was only a matter of time before the lies spread throughout Western Calvendar like an uncontained wildfire...

(So writes Conrad Nightingale)

Lord Bembridge sat alone in the High Counsel Chamber, fixated on the far wall, deep in thought, when a hand lightly touched his shoulder.

"Some wounds are never meant to heal, but your people need you now more than ever. Amanda would not want you to neglect your duties when our future dangles over an uncertain black abyss."

"What's that you say?" asked Bembridge, still in a stupor.

"The Heads of State await you in the Great Hall. Shall we convene the meeting?" responded Alcott.

Lord Bembridge shook his head as though trying to clear his thoughts.

"Yes, John, I shall start the meeting."

The chattering stopped when Lord Bembridge entered the Great Hall. The attack on Stratagem and the after-effects were no longer a secret. Lord Bembridge took his seat and motioned the others to sit with him. When all were seated and the room quiet, Lord Bembridge spoke.

"The rumors are true. Last night, the Xagada attempted to commandeer my flagship, Stratagem. Fortunately, the raid failed, for Stratagem is a formidable warship, and in the wrong hands, it could have easily tipped the balance of power on the high seas.

"Even so, the Xagada are using this event to spread propaganda about an unwarranted attack. I have already gotten reports of disquiet in the streets, and once the news reaches your respective provinces, you will no doubt experience similar situations."

"Then we should return to our homelands immediately!" said Lady Winslow.

"Our united objective remains the same. Despite this recent occurrence, should we disband the Preservation Coalition prematurely, we will be left in disarray and fall like dominoes in a line. Therefore, the quicker we can conclude our business, the better we will be served."

There was a unanimous rumbling and head shaking in agreement.

"Let it be decreed and memorialized by a written treaty that the separate states of Western Calvendar shall act in common for the protection and advancement of each province. Accordingly, each province shall hold and have an equal say in all collective matters, despite its physical size or economic strength. Notwithstanding, each province shall contribute proportionately any required monetary, manpower, and/or natural resources to support all resolutions passed by majority rule.

"Let it also be known that any act of aggression against a member of the Preservation Coalition shall be considered an attack upon us all. If anyone disagrees or requires clarification, please speak."

The room was silent.

"Excellent. Let it be known that the Preservation Coalition has been established on this date."

There was a collective cheer that echoed throughout the Great Hall.

"On to our first order of business – regretfully, a Declaration of War. To ensure our common safety, prosperity, and culture through civil obedience and acceptable behavioral standards, the Preservation Council declares war upon the Xagada Nation regardless of where its citizens may reside. Anyone opposed to this decree, please speak."

Once again, the room was silent. "The Declaration of War has passed."

"Now that we have completed the formalities, it is time to speak of the practicalities," said Lord Driscoll. "I want to know what is the ultimate objective with the Xagada? Are we seeking to segregate our existing communities, or do we intend to exile the Xagada east of the Eskridge Mountains?"

Kivik Runskar said, "If we simply segregate the Xagada, we must constantly police them, taxing our respective administrative resources."

Governor Marston responded, "We face not just an administrative burden if we exile the Xagada to the east; we will be patrolling the borders until they choose to attack. "

"What are you suggesting, Governor Marston?"

"I'm suggesting we rid ourselves of this plague once and for all."

"You mean genocide."

"Yes, I mean genocide; kill every man, woman, and child of the Xagada Nation."

Immediately, a dispute erupted. "I, for one, won't even consider that alternative," yelled Lord Driscoll.

"Not fifteen minutes ago, you swore allegiance to the Preservation Coalition and to abide by majority rule. Yet, the moment your standards are challenged, you act like an intransigent child not getting its way. How can you be trusted?" responded Governor Marston.

"You dare question my integrity?"

"Enough!" interrupted Lord Bembridge. We may not always agree on every issue, but we must hear and respect one another's view."

"You, Lord Bembridge, more than anyone, have suffered directly at the hands of the Xagada; what say you?" inquired Lady Winslow.

"I have sworn a personal oath to find and punish those responsible for the murder of my beloved wife, and I shall not rest until that debt is paid in full. On the battlefield, I vow to kill every Xagada who refuses to surrender unconditionally.

"However, if ours is the morally superior cause, we must be cautious not to debase ourselves beneath any actions of our enemy; we are better people than the Xagada. I cannot slaughter innocent people who pose no threat. Therefore, I vote for exile despite the burden it may bring. Who else stands with me?"

All but Governor Marston raised their hands, but not to be caught in the same trap he had accused Lord Driscoll of, he reluctantly agreed.

"I hope we won't regret this decision; how do we go about it now?"

An initial plan was devised for each Head of State to return to their respective provinces and to begin isolating the Xagada from the general population.

Lacking any formal structure to their government in Thammarat, it was hoped that the Xagada would be caught off guard and quickly moved to holding camps until sent eastward.

SUSPICION EVERYWHERE

The recent monumental change in the political landscape was a lot for the commoner to understand. Between the Xagada propaganda and the newly formed Preservation Coalition's Declaration of War, riots broke out in all major cities in Western Calvendar. Unfortunately, things were no better in the countryside, where longtime neighbors were suddenly at each other's throats. The only hope of stemming the violence was to enact martial law, establish a very restrictive travel policy, and put a curfew in place...

(So writes Conrad Nightingale)

The restrictive travel policy and curfew proved quite effective, as it sufficiently contained the Xagada, allowing the soldiers to scoop up entire families in the dead of night. Another effective measure was to snatch up the children and wait for the parents to turn themselves over to the authorities to be reunited. Although this tactic seemed especially cruel, the mere thought of splitting a family apart created considerable leverage.

In less than a week since the proclamation was announced, nearly all the Xagada in Western Calvendar were in holding camps where they could be controlled. Still, small pockets of resistance were difficult, and the havoc they created often proved deadly. On the tenth day of the 'Roundup', as it came to be known, Lord Bembridge received an important message: The Xantara requested a meeting under a flag of truce.

The meeting was set; the concerned parties would meet at Celesta, a place of sacred significance where enemies could parley without fear of retaliation.

***

A cold drizzle permeated the steel gray sky as if to emphasize everyone's somber mood as the parties gathered under makeshift tents. When it was time, each Head of State moved toward a single fire at the center of the gathering.

Lord Bembridge broke the silence. "Kayla Rycroft, Xantara of the Xagada Nation, you have requested this audience. What is it you have to say?"

The Xantara stared across the fire directly into Lord Bembridge's eyes.

"I say, shame on you all, especially you, heir of Roderick the Righteous. The spirit of your great-great-great grandfather must be in agony because of your actions. It's a disgrace that you and this so-called Preservation Coalition would declare an unprovoked war upon the Xagada people. Shame upon you all for leveraging children to accomplish your objective. And what exactly is that objective? Would you care to share that with me?"

"For generations, the Xagada have moved in and out of Western Calvendar, preying upon our best intentions and conning their way to easy living off the hard work of our citizens. Over the past generation, your people have migrated amongst us and become part of our communities. However, rather than assimilate, you brought your deplorable ways with you, tearing at the very fabric of our culture. It is time for the Xagada parasites to return to their home."

"Things are not exactly as you describe; Western Calvendar has also become our home over the past generation. Do you expect us to abandon our shops and our houses without compensation?

"The Preservation Coalition will allow you to live; is that not compensation enough?" said Governor Marston.

"Is this how you all feel?" Kayla Rycroft looked about the circle. Nobody showed any sign of dissent. "Then, you have left me no choice but to agree to your demands. I ask, but one thing, let us both stand down. Allow us the opportunity to leave in peace. If you agree, there will be no Xagada west of the Eskridge Mountains within three days."

Lord Bembridge looked at each member of the Preservation Coalition in turn; all but one had acquiesced. "So be it, Xantara. The treaty shall be drawn up today. Once signed, your people will be free to take what they can carry on their backs and be gone. We expect no trouble of any type, lest the treaty is broken, and we go to war."

"I give you my personal assurance that there will be no trouble."

"Your personal assurance gives me no comfort. After all, there is still a separate matter concerning your son-in-law and granddaughter."

For what it is worth, I knew nothing of my son-in-law's plan to infiltrate your inner circle, nor would I ever condone my granddaughter's participation in such a scheme. I have not seen my sweet grandchild since she left on that fool-hearted mission. And as for that worthless shit, Tobias Rycroft, if I had him I would gladly turn him over as a token of my sincere wish for peace."

On this highly personal matter, Lord Bembridge's mind was made up.

"The Xagada have a dubious knack for lying so convincingly." The circle broke, and everyone returned to their respective camps until the treaty could be memorialized.

Immediately, Lord Bembridge called the members of the Preservation Coalition to his tent to discuss this latest turn of events.

"I, for one, think this peace accord is too easy. I don't trust the Xagada, but I'm sure that comes as no surprise to any of you."

"Lord Bembridge, you are both cautious and sophisticated in the ways of diplomacy. You are beginning to persuade us. I think we better prepare for the worst, just in case."

***

After the document was signed, the word of the treaty went throughout Western Calvendar. There would be a three-day truce to allow the Xagada to leave, and no trouble of any kind by either side would be tolerated. Anyone foolish enough to break the truce did so at the forfeiture of their life.

It took less than three days to complete the exodus. For once, the Xantara was good to her word. Even so, soldiers of the Preservation Coalition, including members of Lord Bembridge's Ranger Regiment, escorted the Xagada men, women, and children as far as the Virox Divide; from there, they were on their own.

At long last, there was a feeling of peace in Western Calvendar, but for how long it would last, nobody knew.

CHAPTER 20

RETALIATION AND RETRIBUTION

Once she had her people safely back in Eastern Calvendar, Kayla Rycroft quickly implemented her plans to attack Western Calvendar. Her ally and cohort, Blox Nye, Supreme Commander of the Orc, had amassed nearly fifty thousand blood-thirsty orcs on the southern slopes of the Sawtooth Mountain range. Combined with almost thirty thousand Xagada from Thammarat and an additional ten thousand recently exiled Xagada, it was a formidable army...

(So writes Conrad Nightingale)

"Blox Nye, let us gather our respective commanders for a final briefing." Once everyone was gathered within a secure room of Kayla Rycroft's large home, a map was rolled out on a long table. Gregor, who was always attentive, helped the Xantara stand up and get a better perspective. Supreme Commander Blox Nye started the briefing.

SNORT... "Two days ago, Orc Reconnaissance Patrol watched Xagada march home." HARRUMPH...

"We saw no one," responded the Xantara.

SNORT... "That point, not see them. Patrol spy on Coalition. Get intelligence. Report tomorrow morning." HARRUMPH...

"I look forward to the report, Supreme Commander. And, what of our combined capabilities?"

SNORT... "XaOrc, ninety thousand. Control battle by numbers. Have big weapons for attacking Bembridge Castle." HARRUMPH...

The Xantara added, "Not to mention our newly equipped war wagons." Like Stratagem, the wagons had been equipped with giant pivotable crossbows. "Never let it be said the Xagada don't learn from their mistakes."

SNORT... "We win war." HARRUMPH...

"Yes, my friend, we will win this war. Just one important detail – I want Lord Bembridge taken alive. That insolent dog will pay for his disrespect. Understood?"

snort... "Understood." harrumph...

SPYING ON SPIES

The Orc Reconnaissance Patrol would not be returning with the anticipated report, for they did not have the training or stealth of Lord Bembridge's Ranger Regiment, who secretively followed the exiting Xagada into the Virox Divide. Not expecting an encounter, especially while still within the confines of the Eskridge Mountains, the orcs let down their guard. Once spotted by the Rangers, the orcs were at their mercy...

(So writes Conrad Nightingale)

Lieutenant Higgins and his men crouched low behind an outcropping of trees and watched as the orc patrol advanced. The orc wore no distinction of rank on their clothing.

"Can anyone make out the chain of command?"

"Looks like the one barking the orders is the boss," responded Sergeant Lockwood. No one else offered any alternative suggestion.

"Well then, he dies first. We want to take the second in command back to Bembridge Castle for questioning."

"Why is that?" asked Private Mallory.

"Because the orc leader will want to demonstrate his dominant role, and although he will eventually break, it may take too long. Whereas the second in command will consider himself thrown into an untenable position for which he isn't ready to accept. He will likely chatter to save himself any discomfort."

"I mean no disrespect, Sir, but with that logic, shouldn't we seek out the lowest rank?"

"Tell me, Private, WHAT do you know about our mission?" The point was made, and Private Mallory couldn't help but blush. "Back to the original question – whom do we take alive?"

"My bet would be on the big dumb looking one," injected Corporal Sanders.

"They're all big and dumb looking," chuckled Lieutenant Higgins. "Try to be more specific."

"He is a head taller than the rest and looks twice as wide; he has a heavy black beard, and his hair is tied back with trinkets."

"That's a description we can work with; does everyone see the orc that Sanders is describing?" The team members looked and responded affirmatively. "Good. Feel free to soften him up, but whatever you do, DON'T kill him. Sergeant Lockwood, take three men and flank behind the orc patrol. No orc is to escape! The rest of you spread out and remain hidden. We strike upon my lead."

The orc patrol continued to make their way toward Western Calvendar, often seeking the easiest path, for they were still miles from the opening to Virox Divide.

Little did they know they had been surrounded by the Rangers, who remained concealed to all but the most highly trained eye until Lieutenant Higgins stepped out from behind a tree, his sword raised and ready.

"Hello," he greeted the bandy orc in the front of the pack. It was the last word the orc heard as Lieutenant Higgins' sword slashed across the orc's neck.

Before the rest of the orc squadron could respond or seek cover, they were cut down by a flurry of arrows. Several orcs at the back of the squad turned to run but soon found themselves face-to-face with Sergeant Lockwood and his men. Perhaps because they had been taken off-guard, the orc patrol gave little resistance.

Within minutes of the initial kill, the only orc standing was the big brute with a heavy black beard and long hair tied back with trinkets, and he didn't look like he was going to come easily. He lifted his spiked warclub, crouched low like a cat ready to pounce, and gave a deafening shriek.

Much to the orc's dismay, no Ranger accepted the challenge; they just stood there mocking him. Infuriated, the big orc charged toward Lieutenant Higgins, who casually stood there laughing.

Off to the side, Private Mallory let loose an arrow piercing the orc's forearm, causing him to drop his weapon. Another arrow whistled in from the opposite direction, hitting the orc in the thigh and dropping him to the ground. Even in this weakened state, it took three Rangers to hold him down until he was sufficiently bound.

Once back at Bembridge Castle, the orc's hands and feet were shackled tightly to the dungeon wall, where he was left waiting in the dark.

***

At the break of dawn, the Master Inquisitor, Thea Tifton, entered the dungeon alone to face the prisoner. A single torch was placed into the wall sconce, but it was all the light needed to make out the various implements of torture necessary to extract information. Tifton dragged a stool in front of the orc and plopped down. The woman was disheveled and anemic, and her sunken eyes stared blankly into space.

"My name is Thea, what's yours?" The orc didn't respond; he just stared in disbelief.

"I get that same look every time I'm asked to speak to a prisoner, and I know exactly what you're thinking." She giggled as if she alone was privy to some untold joke.

"'How is this frail woman supposed to extract any information from me?' You know, I'm not exactly sure how I do it, but I always seem to get what I'm looking for," again, she let out a giggle.

SNORT… "Eat shit and die, human. Me no talk." HARRUMPH…

"Yuk! That doesn't sound very appetizing. By the way, how are your wounds? Those Rangers can be brutal when they want something." Tifton held up her hand. "Sorry, you don't have to answer that question because I really don't care. In fact, I don't care anything about you. I do, however, want to know why you were spying on the Preservation Coalition?"

The massive orc didn't respond.

"Not ready to talk yet? That's okay. I'm sure I have a remedy for your silence somewhere around here." Tifton started to meander about the dungeon. Occasionally, she would linger, pick up a tool, and stroke it with a perverted passion. She could see out of the corner of her eye that the orc was growing nervous.

"I've been told that orcs have a very high threshold for pain. Is that true?"

SNORT… Fuck you, crazy bitch." HARRUMPH…

Thea Tifton picked up a sharp slender knife and cut the back of her scarred forearm. For her, this was a ritual, one that she had been through many times; the torture was about to begin. She sucked on the cut. The blood had a sweet metallic taste, and she enjoyed it.

"There was no need to hurt my feelings and make things personal. We were having such a nice conversation, and you ruined it. I was lying when I said I didn't know how to extract information. I know exactly what it takes." She selected a long, slender knife and turned toward the orc.

"Unfortunately, I don't have enough time to play with you and test your proclaimed endurance, so regretfully, I'll need to 'cut' straight to the point." She chuckled at the pun. "Do you know what this blade is used for?"

Walking over to the orc, she carefully traced her finger over his trembling body.

"There's the spot." She removed her finger and slid the knife deep into his side, where she left it impaled. The orc buckled and screamed in pain.

"Now, I'm going to ask you some questions, and every time I think you're lying, I'll give the knife a slight twist." To emphasize her point, she gave the blade handle a slight bump. The orc's reaction was immediate.

As anticipated by Lieutenant Higgins, it wasn't long before the orc told all he knew of the pending XaOrc battle plan to conquer Western Calvendar.

TIME IS OF THE ESSENCE

With the vital information coerced out of the orc prisoner, the Preservation Coalition could now put in place defenses, as well as plan a counterattack. That is, if there was enough time...
(So writes Conrad Nightingale)

As quickly as Lord Bembridge could reassemble the Preservation Coalition, he told the other Heads of State about the Xagadas' plan to attack Western Calvendar with the orcs' help.

"We have made a critical mistake thinking that the Xagada were nothing more than a loosely structured band of nomads. The Xagada/Orc alliance and imminent timeline suggest this attack was long in the planning, and we are caught flat-footed. From the size of their combined army to their advanced weaponry, it is clear this will be a battle for the future of humanity," he said.

All hopes for a peaceful settlement were gone in a flash.

"Do you have any details of their attack?" inquired Lady Winslow.

"We expect the XaOrc army to approach through the Virox Divide. We have also learned from the interrogation that the XaOrc plan to break off a large contingent force to take siege of the city of Roderick and Bembridge Castle while the main XaOrc army keeps us busy on the battlefield."

"That's bad news, for orcs will tear down every stone in Bembridge Province and kill anyone they find. You'll need to stay and protect your homeland," said Lord Driscoll.

"Your assessment of orc battle tactics is correct, Lord Driscoll, but I will not abandon the rest of the Preservation Coalition in its greatest moment of need. Never has Bembridge Castle fallen, and let it be known that I'm making plans to ensure it does not fall under my watch."

Lord Bembridge continued, "The Orc Reconnaissance Patrol is due to report back tomorrow morning. When they don't return, we must assume that the XaOrc leadership will surmise that they have been killed or, worse, captured, which means the attack will no longer come as a surprise. In any case, they will begin to march."

"Perhaps stopping the Orc Forward Recon Patrol is enough for them to delay the attack."

"Doubtful. Once set in motion, war is like a juggernaut, harder to stop than it is to start. We only have a few days' advantage to reach the Konosha Plain with our combined forces. So go now, make haste, and gather your troops; we meet next at the Virox Divide."

***

After the Council Chamber emptied, Lord Bembridge asked Minister Alcott to sit with him. "John, you have already done so much in service to the House of Bembridge, but regretfully, I must ask for more."

"No need for regrets, my Lord; I serve at your pleasure."

Lord Bembridge smiled. "You are a good and loyal friend, John. Unfortunately, the mission I have planned for you is dangerous."

"I'm intrigued; tell me more."

"The alliance between the Xagada Nation and Orc Clans is too large to defeat without the involvement of every able person on the plain of Konosha. That means the city of Roderick and Bembridge Castle will be unprotected. I need help if I hope to save Bembridge Province," he said.

"I want you to leave immediately for the Pillars-of-the-Sky, John. This mission will require you to skirt past the enemy. Once at the Pillars, you must convince the Creel that it is in their best interest to join our cause."

"There is no convincing the Creel of any cause," John said. "As mercenaries, they are only interested in payment, and under the circumstance, the asking price will be high."

"Negotiate the best deal you can, but make sure you secure a contract to protect Bembridge Province in my absence."

"I will leave at once, my Lord. Be safe and try not to kill all of those bastards before my return."

SEEKING ASSISTANCE

Johnathan Alcott served as a commando in the Ranger Regiment for most of his adult life, and his tracking skills were finely honed. As such, he was adept at finding the path of least resistance when making his way through unknown territory. Even on the rare occasion that he lacked the necessary skill, his constant companion, Adak, would find the best way. He needed to make his way undetected over the Eskridge Mountains and reach the Pillars-of-the-Sky as quickly as possible. Many lives depended upon his successful and expeditious negotiations with the Creel...

(So writes Conrad nightingale)

Johnathan left immediately after his conversation with Lord Bembridge, and choosing the proper route was critical, for there was no time to waste. The quickest route from Bembridge Province to the Pillars-of-the-Sky is via Serpent's Gulch, but that twisted terrain comes with its issues, not to mention the risk of running into forward XaOrc patrols.

The Virox Divide was out of the question, as this way was the primary route for the XaOrc invasion. Traveling as far south as the Pennon Pass to skirt around the Eskridge Mountains would take too long to reach his destination. Alcott had no choice but to go up and over the range; it would be arduous. He would travel light and travel fast.

Fortunately, Tess was already fed and groomed for whatever the day's activities. She was a good horse, and Alcott knew she would carry him until she dropped, if necessary. As for Adak, he was always ready for a romp through the highlands.

After galloping Tess for most of the day, when Alcott was approximately twenty miles south of the Virox Divide, he turned due east into the Piedmont and began to climb the lower slope of Mount Rannell. Tess continued giving her all, but she was getting exhausted; her body was lathered in sweat, and her mouth was frothed from a lack of water.

When they finally approached a stream, Alcott dismounted and removed the saddle and tack. Tess lowered her head toward the cool running water and drank deeply. While she drank, Alcott wiped her body with a damp cloth.

"There is no finer horse in all of Calvendar," he spoke to her as though she could understand. "You have carried me faster and further than I had hoped, but it is time we part. Travel easy on your way home, Tess." Alcott gave her a loving slap on the flank, and off she trotted.

"It's just you and me now. Adak. Are you ready?" Adak cocked his head as if it was simply a rhetorical question, then he turned and bolted; Alcott followed at a slow but steady jog.

As good a shape as Alcott was in, after a full day and night, the pace was taking its toll. As for Adak, he hadn't broken a sweat, for kolgarrs' have incredible endurance and can run a deer to death. As time progressed and the terrain became more challenging to traverse, Alcott found himself having to stop more often to rest. Occasionally, he would fall asleep only to be awakened by a slobbery lick from Adak. If he failed to respond, a nip on the end of his nose was all it would take to bring him wide awake.

By the early afternoon of the second day, Alcott broke through a clearing where he saw Adak sitting looking out over the horizon. In the distance loomed the Pillars-of-the-Sky, a large grouping of monolithic towers strung together by an elaborate highway of suspended bridges. With luck, he should be there before sundown.

By late afternoon, the first massive structure was within a quarter mile. Alcott told Adak to stay back and keep hidden while he proceeded alone. Once he reached the base of the first tower, he cupped his hands around his mouth and yelled into the sky.

"I am Johnathan Alcott, bearing an important message from Lord Bembridge for the leader of the Creel!" He waited several minutes, but there was no response. Walking further into the circle of pillars, he tried again.

"I'm Johnathan Alcott, on an urgent mission from Bembridge Province. I must speak to the leader of the Creel at once!" Again, there was no response. This went on until just before dusk.

"Please, I implore you, I must speak with the leader of the Creel; it is a matter of life and death!"

"An urgent meeting regarding a matter of life and death – that sounds very grave indeed," came a voice behind some shrubbery. Stepping forward was a shirtless muscular man, his tan body bearing many scars, his long black hair tied in a single braid.

"I am Logan Trask, leader of the Creel. What do you want of me, Johnathan Alcott of Bembridge Province?"

"Is there somewhere we can sit and speak?"

"You can sit here on the ground and speak. If you require privacy, I assure you it's just the two of us."

Alcott looked about suspiciously, "It's unusual for a leader to place himself in peril without protection."

"I never claimed to be unprotected. I caution you that any aggressive move toward me will be met with a phalanx of arrows sent from the sky. You'll be lucky to get more than a few steps, that is, if I don't cut you down myself." Logan was calm and emphatic in his declaration, and Alcott was sure he wasn't bragging.

"It's almost time for the evening meal if you have something to say, speak, or be on your way."

Alcott began, "Recently, the independent provinces of Western Calvendar united in a cause to save our cultural integrity, and we exiled the Xagada people back to Eastern Calvendar. In retaliation, the Xantara allied with the orc clans of the Sawtooth Mountains to invade Western Calvendar, which they are doing as we speak. We have discovered that part of their invasion plan is to send a large contingent force to take Bembridge Castle while Lord Bembridge and his army fight on the Konosha Plain.

"Then, Lord Bembridge should withdraw and return home to protect his interest."

"Lord Bembridge will not betray the Preservation Coalition, as he has vowed to stand united."

"It sounds like Lord Bembridge is a man of honor; for that, he has my respect. However, he should prepare for the worse, for his homeland will fall."

"Not if the Creel agree to come to his aid?"

" Are you suggesting that the Creel involve themselves in your dispute?"

"Everyone knows the Creel are for hire at the right price. Let us negotiate."

"If I were interested, why would I bother negotiating? I assume you are here because what you say is true; therefore, Lord Bembridge must be prepared to pay whatever my price. Under the circumstances, that price will be quite high. Are you authorized to accept on his behalf?"

"Regardless of the dire circumstances, I'll accept only if your price is reasonable," responded Alcott.

"Then, here is the asking price, and it is **NON-NEGOTIABLE**. I know of the recent formation of the Preservation Coalition. I am upset that Lord Bembridge would reach out as far as the dwarfs of Remmelic and the elves of Gwaii yet never consider inviting the Creel. It was taken as an affront to my people."

"It was not meant as an insult. At the time, we sought allies, not mercenaries."

"That is the problem. The Creel Nation is not recognized as a legitimate State, and therein lies my asking price. We will join in your battle only if the Creel Nation has full recognition and equal standing on the Preservation Council."

Alcott was taken aback, for he had expected an extremely high ransom in gold. However, there was no hesitation in his response. "I agree and welcome you to the Preservation Council on behalf of Lord Bembridge."

"And, what of the other members of the Coalition? Do you speak for them?"

"I do not," answered Alcott. "But on my life, I will see that it happens."

"I assure you, Johnathan Alcott, that is exactly the case. Now, my new friend, please join me for dinner. You need a hot meal and a good night's rest. We will ride at morning's first light and catch up with the others where they wait."

"Your men have already set out?" inquired Alcott. "Yes,

earlier today when you first arrived. I felt confident that you would meet our price, and there was no time to waste." Logan made a strange-sounding call, and within seconds, a basket was lowered to retrieve them.

"One last thing, shall we leave some food for your kolgarr, or will he fend for himself?" Alcott was duly impressed.

CHAPTER 21

MARCH OR DIE

When the Orc Reconnaissance Patrol failed to report, it was assumed that the Preservation Coalition learned of the XaOrc plan to invade Western Calvendar…

(So writes Conrad Nightingale)

"We can't delay a moment longer; it is time to march!" declared Kayla Rycroft.

SNORT… We ready," replied Blox Nye. Orc lead, Xagada, follow through Virox Divide. Once through, five thousand

XaOrc go to Bembridge Castle. We smash all. No prisoners."
HARRUMPH…

As agreed, the first beat of the war drums rang within the hour, and slowly, the troops began to move out. For an army this large, the march to and through the Virox Divide would take two days. Once through, strategic planning, battle tactics, and luck would determine future timelines and objectives.

A FIGHTING CHANCE

The orc prisoner broke quickly under the skilled hand of the Master Inquisitor. Obtaining the knowledge of when and where the XaOrc army planned to attack, at least, gave the Preservation Coalition a fighting chance to defend themselves rather than being taken completely off guard. Setting out from the various provinces, the combined Preservation Coalition armies wasted no time converging on the Konosha Plain, approximately a mile due west of the Virox Divide. Where wildflowers once bloomed, over forty thousand soldiers now dotted the countryside.

Campaign Headquarters was erected upon a small knoll overlooking the proposed battlefield. The flags of the Houses of Bembridge, Driscoll, Winslow, and the Bohkor and Kermatic territories flew proudly above the tent. Inside, the respective Heads of State went over last-minute details. However, with no apparent battlefield leader, the Campaign Headquarters was in immediate disarray... (So writes Conrad Nightingale)

"We need a commander to lead our combined forces," Governor Marston spoke above the clamor. "And although, as a freeman, I prefer elected officials, a battlefield is no place for democracy. We need an experienced commander giving orders, preferably one who can act under duress and knows first-hand that no battle goes as planned. I suggest Lord Driscoll."

"No disrespect, but we shouldn't rule out the strongest house amongst us," another said. "What say you, Lord Bembridge?"

"I say heavy is the burden of he who leads others in battle. I have fought alongside Lord Driscoll several times and know him to be a tactical and decisive leader. I, for one, will be honored to fight under his direction. If there are no others for consideration, what are your orders, Field Marshal Driscoll?"

***

Although Field Marshal Driscoll was familiar with this region, he studied the map before him, looking for any tactical advantage the terrain might yield.

"The alliance between the Xagada Tribe and Orc Clans has culminated in an army that outnumbers us two to one. Though we are a superior trained army, the sheer number of combatants will pose a significant problem. Therefore, we will strike the first blow here," Driscoll said, pointing to a spot on the map.

"We must do whatever it takes to contain the XaOrc army within the canyon for as long as possible, reducing their numbers and hopefully demoralizing them in the process. Once they break free - and they will break free - we need to keep them against the mountains to limit their maneuverability.

"I want an initial force of five thousand troops to meet the XaOrc army at the narrowest pinch point in the Virox Divide. Those troops will hold back the advancing XaOrc army for as long as possible," Driscoll finished.

"Since the House of Winslow lies nearest to the canyon opening at Virox, we shall hold the XaOrc army at bay," said Lady Winslow.

"The honor of first blood shall be yours," responded Field Marshal Driscoll. "Lord Bembridge, we will also need your Rangers; they must create a diversion for our forces to retreat at the appropriate time.

"I'll send my Ranger Regiment into the mountain passage to look for any pinch points where they can create difficulties for the enemy," responded Lord Bembridge.

"We also learned that once through the Virox Divide, the XaOrc intend to break off a significant contingent force with war machines and head them toward Bembridge Province. The intermittent woodlands will require them to take the road northwest," Driscoll continued.

"I intend to slow, if not stop, that march. I want lines of sharpened pickets interspaced with oil-filled ditches ready to be set ablaze. Many a freeman from the Tanglewood Forest know their way around an axe, Governor Marston. Care to take on this assignment?"

"Consider it done, sir," Marston replied.

"I appreciate the support for Bembridge Province, but don't jeopardize the overall battle for one State. As I've said,

I have already set in motion my plans for the protection of my homeland," Bembridge said.

"That is good to hear, and I sincerely wish you well, Walter. Nevertheless, we'll contain and push the XaOrc army southeast, leaving them no way to escape except via the Pennon Pass into Bessemer, the Valley of Dragons."

There was a pregnant pause in the conversation before Marshal Driscoll's final words, "We've arrived a day earlier than the XaOrc, but there is still no time to waste. Let's get to work setting the trap."

BUYING TIME

It was a good overall plan, and Lady Winslow took command of the first assault; she wouldn't have it any other way. The next day, five thousand soldiers moved into the Virox Divide approximately three miles until they reached the narrows, with two consecutive switchbacks and high cliffs banking on either side. This terrain would allow the Preservation Coalition troops to remain hidden until the last second. One thousand archers were ordered to the front line; each soldier carried as many arrows as they could bear within multiple slings. Their objective was straightforward: once given the signal to start firing, launch as many arrows as deep into enemy lines as possible. After spending their rounds, they were to move to the back of the line and be replaced by the infantry. The infantry was armed with long lances to penetrate any advancing threat. When the lances were no longer effective, each soldier carried a short sword, ideal for close-quarter fighting…

(So writes Conrad Nightingale)

By now, the XaOrc army was not far away, and you could feel the earth vibrate as their considerable numbers marched in unison. Lord Bembridge immediately ordered his Ranger Regiment to seek higher ground and look for any means to slow the advancement when it came time for the PC troops to retreat. There was nothing more to do but wait.

Two hours later, forward scouts reported that the enemy was within a mile of the narrows. They advised that the enemy seemed endless, and the sight of the ugly armored orcs gave even these veteran commandos a chill. Lady Winslow turned to her troops and spoke loudly for all to hear.

"Take heart! Orcs bleed, and they die, so let's take a huge bite out of them! Hold fast and wait for my signal!"

The troops waited as ordered. There were no heroes longing for battle; everyone was scared, and soon, the pounding of their heartbeats merged with the din of the XaOrc war drums. A forward scout darted into view, "They're within a hundred yards."

Lady Winslow drew her sword and held it high above her head, "Now!" she yelled, bringing her sword to the ground. The first line of archers ran into the open, crouched low, and let their deadly cargo fly. Again and again, arrows flew forth. Caught completely off guard, the XaOrc soldiers screamed in pain and fell before the onslaught. However, those in the back kept coming, marching over the dead and dying.

When the last arrow was notched and launched, the archers retreated, replaced by the infantry. Shields raised and lances lowered, they created a nearly impenetrable wall closing off the narrow. But the XaOrc army pushed forward in an almost hypnotic state, impaling themselves upon the extended pikes.

Close-quarters hand-to-hand combat came next. The orcs were ferocious fighters, single-minded, and not afraid to die. They continued to push forward, flails slinging over the defensive shield wall, now giving better than they got.

Lady Winslow's company began to take too many casualties to remain in place; it was time to withdraw. She hoped Lord Bembridge's Ranger Regiment had found a way to slow the XaOrc advance from on-high. The trumpets blew the call to retreat; the troops turned and, on the run, headed for the Konosha Plain.

But this only encouraged the orcs, who hastened their attack. However, as the orcs squeezed through the narrows, there was a loud rumbling from on high. Looking up, an avalanche of rocks poured down upon them. When the dust cleared, several hundred more orcs lay dead among the rubble. The Ranger's attack from above had slowed the orcs' advancement long enough to allow for a clean getaway.

***

Once back at the Campaign Headquarters, Lady Winslow estimated her company had killed approximately ten thousand orcs at the narrows while suffering just north of one thousand PC soldiers lost or wounded. "The loss of any of our soldiers is devastating, but a ten-to-one victory is an acceptable return.

"Well done, Lady Winslow. You have not only shown the XaOrc army of our superior fighting skill but have also bought us precious time to ready our defenses," exclaimed Field Marshal Driscoll.

"I don't think the orcs give a damn about superior fighting skills or tactics; they are a brutal single-minded force, more afraid of their command structure than us," said Lord Bembridge.

"Then, when they get here, we will have to be as brutal in our resolve," responded Governor Marston.

CHAPTER 22

THE CLEANSE

For the past couple of days, Alcott had existed on beef jerky, water, and intermittent naps of no more than two hours. So, after a full hot meal, when he laid down on a feathered mattress and pillow, he was unconscious for a solid eight hours. When he awoke just before daybreak, Logan Trask was already outside waiting…

(So writes Conrad Nightingale)

"Rested and ready to go, I hope?" asked Logan.

"I haven't felt this good in days," responded Alcott.

"Then, let's not waste more time; horses are waiting for us below. Follow me."

Logan gave his wife a passionate kiss goodbye as if it would be his last. Alcott grabbed his sword and nodded his thanks to Katherine as the two were lowered in a basket. Once below, they mounted their horses and galloped off into the pre-dawn morning.

***

When the sun was shining directly overhead, they came upon nearly one thousand Creel waiting outside the eastern entrance to the Virox Divide. As they dismounted, a man approached.

"This is my Captain, Travis Yarborough. Travis, this is Johnathan Alcott, an emissary from the Preservation Coalition." The two exchanged nods.

"What have you learned, Travis?"

"The XaOrc army started through the Virox Divide two days ago. They're moving steadily and, barring unforeseen circumstances, should be through the divide by now."

"Knowing Lord Bembridge as well as I do, I think he will have a few surprises to slow the enemy.

"Actually, their advancement stopped yesterday afternoon. Perhaps he sprung one of those surprises already."

"No time to waste; sounds like we are going to cut things close. Get the men mounted, Captain; we ride for Serpent's Gulch."

"What do we do with the boy hiding in the tree, listening to us?" asked Alcott, wondering if the others were even aware of his presence.

"Ah yes, the little bird." Logan turned and walked several steps toward a large oak tree covered with thick moss, a pretty good hiding place to an untrained eye.

"You, up in the tree, come down. We need to talk." There was no response, not so much as a leaf fluttered.

"All right then, I'll have my archers shoot you out of the tree." The boy saw two archers notch arrows, ready for the command; it was all the coaxing he needed. However, as soon as the boy's feet reached the ground, he darted like a fox on the run. Instantly, two warning shots hit just inches in front of his stride; the boy slid to an immediate standstill.

"No more games, boy, come here!"

The young boy walked boldly up to Logan until they were face-to-face. His slender body shook involuntarily. He was frightened; nevertheless, he stared deep into Logan's eyes and proclaimed his identity.

"I am Ryker Drake, son of Walker Drake and a proud Xagada."

"I am Logan Trask, Leader of the Creel Nation." The two held one another in their respective gaze.

"Where is your father now?"

Ryker straightened his back along with his resolve.

"He is serving the Xantara on the front lines of the great XaOrc army. You may meet him soon enough."

"Too young to fight, so your daddy left you behind to be the man of the house until his return; is that it? What would your father think to hear you abandoned your mother to become a spy?"

"My mother is dead. Besides, I'm no spy," spit Ryker. "I'm a patriot!"

"I admire your distinction, but unfortunately for you, I don't share your characterization. You have undoubtedly heard our plan and feel obligated to share this information with the XaOrc, so what am I to do with you?"

"Whatever you normally do with your prisoners, I suppose."

"That's a problem, Ryker. The Creel Nation does not have the manpower nor resources to keep prisoners alive; therefore, we do not take prisoners. You understand what that means?"

Ryker Drake went pale, and his eyes began to well up; he was about to meet the spirit of death.

"Perhaps there's another way; are you a betting man, Ryker?" This question got everyone's attention. *What is he up to,* thought Alcott? "I'll bet you can't get to the Xantara in time to warn the XaOrc Army of the Creel's plan to protect Bembridge Province. Of course, if you do, you will be treated as a great patriot and rewarded appropriately."

"And, what will you gain by the wager if I don't arrive on time?"

"I want your oath that if the war does not go well for the XaOrc, you will come to the Pillars-of-the-Sky on your eighteenth birthday and join the Creel Nation. We can always use strong, honorable men such as yourself." There was no way the boy could reach the XaOrc in time, but Trask was giving him some purpose and dignity.

"Agreed."

"Captain Yarborough, give Ryker Drake back his horse." Turning to Ryker, he continued, "Next time you're out spying, hide your animal before yourself. Once we found him, we knew to continue looking until we found you. I hope your horse can run, as well as he can pull a plow. Good luck, Ryker Drake."

"I believe you to be an honorable man, Logan Trask. I do hope you don't die suffering." Off trotted Ryker through the Virox Divide while Logan Trask led his men, full gallop, for the Serpent's Gulch.

NOTHING BUT AN INCONVENIENCE

The XaOrc Army had suffered a defeat at the narrows, but it was not enough to stop their forward momentum. By early morning, the army had spread out across the mouth of the Virox Divide, where they had stopped and made camp. Inside the XaOrc Campaign Headquarters, final discussions were held for the mission to capture Bembridge Province. Assembled before the Xantara and the Supreme Commander were the joint captains and supporting officers of a contingent force of five thousand soldiers assigned to take the city of Roderick and Bembridge Castle...

(So writes Conrad Nightingale)

All stood quiet as Gregor led the Xantara to her chair; once seated, she began speaking barely above a whisper.

"Some may see yesterday's skirmish in the narrows as a defeat – nothing can be further from the truth. We have shown the Preservation Coalition that despite ambush tactics, their puny force is no match for the mighty XaOrc Army."

The tent was immediately filled with cheers and calls for victory. The Xantara held up her hand, signaling for silence; once quiet, she continued.

"The real battle begins today, and the PC has no idea what to expect, but they will find out soon enough." Again, the cheers began.

Supreme Commander Blox Nye made his way to the war table at the center of the tent. Carved pieces were placed on a map, showing the locations of the respective XaOrc forces. The map showed an unobstructed route leading directly to Bembridge Province.

SNORT… "When war drums sound, we meet enemy on battlefield. Kam Otez leads contingent force. Destroy Bembridge Province… HARRUMPH…

The Xantara couldn't raise her voice above the din as she frantically squeezed Gregor's arm to intervene on her behalf. Understanding the orc's propensity to destroy everything in sight, he yelled.

"The Xantara wants to emphasize that the objective is to capture and hold the city, not destroy it!"

The Xantara smiled at Gregor and patted his arm. Now that she had everyone's attention, she continued.

"Don't look so dismayed. The Orc Clans will be well compensated in treasure for your efforts; try not to burn every timber and pull down every stone when capturing the city and castle, for we plan to make it the new capital of the XaOrc Nation."

Of course, she was lying, but her assurances seemed to placate even Blox Nye. "We don't anticipate any resistance, but should it occur, protect your Xagada brethren, for they have lived within Roderick and can guide you accordingly."

SNORT... No worry, orcs' tiny brains understand. We follow plan. Protect Xagada little brothers HARRUMPH... The orcs howled in laughter.

Kayla Rycroft was being mocked. Although she did not respond, her icy glare spoke volumes — this was a fragile alliance.

DUTY BOUND

The small boy bouncing atop a large workhorse as it trotted along was comical to behold. It isn't easy to get a horse whose only purpose in life is to amble along pulling a plow, now to run, regardless of the emergency. Nevertheless, Ryker Drake wouldn't give up, frantically kicking at the sides of the animal until his ankles were bruised. More than once, Ryker thought it would be quicker to get off the horse and start running himself, but then the horse would break into a trot for a short distance. On and on, the cycle repeated itself since he departed with the Creel earlier this morning...

(So writes Conrad Nightingale)

"Come on, Elias, faster. The XaOrc need our help. Dad needs our help. Don't give up on me."

A big orc stepped out from hiding in the brush; he spread his arms wide, bringing Elias to an abrupt stop. SNORT... Hold, boy. Where you goin'?" HARRUMPH...

Ryker was startled by the unexpected encounter; truth be known, alliance or not, the sight of any orc, especially one this size, scared him.

SNORT… "Where you goin', boy?" repeated the orc. HARRUMPH…

"Let me pass. I have important information for the Xantara; it's a matter of life or death. Now, let me pass! Ryker demanded."

SNORT… "No, boy. No, let you ride into XaOrc Headquarters; cost me my head." HARRUMPH…

In any standoff, there are many factors to consider, such as time being of the essence or one's willingness to endure physical discomfort. In this case, Ryker was sure the orc would, if necessary, end his life, and precious time was quickly running out.

SNORT… "Know how to settle. Tell me. HARRUMPH… SNORT… If important, I take you to Xantara. HARRUMPH… SNORT… If not important, you go home" HARRUMPH… Ryker knew he had no choice, and he told the big orc about his spying on the Creel, leaving out any details of getting caught.

SNORT… "Boy right, important information, valuable information." HARRUMPH…

"Then take me to the Xantara at once; we have no time to waste."

SNORT… "No. Me take information. Get down off horse." HARRUMPH… Ryker had been tricked. He kicked Elias in this side with all his might; the horse immediately jumped, but the big orc held his bridle tight.

SNORT… "Me say down." HARRUMPH… The orc threw the boy from the saddle with his free hand. Ryker Drake hit the ground with an audible thud, striking his head on a rock. He let out a moan. Once the orc mounted, he looked down at the child.

SNORT… "You no look good. Put out of misery. Right thing to do." HARRUMPH…

The orc walked Elias back and forth over Ryker until the life was crushed out of his tiny body.

Then, the orc rode for XaOrc Headquarters as though nothing unusual had happened. At a slow but steady pace, he should arrive before the evening.

CHAPTER 23

THE SPOILS OF WAR

True to their plan, once the war drums sounded, a contingency force of one thousand Xagada soldiers led by four thousand orcs, along with several catapults and a sizeable battering ram, immediately turned northwest toward Bembridge Province. As anticipated by Field Marshall Driscoll, the tree line funneled the XaOrc contingent force toward the roadway, where they encountered a gauntlet of sharpened pickets and pitch filled ditches barring their way.

However, these obstacles didn't stop the single-minded orcs from trying to reach their objective. First, the XaOrc pushed through the picket lines, using the fallen bodies of their brethren to blunt the points. Then, their logistical backup team began to cut down the obstacles while under the fire of PC archers. Hundreds fell, but the orcs did not give up. They advanced foot by foot, yard by yard, until finally, within the entanglement, the PC shot burning arrows, setting the oil ablaze from a safe distance. The smell of burning flesh was nauseating, but still, the orcs did not stop advancing. Finally, Governor Marston's freemen gave way, rejoining the main company, already under heavy attack…

(So writes Conrad Nightingale)

By evening, the XaOrc contingent force had moved out of sight, and both main armies had lost many soldiers on the battlefield with little notable progress. As the sunset faded and the sky grew dark, there seemed to be a natural break in the hostilities, but this was no truce.

On the contrary, those who foolishly entered the battlefield, even with the intent of treating the wounded, were quickly brought down by sniper arrows.

A NECESSARY RISK

After separating from Ryker Drake, Logan Trask, Captain Yarborough, and Minister Alcott led the Creel through the treacherous Serpent Gulch. Although a shorter route through the mountains to their destination, the dry riverbed was narrow, full of twists and turns, and it slowed the horses down to no more than intermittent lopes. To make matters worse, the weather was a concern because an afternoon thunderstorm was not unusual during this time of year, and should that occur, it could prove disastrous if floodwater caught them within the confines of the canyon.

Colder winds blew ominous-looking clouds out of the Sawtooth Mountain range, and occasionally, distant claps of thunder could be heard; it was nerve-wracking. Nevertheless, this was the plan, and the thousand-plus Creel moved in single file with precision...

(So writes Conrad Nightingale)

Luck was on their side, and the inclement weather stayed to the north. By mid-afternoon, the Creel banded together, safe and sound, at the northwest entrance to the canyon.

"We made it through the gap and in good time to boot," said Logan. "Guess that means young Ryker didn't deliver his message in time to make any difference. And, you thought I would have to kill him," he laughed.

"You handled the situation like a father," responded Alcott. "I suspect you'll be seeing Ryker on his eighteenth birthday." Had they known the truth, their hearts would have been heavy.

"I'm going to ride south and take a closer look." Off dashed Captain Yarborough with two soldiers in tow.

***

While Captain Yarborough investigated the enemy's progress, the Creel continued to Roderick. It was a five-mile run to the outer gates of the city. To those inside the city, the sound of a thousand horses galloping in your direction must have been frightening. Once they arrived, the gate was locked, and nobody was in sight.

"What do you make of it, John? Has the city been abandoned?"

"Perhaps those who were unable to fight have retreated to the castle, where they can try to protect themselves." Alcott rode forward to the base of the gate. "Hello, inside, Roderick! This is Minister Alcott! I have brought reinforcements!"

The gate began to rise, and out came Sergeant Womack, who had a grin on his face and arms flung wide. Alcott dismounted, and the two embraced.

"Glory. Glory to you, Minister Alcott, and glory to your friends."

"Allow me to present Logan Trask, head of the Creel Nation." Trask dismounted and reached for Womack's hand, which he heartedly accepted.

"The night will soon be upon us. Come inside the gate and refresh yourselves.," said Womack. A thousand Creel were greeted warmly once inside the city of Roderick. All were provided with food, ale, and a place to rest peacefully while they could. Watchmen were stationed to keep a lookout for Captain Yarborough and his men.

A couple of hours passed when Captain Yarborough reported back to Logan. Introductions were brief, and the captain responded with his customary nod.

"The XaOrc contingent force has been broken, many have perished on the Konosha Battlefield, and many more were gravely wounded. The orcs are now in command, while the Xagada have been relegated to little more than slaves pulling the catapults and battering ram."

"I'm sure that isn't sitting well," injected Sergeant Womack.

"When should they arrive?" asked Logan Trask.

"They need rest. My guess is they will arrive tomorrow mid-morning.

"That doesn't give us much time to fortify your defenses."

"We won't need to," responded Sergeant Womack. "Why let the XaOrc destroy even a single stone? Instead, we will invite them in." Womack smiled at Alcott, who winked back his concurrence.

Logan Trask and Travis Yarborough would understand soon enough."

PRESSING FORWARD

The surprise blockade was the second time that the XaOrc had suffered a significant loss at the hands of the Preservation Coalition. The XaOrc contingent force had lost at least a third of its soldiers and all its experienced officers. The remaining junior officer who took command was young Kai Kolack, recently given his commission in exchange for his father's significant contribution to Blox Nye's coffer. Though Kai Kolack's position allowed him to be privy to the overall plan to seize Bembridge Province, he was never meant to be in command. However, under the circumstances, he would have to assume the role for which he was so inadequately prepared...

(So writes Conrad Nightingale)

Sergeant Palkir Throm, an experienced non-commissioned officer, reported troop status to Lieutenant Kai Kolack

SNORT... "Over three thousand XaOrc dead or badly injured. All officers but you dead. Only five non-commissioned officers left. HARRUMPH...

SNORT... All slaves to pull war weapons, dead. One catapult lost. Other weapons functional. Your orders?" HARRUMPH…

SNORT… "Assemble team of Xagada to pull weapons. Lieutenant Kai Kolack and Sergeant Palkir Throm exchanged grins. Once ready, we march." HARRUMPH…

SNORT… "If they no comply?" HARRUMPH…

SNORT… "Orc soldiers outnumber the Xagada. Insist." HARRUMPH…

SNORT… "What about forward patrol?" HARRUMPH…

SNORT… "No need. Command says expect no problems." HARRUMPH…

SNORT… "No problems!" HARRUMPH… Sergeant Palkir Throm began to turn bright green. SNORT… "What the fuck you call this?" HARRUMPH…

SNORT… "You have orders! No challenge me." HARRUMPH…

Lieutenant Kai Kolack swung his horse about and trotted away, leaving a highly irritated Sergeant Palkir Throm to do his bidding.

EVER THE SCOUNDREL

While the XaOrc commanders reviewed the day's activities and set strategies for tomorrow's battle, a big orc atop a plow horse sauntered into the back of XaOrc Headquarters. Two guards immediately challenged him...

(So writes Conrad Nightingale)

SNORT... "Hold fast!" ordered one of the guards. HARRUMPH...

SNORT... "I am..." He was cut off mid-sentence by a Xagada officer who was standing nearby.

"You can save the introduction; I know exactly who you are. Stay here; I'll try to get you an audience with the Xantara and Supreme Commander. I assume that's what you want?"

Turning to the orc guards, he gave the order to watch him closely.

"If he tries to follow on his own – kill him where he stands." Lieutenant Esmond entered the headquarters tent and motioned for Gregor to join him. After a short discussion, he returned for the big orc.

Once back in the tent, he announced, "Xantara, Supreme Commander, Olav Tyan wishes to speak with you."

***

"The pig that walks on two legs has served himself on a proverbial platter. Blox Nye, I made the mistake of listening to this one in the past. It cost me my beloved granddaughter. I should have let you kill him on sight. I won't make that mistake again. He's yours."

SNORT… "That mistake. I have valuable information. HARRUMPH…

SNORT… Information that could save many XaOrc lives." HARRUMPH…

SNORT… "No bargain. Talk while you have tongue! HARRUMPH…

SNORT… "No. Money and promise of safe passage, first." HARRUMPH…

"Bold words. What is your price?" inquired the Xantara.

SNORT… "One hundred gold pieces." HARRUMPH…

"One hundred gold pieces is twice what you initially asked for my granddaughter; ninety gold pieces more than you asked for your own life."

SNORT… "Me got cheated," responded Olav Tyan. HARRUMPH…

Blox Nye nearly came out of his chair, and it was all Kayla Rycroft could do to restrain herself.

"You insolent dog!" The Xantara was vexed, but she needed to know why Olav Tyan risked his life coming to see her.

"Gregor, get him his money."

Gregor returned shortly with a large, heavy leather pouch stuffed with coins. Olav Tyan smiled as he hefted the bag up and down, feeling its weight.

"Do you want to count it?" asked the Xantara incredulously.

SNORT… "No, me trust." HARRUMPH…

"Then start talking, and prey the information warrants the cost."

Olav Tyan told the Xantara and Supreme Commander of a surprise Marshal Driscoll had in store to slow, if not stop, the XaOrc contingent force. He also gleefully advised that the Creel were riding to protect Bembridge Province. However, he could provide no details.

SNORT… "Late, donkey shit!" HARRUMPH… Olav Tyan looked perplexed.

"The Supreme Commander is trying to convey that the PC has already sprung their trap on the XaOrc contingent force. Less than a third made it through and are now on their way to Roderick," the Xantara said.

"Under the circumstances, what would you have us do with this information of yours? Give up our advantage and abandon the battlefield to ride to the aid of our brothers? As usual, you have overplayed your hand, Olav Tyan. The information is about as useless as a wax teakettle. I demand a full refund."

Olav Tyan attempted to run out of the tent but was immediately stopped and held in place. Gregor walked over to retrieve the money, but when Olav Tyan refused to let go, Gregor casually drew his knife and cut off the orc's thumb.

Olav Tyan screamed in pain, and those within earshot laughed, for they knew the big orc was getting his due.

"Blox Nye, what is your sentence?"

SNORT… "Olav Tyan goes to front. No weapons." HARRUMPH…

"Sounds like an appropriate end," laughed Kayla Rycroft. "Have an agonizing death, Olav Tyan, but before you go, tell me how you came by this information."

HARRUMPH… SNORT… HARRUMPH… SNORT… HARRUMPH… SNORT… Snorting profusely, Olav Tyan refused to answer; he just held part of his clothing to the bloody stump and glared at the Xantara.

"Lieutenant Esmond says you rode in on a workhorse owned by the Drake Trading Post." Olav Tyan looked surprised.

"Every Xagada that has traveled between Eastern and Western Calvendar has passed through Drake's establishment, and we are all well acquainted with his brand. Since Walker Drake and his men are here serving the Xagada cause, I assume you ran into his son? Did you at least grant the boy a swift and painless death?"

She could see from Olav Tyan's expression that he did not.

"Fucking pig! Death is too good for you."

After Olav Tyan was dragged kicking and screaming to the frontline, Kayla Rycroft beckoned Gregor closer, whispering, "Bring Tobias to my tent." Within the hour, Tobias was quaking before his mother-in-law.

Kayla's crooked finger motioned Tobias down upon his knees, bringing the two face-to-face. "I will give you one last chance at redemption; it is a mission of great importance."

"Yes, I accept. Anything to please you, Mother," responded an exuberant Tobias.

"If you want to please me, stop calling me Mother, you black tongue adder."

"Of course, Xantara."

"It appears the Creel have thrown in with the Preservation Coalition and are presently busy in Bembridge Province. I want you to gather your band of misfits and ride to the Pillars-of-the-Sky with due haste. Kill every last woman and child to show any Creel remaining after this war that the price of their involvement was too high. Do you think you can handle a bunch of defenseless women and children?"

"I won't let you down this time, Xantara."

"If you do, don't come back; run far and hide, for you are as good as dead. Now go!"

CHAPTER 24

HOPEFULLY, LESSONS LEARNED

The next day brought a new twist, with the XaOrc army now pressing the advantage. Xagada soldiers advanced under a bright yellow banner, each wearing a yellow armband to distinguish themselves from the PC warriors. They rushed to the center of the battlefield, trying to distance themselves from the Eskridge Mountain Range and get some space to maneuver freely.

(So writes Conrad Nightingale)

As decreed, Olav Tyan stood weaponless at the front of the line. When the order to attack was given, the soldiers immediately behind the big orc were more than happy to encourage his headway with a sharp poke of their spears. Olav Tyan was caught between the proverbial rock and a hard place. Reluctantly, he marched forward.

The XaOrc had advanced little more than five hundred yards when the PC let loose volley after volley of arrows that fell from the sky like rain.

Everywhere Olav Tyan looked, bodies dropped to the ground, including his wardens. There was no place to escape the onslaught. Suddenly, Olav Tyan had the solution. With his one good hand, he dragged several corpses into a pile and burrowed under like a scared rabbit hiding from a hawk. He laid still for hours as the battle commenced around him.

***

Slowly but surely, the XaOrc gained control of the battlefield. They could now strike in any direction. Field Marshal Driscoll tried to tighten the troops around the XaOrc to contain them.

It seemed to be working for a short time when a new weapon was brought forward – the Xagada war wagons. A dozen large, converted caravans, each drawn by four horses, raced onto the battlefield.

The sides of the wagons were heavily armored, and Xagada archers shot arrows through multiple protective portholes. On top of each wagon, giant crossbows were mounted on pivot plates in the front and back. The larger bolts could fly greater distances and easily pierce any armor, keeping the PC forces back.

Often, a single bolt would take down numerous adversaries. The failed attack on Lord Bembridge's warship, Stratagem, had given them the idea of converting the caravans.

Have a taste of your own medicine, thought Kayla Rycroft, watching from a safe distance.

The wagons formed a tight circle, trapping and killing those caught inside while keeping PC rescue troops at bay.

***

By evening, the fighting had calmed down. The XaOrc had won a decisive battle that could change the outcome of the war.

Only then did Olav Tyan come out of hiding. He had had enough of trying to profit off this war, and he was intent on getting back to his homeland without further consequence to his well-being.

In all their celebration, no one took notice of the lone orc making his way back through the Virox Divide.

COME IN IF YOU DARE

By mid-morning, as predicted, the XaOrc stopped their advancement just outside the north gate to the city of Roderick. The gate itself was left open and unguarded. There was no challenge to stop the XaOrc from walking straight into the city…

(So writes Conrad Nightingale)

SNORT… "Too quiet," said Sergeant Palkir Throm. "No trust. Where people?" HARRUMPH…

SNORT … "Fighting at Konosha," responded Lieutenant Kai Kolack. "Just old men, women, and children here. Probably in castle hiding. We move forward." HARRUMPH…"

SNORT … "No trust!" HARRUMPH… objected Palkir Throm.

SNORT … "Me tired of arguing. Last time challenged. HARRUMPH… SNORT… Take six soldiers and check. Thirty minutes, no more." HARRUMPH…

Sergeant Palkir Throm grabbed a half dozen orcs and entered the city.

SNORT … "Wait for report," he called back over his shoulder.

Once through the gateway, the XaOrc Forward Reconnaissance Team found themselves on a narrow cobblestone street bracketed on each side by tall windowless buildings, their facades decorated with a gargoyle motif. They moved slowly and cautiously to the end of the road.

Five hundred yards to the right laid a dead end; however, at least two adjacent courtyards required investigation. To the left, a large tower loomed over a circle of intersecting roads. The rooftops of three similar towers could be seen disbursed within the city's walls. It would take the orcs time to properly inspect the city for traps.

Having lived within the city of Roderick, the Xagada would have valuable insight, but they weren't anxious to share, considering their recent treatment.

It was taking the Forward Patrol too long. Already incense and impatient, Lieutenant Kai Kolack ordered the rest of his troops to advance. First, a hundred orc, followed by the Xagada pulling the war machines, then more orc soldiers. Sergeant Palkir Throm screamed out to stop the advance, but it fell on deaf ears.

You, shit-for-brains, he thought to himself.

When the street could hold no more, a heavy iron gate slammed down, impaling those below while blocking further access or retreat. Some tried to spread out on the

adjacent street, but it was a bad decision. Shutters on top of the tower opened, and an endless number of arrows flew into the crowd below.

Palkir Throm pushed back through the crowd, determined to kill Kai Kolack for his stupidity, before taking his last breath. Then he saw Kolack through the gate's iron lattice, standing there, his mouth agape at the waylay he caused.

Grabbing a crossbow from a nearby soldier, Palkir Throm took careful aim for he would have to thread the lattice to reach his intended target. He took a deep breath and let the bolt fly, but it was wide of the mark, bouncing harmlessly off the iron while ringing it like a bell.

The sound of the near miss got Kai Kolack's attention, but there was nothing he could do, nowhere, to retreat, for the Creel galloped out of the adjacent tree line; with lances lowered and swords drawn, they cut through the XaOrc that remained outside the walls like ripe wheat.

Sergeant Palkir Throm pushed toward the gate another twenty feet. He notched his bow with an arrow and slowly raised it to eye level; this time, he would not miss.

SNORT … "Die, you fucker!" but he never got the shot off. Above their heads, the gargoyles spit forth molten tar from the pits at Blackpool. The ooze covered their bodies from head to toe — a slow and painful death.

***

True to their custom, the Creel took no prisoners. That evening, the Creel went body to body, putting every XaOrc out of their torment.

"You have completed your task and saved Bembridge Province. Let me be the first to welcome the Creel Nation to the Preservation Coalition, Lord Trask. I will advise the council tomorrow. I know they will be grateful, especially Lord Bembridge."

"We can tell them together, John, since the Creel will be riding for Konosha at first light."

"That is unnecessary, Lord Trask; you have fulfilled the bargain."

"Exactly, so it is absolutely necessary to go with you, for an attack against any member of the Preservation Coalition is an attack against us all."

SUBTERFUGE

The Preservation Coalition suffered a significant defeat on the Konosha Battlefield. The Xagada war wagons had proven themselves a formidable weapon and, accordingly, needed to be taken out of the equation at all costs...

(So writes Conrad Nightingale)

Field Marshal Driscoll looked around Campaign Headquarters before stopping his gaze on Lord Bembridge.

"Walter, I regret we must call upon your Ranger Regiment to perform the impossible once again."

"My men stand ready to serve. What do you propose?

"Can your men use the cover of night to breach the enemy line and rid us of these war wagons?"

"Sabotage is one of their many talents. Leave it to us." Lord Bembridge turned and exited the tent. Nobody knew what he planned, but they all knew the Ranger Regiment was their only hope.

***

The night cooperated, throwing a heavy blanket of clouds over the stars and moon above. In the wee hours of the morning, fifty rangers cloaked in black with the exposed parts of their bodies painted with mud crawled on their bellies toward the circle of war wagons. The plan was straightforward – infiltrate the enemy, tie the wagons together, and then scare the horses into bolting. Once underway, the war wagons would tip over, trapping those inside the circle long enough for the Rangers to run like hell back to their lines.

Late that night, the Rangers crawled slowly, ever so quietly, toward the enemy's war wagons. If the fallen blocked their way, they washed over the bodies like a gentle wave, never breaking formation. It took better than an hour to move a quarter mile, but no one within the XaOrc camp heard them coming.

The war wagons were still in a tight circle formation and guarded on their perimeter by a handful of exhausted soldiers; they were nearly asleep on their feet. Lieutenant Higgins used hand signals to order his men to kill the guards. Silently, they slithered through the grass like poisonous snakes until they were within feet of their prey, then they struck from behind, covering the mouths of their victims as their daggers pierced deep into the kidneys, then sliced across their exposed throats. The skilled Rangers even lowered their bodies to the ground to muffle the sound of the fall. Inside the circle, the snoring and grunting of tired Xagada and orc troops continued unabated.

Remaining bent low, the Rangers set about tying the war wagons together in a segmented pattern. Occasionally, a horse would shift in discomfort, and the Ranger's choreographed dance would seize momentarily until calmness returned. The intricate web was completed in minutes. The troopers stood by the horses, awaiting the final signal.

Lieutenant Higgins screamed out the order, and the Rangers yelled a battle cry, slapping the flanks of their respective horses. Startled, the horses bolted in all directions. As they ran, the ropes grew taunt, tipping the war wagons on their sides. Many inside the circle were crushed under the weight of the large wagons or trampled by the stampeding horses, while others rushed around in chaos.

By now, the enemy front was awakened from the clamor, and wasting no time, Lieutenant Higgins ordered a swift retreat. The Rangers ran through the dark toward their line of defense. The quarter-mile trek back took much less time.

Neither side got to sleep the few remaining hours before sunrise. As the sky brightened, you could see the wreckage in the distance; no single war wagon remained intact.

CHAPTER 25

DISGRACE AND VALOR

Kayla Rycroft was right about one thing; there wasn't any level her son-in-law wouldn't stoop to ingratiate himself. This was his chance to get back into the Xagada's inner circle, and he didn't care who got hurt or killed in the process. Rycroft rounded up eleven men for what he said would be an easy but critical assignment while staying far away from the mayhem playing out on the Konosha Plain...

(So writes Conrad Nightingale)

The height of the monoliths within the Pillars-of-the-Sky not only kept its occupants out of immediate danger from below but also served as observation towers. There was little to no chance that anyone could sneak up unseen. Therefore, to carry out his dastardly deed, Rycroft decided to take a straightforward approach; he would enter the stronghold under the guise of reporting on the Creel's progress in battle. Still not knowing if any men were left behind, Rycroft and his gang approached slowly under a white flag. When he reached the bottom of the first monolith, he called out.

"Hello! We come bearing news of the battle."

A voice from somewhere above called back; it was a female voice. "Does it take twelve strong men to bear a single message?"

"These are dangerous times, my lady; one never knows who could be lurking around any corner. May we come up and speak to the men in charge?"

"All our men have left for the battle, but you may come up and speak to me. My name is Katherine, and I am the wife of Logan Trask, leader of the Creel. I will send down a basket. We are anxious to hear how the battle fares."

As the basket was lowered, Rycroft grinned and proclaimed to his men how easily the Creel were duped. When the basket reached the ground, another voice rang out from above.

"Load only six men at a time!" Rycroft sent six of his men ahead to ensure everything was all right before he put himself in danger. Slowly, the basket began to ascend, its ingenious pully system allowing one small woman to lift the full basket on her own. Once the first six men disembarked, the basket was lowered for the second group. When everyone in Rycroft's group had reassembled, the woman motioned them across a swinging bridge to a larger monolith. To the uninitiated, it was a precarious position to be in; they hesitated and then noticed a man casually approaching from the other side. Rycroft turned his attention toward the woman working the basket.

"I understood there were no men left behind, only the women and children?"

"That's true. Skylar is the son of Logan Trask, and although big for his age, he is just a boy of fourteen years, not old enough to go fight with the men."

Big wasn't an accurate description, thought Rycroft. This so-called boy already stood six feet and looked to be every bit of a hundred and eighty muscular pounds. As Skylar approached, he smiled and greeted Rycroft and his gang.

"Well, met, friends. My mother and the other elders await you in the Council Chamber. Follow me, and don't be afraid; the bridge will easily bear the weight of us all."

The group started to move gingerly across the expanse as the bridge began to sway, causing some to grab tightly to the rope railings while others dropped to their hands and knees. Skylar turned and laughed at the spectacle.

"If the height bothers you, fix your gaze on the horizon, and don't look down." On he walked while the others did their best to follow. When Skylar reached the middle of the walkway, he bent down and casually attached a coil of rope to a mechanism around his waist.

"Gentlemen, this is where we must part ways," with that, he leaned over the rail, repelling himself to the ground.

"It's a trap! Go back!" shouted Rycroft. However, when they looked back, they saw the tiny woman attendant smiling and shaking her head no. She appeared to be holding a lynchpin that supported the bridge to the cliff face.

"Forward! Move forward quickly!" shouted Rycroft, but as they turned, they saw another woman holding a lynchpin on the other side.

"Don't move!" the woman commanded. It was the voice of Katherine Trask. "Tell me the real reason for your visit, and if you lie – you die."

The men were a bundle of nerves; some lay in a ball and whimpered at the prospect of falling to their deaths. "Tell her," they begged Rycroft. "Maybe she will have mercy?"

"I already told you," responded Rycroft. "We are here to report on the battle."

"And how is the battle going?"

"Badly at first, but the Creel have turned the tide in favor of the Preservation Coalition."

"Imagine that; a thousand Creel fighters have affected the outcome of nearly a hundred thousand soldiers. The Creel are indeed skilled fighters but not that good."

Katherine gave a signal, and arrows flew from a place of hiding. Several of Rycroft's men were struck.

"In case you haven't noticed, you are in a difficult position. Time to start telling the truth."

"All right, the Xantara sent us to kill anyone left alone in the Pillars-of-the-Sky. She means to send a message to those who fight against her. That is the truth; I beg you to have mercy. You can take me prisoner. I have value. I am the son-in-law of the Xantara."

"And what of your men?"

"Do what you like with them, but don't kill me!"

"What kind of leader are you? You are a coward and disgust me to my very core."

Katherine pulled the lynchpin, and her side of the bridge broke free; swinging in a large arc, the momentum flung Rycroft and his men to their deaths below.

ALL OR NOTHING

The raid by Lord Bembridge's Ranger Regiment was highly successful, but there was no time for celebration. No longer did either side hold any tactical advantage, and from this moment, it would be a battle of brute force and attrition. Across the battlefield, the XaOrc Army could be seen amassing their combined might. They intended to march forward and not stop until the Preservation Coalition was decimated...

(So writes Conrad Nightingale)

The previous day, runners were sent throughout the countryside, calling every able-bodied person to stand with the Preservation Coalition. Hundreds of men, women, and teenage children answered the call, bringing with them pitchforks, hammers, scythes, and any other tools of their trade that could harm the enemy. Still outnumbered, the PC Army would have to stop the XaOrc Army by any means necessary or face defeat.

It was midday when the signal was given, and the two great armies merged for the final time. Arrows crisscrossed the sky as the armies marched forward. When they finally met, there was a giant clash of metal against metal. The din could be heard for miles. Combat was challenging at close quarters, and under the crush of pushing bodies, one could be easily injured by their brothers-in-arms as that of the enemy.

Yet, Lord Walter Bembridge, the people's champion, stood in the thick of the battle. Together with his bodyguards, the Impregnables, they slashed their way deep into the enemy line. His endurance seemed to have no end, and any that came within the reach of his sword fell to his blade.

Similar scrimmages broke out all over the Kenosha Plain. Blood and guts slicked the grass, making it hard to keep one's footing while swinging weapons of war. Yet swords and battleaxes, pitchforks, and sickles still managed to find purchase, smashing heads and cleaving body parts. So many bodies had been ripped to pieces that it was impossible to determine which arm or leg belonged to which torso.

***

They had given their all, but by late afternoon, things looked bleak for the Preservation Coalition. Back at Campaign Headquarters, there were murmurs regarding surrender.

"If Lord Bembridge was here, he would have your head for speaking of surrender!" yelled Field Marshal Driscoll.

"But he is not here; he is out fighting on the battlefield instead of commanding the forces with us. For all we know, he is dead," Alcott said.

"Whether he is dead or not, I will not surrender to an army of orcs and degenerates. What do you suppose they will do with us? Orcs don't take prisoners, and likely those of us that live will be sold in the Berwo slave market."

A soldier ran into the tent, shouting, "They're here! The Creel are here to save us! They're riding through the battlefield at full gallop, cutting down the XaOrc! The enemy is in full retreat!"

The Overlords rushed outside the tent to witness the spectacle. XaOrc soldiers scattered in every direction but to no avail; they were brought down at a dead run. Within minutes, the remaining XaOrc dropped their weapons and, running as fast as they could run, retreated straight up the mountainside. No one wanted to be caught in the open, which meant certain death.

The Creel reined in their horses and awaited orders.

"What do you want us to do with this scum, Johnathan Alcott?" Lord Trask asked. "It's your decision. Will it be life or death?"

"That is for the Preservation Coalition to decide, and as an equal Head-of-State, you'll have more to say in the matter than me," Alcott said.

Lord Trask smiled. "Until a decision can be made, round up the remaining XaOrc and hold them together."

The storm that had been chasing them finally caught up. It began to rain, and while the members of the Preservation Coalition, including the newest member representing the Creel Nation, met inside Campaign Headquarters to determine the fate of the XaOrc.

Lord Bembridge knelt alone in the rain surveying the death and destruction. Johnathan Alcott walked up to join his friend.

"You did well, John. You and the Creel saved us all. Thanks to the gods, you decided to leave Bembridge Province and come to our aid."

"That was Lord Trask's decision alone. When I told him he had completed our agreement and was now an active member of the Preservation Coalition, he looked at me and said, "Any act of aggression against a member of the Preservation Coalition shall be considered an attack upon us all."

"It seems I have misjudged the Creel; they are an honorable people, and I owe Lord Trask an apology and a debt of gratitude. I'll have to tell him when we have an opportunity to meet."

"You can tell him now; he waits inside with the other Overlords." As Lord Bembridge and Johnathan stepped into the tent, those inside dropped to one knee.

"All hail, King Bembridge! Long live the King!"

Lord Bembridge, – now *King* Bembridge—stood dumbfounded.

"What is the meaning of this?" he whispered to Alcott, who knelt below him.

"The vote was unanimous, Your Grace. You are the first King of all humans in Calvendar, wherever they reside. May we rise, Your Grace?"

His subjects stood and came forward bearing good tidings with hardy handshakes and hugs. "My Grace, may I present Lord Trask of the Creel Nation," introduced Alcott.

Lord Trask knelt. "My King, I am honored to meet you finally."

"Please stand, Lord Trask, for I am honored TO MEET YOU. I owe you my apology for the grave oversight of not inviting the Creel Nation to the formation of the Preservation Coalition. I also owe you an eternal debt for saving Bembridge Province from annihilation."

"There is no debt between us, for the contract has been paid in full. Now, there is only friendship and my oath to serve you faithfully." The two men embraced.

"My Grace, what are we to do with the prisoners?" questioned Field Marshal Driscoll; the room fell silent.

"The Xagada were already in an alliance with the orc and planning an attack when the Xantara gave us her word that she would take her people east and never return. It was only by luck that the Rangers captured the orc forward patrol, and we learned of the pending battle in time to take defensive measures. The orc cowards have run for their homes in the Sawtooth Mountains.

"However, let it be known throughout Calvendar that there is a kill bounty on any orc that dares to come out of the mountains.

"As for the Xagada, the Preservation Coalition has already ruled against genocide. Nevertheless, for the next generation, no Xagada will casually slip in amongst our citizens.

"Tomorrow, every man, woman, and child of the Xagada Nation, including those still in Thammarat, shall be branded on their forehead with an X for all to see.

"That is my ruling; let the identification process begin with the Xantara herself."

***

The next day, fires were built, and branding irons bearing an X were forged. Heavy blocks would be set on either side of the prisoner's head to hold it in place while the white-hot iron seared the skin. As ordered, Kayla Rycroft was brought to the front of the line.

She glared as King Bembridge approached. "Is this how the new King treats his subjects, even those who have surrendered and asked for mercy?"

"No, this is how the King treats those who break their word, returning to prey upon the innocent." The King held forth his hand for the branding iron as the Xantara's head was placed between the blocks. He leaned forward and whispered.

"I will leave you unmarked if you turn over your son-in-law and granddaughter."

The Xantara tried to spit, but it fell back into her face.

"Fuck you! I sent that good-for-nothing asshole to kill everyone remaining at the Pillars-of-the-Sky or run for his worthless life if he failed. He never came back, so who knows what happened?

"As for my granddaughter, she is still lost to me. Now do what you must, you piece of shit."

Kayla Rycroft screamed as King Bembridge held the iron tightly against her forehead. The skin blistered and burned until she fainted from the pain. When the iron was removed, she bore the mark of shame.

As she was removed from the blocks, one of the guards noticed she was no longer breathing; her heart had given out during the process.

"Throw her body aside, face up, for the other Xagada to witness. Hopefully, it will instill them with fear. Bring the next Xagada forward." King Bembridge handed the branding iron over to one of the soldiers.

***

Moving over to Lord Trask, King Bembridge asked if he had heard the Xantara's dying words. He shook his head yes. "Go, see to your people. I will send reinforcements as soon as possible."

"My thanks, but all those men for a small band of Xagada thugs; that won't be necessary."

"Well, I, for one, will ride with you! That is, with your permission, my King?" said Alcott.

"Granted, and John, make sure Tobias Rycroft's death is painful." Turning to Lord Trask, he shook his hand. "Our best wishes go with you, Logan. I pray you will find everything is all right."

CHAPTER 26

HOW WENT THE WAR

Cutting straight through the Virox Divide allowed the Creel to reach their home quickly. On the morning of the second day, the Pillars-of-the-Sky stood silhouetted in dawn's pink and magenta colors. Their hearts sank when they could see one walkway hanging precariously down the side of the cliff face. Lord Trask spurred his steed forward...

(So writes Conrad Nightingale)

Skylar greeted them as they approached the first monolith, smiling as if nothing was out of the ordinary.

"Hello, Father; how did you fare?"

"We lost fourteen men; another thirty-eight were injured."

"I will see to their needs at once." Skylar began to walk away.

"Skylar! It looks as though you may have encountered some trouble while we were away?"

"Nothing much to get excited about. Mother can fill you in on the details. She's at home baking."

***

"Come with me, John." The two entered a nearby basket, and Logan signaled to bring them up. When they reached the top, they crossed several bridges to Logan's home. When they entered, Katherine rushed into her husband's embrace.

"Well met, husband. I trust it was a success?"

"To be sure. You now address Lord Trask of the Pillar-of-the-Sky Province, an equal member of the Preservation Coalition."

"Oh my, impressive indeed, but don't let your head grow too big to fit through the door," Katherine laughed, then noticed Alcott standing there.

"Greetings, John. I see you have returned my husband safe and sound. I guess I won't have to come for you after all." She giggled an infectious laugh, and Johnathan blushed. She reminded him so much of Ingrid, whom he missed dearly.

"I just finished baking. Sit and rest. I will bring you warm bread and cheese to snack on and fresh ale to wash it down. How does that sound?"

As she scurried about preparing the meal, Logan asked. "Lady Katherine, we noticed one of the walkways hanging. Did you have trouble?"

The sound of her new title took her aback, "Lady Katherine, I'll have to get use to that." Like Skylar, Katherine seemed to think it was no big deal.

"Well, some Xagada scoundrel came around with a band of scallywags, claiming he was here to report on the battle's progress. That would be a first; you sending me a message of how you're doing." Katherine empathized that point with a cold stare; now it was Logan's turn to blush.

"Anyway, that weak ruse and a guard of eleven men was a dead giveaway, so I allowed them to come up for a chat. Once on the walkway, the big dumb one played his hand."

"Do you recall his name?" Alcott asked anxiously.

"Not really, but he said he was the son-in-law of the Xantara as if that means anything."

Alcott stiffened in anticipation of finally catching up to his nemesis.

"I need to ask Katherine, what happened? Did you send him away? Do you know where he is now?"

"Yes, I sent him away and know his exact whereabouts. Once I had the lying bastard and his gang trapped in the middle of the skywalk, I pulled the lynchpin on the cowards and sent them to their deaths. As for where he is now, he is just a pile of ash used to fertilize our crops."

The color ran from Alcott's face knowing he would never get revenge on Tobias Rycroft.

"I can see this comes as bad news, my friend. What did this man mean to you?" asked Katherine.

"Tobias Rycroft raped, tortured, and murdered my wife. I've been hunting him for months."

"I'm sorry, John. Had I known, I assure you I would have taken him alive."

"No need for apologies, Katherine. Trying to take Rycroft alive could have been catastrophic for everyone here. You have done Calvendar a great service, eliminating the scourge known as the Xagada Butcher."

JUBILATION

The citizens of Western Calvendar had paid dramatically in terms of debilitating injuries and loss of lives to preserve their cultural integrity. The months following 'The Cleanse' were a time of grief and mourning...

(So writes Conrad Nightingale)

King Bembridge was not immune to the devastation but needed to compartmentalize his feelings long enough to bring peace and stability back to the people. He began by taking time to restructure the High Council, getting representation and ideas from all the provinces within his newly formed Kingdom.

Today was the first official meeting. As King Bembridge and his new Chancellor, Kivik Runskar, entered the Council Chamber, they all rose from their seats, showing due respect. King Bembridge sat and motioned the others to join him; once the room quieted, the King addressed the members.

"You have all taken an oath of fidelity and obedience to serve me. However, and this is an important distinction, your loyalty must also extend to serving all the people of Calvendar. I will not tolerate do-nothing sycophants, and I will not tolerate anyone using their stature on this High Council to oppress the very citizens they serve. All ideas of merit will be heard and carefully considered.

"Once I have rendered a final decision, you will be expected to carry out my ruling without further deliberation. Am I clear?"

As was King Bembridge's way, he went around the table, stopping on each member to hear their affirmative reply.

"Excellent, then we shall discuss our first order of business — the Kingdom's present state of being. Who wants to start the conversation?"

"As the Minister of Interior, allow me to state the obvious," said Garrett Cunningham from the Kermatic Territories.

"The toll of the war weighs heavily upon our people, who subsequently have become paralyzed and cannot seem to move forward. We must provide them a reason to celebrate our victory."

"I agree," said Sloan Breckenridge, the Minister of Finance, whom Lady Winslow nominated.

"Walter, please accept my nomination not simply because I'm your mother-in-law but also because I am your loyal subject. A woman instinctively knows how to manage money."

"The individual provinces are a shadow of their former selves," continued Sloan. "The newly formed Kingdom opens a world of possibilities; that is the message we should send."

"And how do we send out that message so it will be embraced?" asked the King. Soon, everyone was offering ideas for consideration.

"Perhaps we can establish a park on the Kenosha Plain, where everyone can collectively mourn each year. We can build a great monument to celebrate and remember our brave fallen brothers," proposed young Gilmore Hathaway, the appointed Minister of Records after Hayden Radcliff passed from old age.

"Let's not forget those who still live and carry the scars of war. We should begin awarding metals in publicly held ceremonies to those who served the Preservation Coalition with distinction. These heroes can be everyday reminders of our combined victorious effort," put forward Burns Ellsworth, the newly appointed Ambassador to the Dwarf and Elven Kingdoms.

"I am pleased with all these suggestions. Sloan, as my Minister of Finance, take the lead on a committee and provide some cost details regarding implementation. Oh, and be forewarned, I don't want any mention of needing to increase tax revenue. This meeting is adjourned."

***

Johnathan Alcott approached King Bembridge with a greeting and indicated they needed a moment to talk. "Your first meeting of the High Council was encouraging and productive. You must be pleased?"

"I am pleased with everything but one thing – why did you refuse my request to become Chancellor?"

"I already have two positions that suit my particular skillset; you made me both High Marshal and the Minister of Justice?" he said facetiously.

"I did, but we need more than one marshal to ensure security throughout the country, and it's time you concentrate more on your Minister of Justice role. I'm considering implementing a civil policing organization, a group recognized throughout Calvendar to uphold the law. What do you think about reorganizing the Ranger Regiment into Deputy Marshals?"

"I can't fault the logic as long as I don't have to assume a new title," chuckled Alcott.

"So be it. When you stop laughing, advise your deputies of their new role and mission. Oh, and one last thing" …

"Yes?"

"Priority number one is bringing the fugitive, Eleanor Rycroft, back to Bembridge Province to stand trial."

CHAPTER 27

NEW DANGERS THREATEN

Over the years, Johnathan Alcott helped King Bembridge bring to fruition his vision for a society where everyone, regardless of their station in life, is subject to the same rule of law.

To accomplish this objective, Alcott appointed Spencer Fleming as High Marshal; he strategically placed Law Enforcement and Special Operations Depots throughout Calvendar; and Deputy Marshals were empowered to go anywhere within the King's jurisdiction to quash civil disobedience while bringing the accused in to face trial.

Although they held significant authority, a Deputy Marshal's responsibility to protect and serve was not taken lightly, for every public servant knew that taking advantage of their oath of office would not be tolerated by either Marshal Fleming or Minister Alcott. Abuse of their position was a sure way to find themselves on the wrong side of Blackpool Penitentiary's granite walls...

District judges who understood and agreed with King Bembridge's overall vision were appointed and quartered in every province to resolve infractions quickly and equitably. The newly formed judicial system was respected and ensured all citizens peace and prosperity. Through a newfound sense of brotherhood, major crimes seemed to be a thing of the past, that is, until 'Bloody Thursday,' as it would come to be known.

(So writes Conrad Nightingale)

It was a cold, wet, early winter afternoon when word reached Minister Alcott that a small village in the Kermatic Territory had experienced a senseless killing spree.

Perhaps more disturbing was the news that several Deputy Marshals were killed attempting to apprehend the perpetrators. Deputy Marshal Preston survived the melee, but he was mortally wounded and not expected to live more than a week; he had a message for Minister Alcott's ears alone.

Alcott replied via carrier pigeon that he was on his way with due haste and to make Deputy Marshal Preston's final days as comfortable as possible. Then, traveling with the same intensity he had done years ago to reach the Creel during 'The Cleanse', Alcott made it to the Law Enforcement and Special Operations (LESO) Office No. 7 in record time.

As Minister Alcott approached the bedside of Deputy Marshal Preston, he could see the man was in great pain, trying desperately to hang on long enough to speak to him; it was as if he had been compelled to do so. Preston's torso was tightly wrapped with a thick bandage, for which the principal purpose was to keep his insides from spilling. He was pale from the loss of blood, and labored breathing caused his body to heave slightly with every breath.

When Preston's glassy eyes fell upon Minister Alcott, the moaning stopped, and he reached for Alcott's hand. Deputy Marshal Preston's grip was surprisingly firm as he pulled Alcott closer. Through pasty lips, he whispered.

"Remember, I promised you a long and painful death. I'm coming to fulfill my promise, Longshanks." And then, Deputy Marshal Preston found the peace he so deserved.

No other person attending the dying young man heard the exchange, nor would they have understood, but the message had a profound effect upon Alcott.

"I promise you a long and painful death," was the exact threat Tobias Rycroft made at their first encounter in the high desert of Jadhar so many years ago. Not to mention that Rycroft was the only person who ever dared call him 'Longshanks,' but how can this be possible? Rycroft had died at the Pillars-of-the-Sky during 'The Cleanse', or so Katherine Trask had told him. Had she intentionally misled him, and if so, why?

So many questions rushed through Alcott's restless mind, and now, more than ever, he needed the answers.

I will find you, you cock sucker, and I vow I will end this nightmare once and for all!

Minister Alcott looked to Jacob Colburn, one of the few remaining Deputy Marshals at LESO 7.

"Once word of the killing spree spreads through Calvendar, there will be panic. High Marshal Fleming is close behind me, and he brings reinforcements with him. Until he arrives, you are in charge. You and your men do what you can to keep the peace."

"Aren't you staying?" asked Jacob sheepishly.

"I have a fugitive to hunt. I'll be leaving at morning's first light. Advise Marshal Fleming of my intentions when he arrives; he will know what is required." Alcott turned and stormed out of the room.

***

It was another bleak, dreary day when Alcott rode south into the Kermatic Territories; his pace was steady and determined. Soon, Tanglewood Forest stood before him like a giant fortress wall impeding his progress. These woods were ancient and dense, and it would take all of Alcott's considerable experience to pick up a trail.

He continued riding along the frontline of trees until he reached a natural break, cut by the Bersa River. This is where Rycroft and his gang could gain access into the forest.

Follow the river long enough, and you find his hideout.

Deeper and deeper he went until he came upon a clearing, a perfect spot for Rycroft and his men to hold up. However, there was no sign of Rycroft or any other life form. The silence was disconcerting, and every fiber of Alcott's body tingled. He found himself wishing for Adak's companionship; Adak's keen senses would ferret out any concerns, but the faithful kolgarr had vanished shortly before 'The Cleanse'.

After surveying the area carefully, Alcott finally assured himself that everything was okay; he would camp here for the night. Although plenty of wood was lying on the ground for a warm fire, Alcott didn't want to give away his pursuit, so it would be a dinner of jerky and extra blankets on this cold night.

***

"Caught sleeping again, I see." Alcott was startled awake. Before him stood a man he didn't recognize, yet somehow, he knew it was Tobias Rycroft, stinking as ever.

"What the crux?"

Alcott quickly looked about the opening. The two were alone under the light of the stars. He jumped to his feet, quickly drawing out his hunting knife and holding it only inches from Rycroft's face.

"This time, you won't get away, nor will you be taken prisoner. You will die!"

"Oooooo, so scary. How did you put it to me when we first met? Are you going to fight or just fan me to death with that knife?"

Alcott lunged forward, pushing his knife into Rycroft' soft exposed throat, the blade made purchase, but Rycroft just stared back, laughing. Alcott struck out repeatedly, puncturing the body like a pin cushion but to no effect.

"Unbelievable!"

"Oh, you better believe it," responded Rycroft. Maybe it's your weapon? Let me try." Rycroft twisted Alcott's wrist, causing him to loosen his grip on the knife, which he grabbed away. Rycroft swiped the blade across Alcott's face, cutting the skin effortlessly.

"No, the blade is good and sharp. What do you suppose it could be?"

"Why are you playing these games?" came another voice behind Alcott's back.

Alcott was startled and turned to see who spoke. Though unrecognizable, the man's stance and arrogant demeanor immediately identified him as Nigel Oswalt. Alcott was utterly befuddled.

"I enjoy playing games," snarled Rycroft. "Especially ones that I can't lose." Rycroft never took his eyes off Alcott.

"Just don't kill him before I get some payback."

"Although I began questioning Lady Katherine's account of your death at the Pillars-of-the-Sky, I witnessed this sniffling asshole's final demise, caged above the square. I don't know how the two of you managed it, but it appears the specters of Tobias Rycroft and Niles Oswalt now stand before me in someone else's bodies?"

"You're not as dumb as you look, Longshanks. Yes, that bitch at the Pillars-of-the-Sky pulled the bridge from under me. I'll drop in on her when I'm through here." Rycroft gave out a laugh.

"Do you get it? I'll drop in on her. Even that idiot kory friend of yours would find that pun funny, that is, if I hadn't already snapped his neck."

Alcott could take no more, and he dove at Rycroft, or whoever he was, taking him to the ground.

"Enough!" yelled Rycroft. "Hold him!"

As if the trees themselves began to change, a dozen of Rycroft's henchmen stepped into view. Their bodies were in various states of decay, and they reeked of death. Several grabbed Alcott, dragging him to a nearby tree and binding his hands and feet. Once immobile, they stripped him of all clothing. Rycroft handed Alcott's hunting knife over to Nigel.

"Chancellor Oswalt, I believe the first cut is your honor."

Oswalt approached with a malicious gleam burning deep within his eyes. He looked over Alcott's stretched-out body and made the initial incision down the center of his breastbone. Alcott screamed in anguish as the knife's edge was placed just below the surface, and his skin slowly peeled away. This went on throughout the night, each apparition taking his turn, being ever so careful not to deliver a death stroke.

After hours of prolonged agony, all things Nigel Oswalt and Tobias Rycroft consumed Johnathan Alcott's last conscious moment.

As he gasped for air but found no relief and the light faded from his eyes, all Alcott could sense was the stench of Rycroft's breath as he leaned in close and whispered.

"Rot in hell, Longshanks."

The blade was sharp, and when wielded in Rycroft's expert hand, it cut deeply across his victim's stomach, Rycroft's signature killing move.

As Alcott's intestines spilled forth, he found the act relatively painless compared to the past few hours being flayed alive. At first, the countryside began to spin, Alcott's vision was reduced to pin-picks of blurred light, and finally, his body convulsed as he fought for air only to aspirate on his blood.

Within minutes, everything Alcott knew or felt in his lifetime was gone.

***

Shortly after sunrise, Marshal Fleming and six of his Deputy Marshals rode into the clearing. They had been following signs left behind by Minister Alcott, but unfortunately, they arrived too late. Sometime during the night, Alcott drew his last breath. Tobias Rycroft had kept his promise – it was a long and painful death.

It was a gruesome sight, and even these battled-hardened veterans of the former Ranger Regiment were sickened by seeing their Commander displayed in such a manner.

Once they had an opportunity to recompose themselves, they buried Minister Johnathan Alcott in the clearing where he met his end.

CHAPTER 28

IT'S NOT YOUR TIME

No longer troubled by the burdens of life Johnathan Alcott was at peace. When he awoke, he found himself being held ever so gently. It felt good and comforting; he didn't want the feeling to stop. Then, his eyes adjusted, and he saw her face — it was Ingrid...

(So writes Conrad Nightingale)

"What am I going to do with you?" she said. "I ask you to clean up for dinner, but I find you napping by the brook." Johnathan was sure he was looking at Ingrid, but how could that be?

Has this all been nothing but a bad dream? he wondered, but it didn't matter – nothing else mattered. He and Ingrid were both alive and home together.

"Come on, sleepy head, our dinner guest is already here."

Perplexed, Johnathan followed Ingrid into the house.

***

Rocking on the front porch was a distinguished gentleman, strong of stature, with wavy silver hair and violet eyes. He stood to greet Johnathan.

"I see Ingrid found you," he smiled warmly and held forth his hand.

Johnathan returned the greeting, wondering when or where the two had met.

"Don't you recognize your old companion?" was the man's nonchalant response.

"Adak?"

"Yes, John, it's Adak. Although in human form, I go by the name of Conrad Nightingale. In fact, I've been writing your story."

Whatever was happening, it was all coming too quickly for Alcott to assimilate, and he was becoming increasingly anxious.

"Try to remain calm; there is much to discuss, and all will be revealed soon. Let's go inside out of the sun and have a refreshing drink."

The three of us entered Albem and sat around the kitchen table as though nothing was unusual. We drank the cool lemonade, not speaking but looking at one another with unspoken compassion.

When our cups were drained, Ingrid jumped up, anxious to serve the venison stew and freshly baked bread she had been preparing all day.

"I hope you two are hungry. Eat your fill; we have plenty," she remarked while ladling the stew into giant wooden bowls.

"John, pour us some more lemonade, will you, or would you men prefer something stouter?"

We continued exchanging niceties while reminiscing, even during the meal. But the fundamental subject I knew was coming, remained unaddressed for the moment, until the awkward pause finally arrived.

"No, you're not dreaming, John," I, Conrad, finally proclaimed what I already knew Alcott was thinking.

"There is no easy way of telling you, so I'll get right to the point. – You are dead, but not in the sense of being truly gone. Instead, you have passed into another realm of reality; some refer to it as the Twilight."

"You mean purgatory?"

"For some, it can be a dismal place from which there is no escape. For others, it is merely a waiting room where they gather their thoughts and perhaps finish something important before moving on to their final destiny. Allow me to explain. . ."

After giving me his undivided attention, Johnathan tipped back his head and briefly closed his eyes, unable to come up with the appropriate words to express the sheer exhaustion he was experiencing. Yet, he made it clear that he would not go on another day carrying the burdens of others. He was utterly devastated, so I provided counsel, hoping he would find solace in my advice.

"Helping those who can't help themselves and everything that comes with such a daunting responsibility is out of your control; it is simply part of your destiny."

I meant to free him from the weight of his obligation, but apparently, I had accomplished the exact opposite.

Johnathan paced like a caged animal, ready to lash out at any moment. Stopping abruptly, he slapped his chest. This time, he had no problem finding his words, which were succinct and to the point.

"There is only one master of my destiny; that's **ME**!" Taking a deep breath, he dismissed my counsel with a wave of his hand.

"I no longer choose to walk this path, and I'll hear no more on the matter."

It was a foolhardy statement made by a proud man under considerable duress, notwithstanding he would learn soon enough that one's fate is… inevitable.

"To think that one is the master of his destiny is foolhardy. Although you choose the path upon which you travel, your destination has been preordained. You are who you are meant to be, and there is no avoiding the inevitable. John, helping those who cannot help themselves was your purpose in life and now in death."

"Destiny can be damned!"

"If you truly believe that, then I fear the Twilight will become your purgatory," I said.

"I can accept things here as long as Ingrid is by my side," Johnathan replied.

"The truth is, Ingrid does not belong here anymore than you, but she refuses to move on without you," I told him. "Would you condemn her to an eternal life of emptiness to avoid your responsibility?"

Alcott was angered by Conrad's assertion that he would jeopardize Ingrid's happiness under any circumstance.

"Tread lightly, old friend!"

I raised my hands in a surrendering gesture.

"This is an emotionally charged conversation, but remember we are friends, and together, we will find the correct path forward. Try to understand that significantly more is at stake than our three destinies. Let me explain.

"Under the guise of the civil war, a deity by the name of Vennick upset the natural balance between life and death when he opened a gate to the Underworld, unleashing all manner of specters, demons, and monsters upon Calvendar.

"Nearly impossible to stop, if left unchallenged, this evil incarnate will terrorize and destroy all that is good. John, you know what I'm saying to be true from your own recent personal experience," I said.

"Yes, I know this evil cannot be stopped because I fought the wraiths of Nigel Oswalt and Tobias Rycroft. I battled these specters with all my skill and every fiber of my being only to find myself at their mercy – mercy which never came."

"I'm sorry I wasn't there to help you," I said. "However, you didn't lose the battle to the wraiths due to a lack of skill but rather because of a lack of knowledge. To the uninformed, wraiths can be quite disturbing, but they are merely apparitions without substance," I told him.

"I beg to differ. What I encountered was very real indeed, as was my knife that they used to filet the skin from my body."

Johnathan saw Ingrid begin to cry from the corner of his eye; he had upset her and was immediately ashamed of using such graphic language.

"Bent on revenge and chaos, Nigel Oswalt, Tobias Rycroft, and a dozen of his men were among the first apparitions to escape back into the land of the living. However, without any corporeal structure, they quickly learned that wraiths are little more than cold wisps of air.

"It probably won't come as a surprise to learn that Oswalt is as clever in death as he was in life, for he deduced the need for a human host. Unlike demons, wraiths lack the power to possess the living against their will. Nevertheless, Oswalt tried to make it happen. After numerous attempts, when all seemed lost, Oswalt had an epiphany; he needed only to wait for a living body to die. Once the corpse was unoccupied, assimilation was as easy as slipping into a new pair of boots. The only problem is that the corpse decays, requiring the wraith to seek new vessels constantly.

"It wasn't long before Oswalt learned of an old villager in his final throes of life. That night, Oswalt visited him. I suspect the mere sight of this ghostly visit was enough to frighten the fragile man to death. Once inside the old man's body, Oswalt set about finding a more suitable host. With a kitchen knife, he stabbed the son asleep in the adjacent room.

"This time, he found results were much better — he now possessed the strength and speed of a younger man. And so, it continued until Rycroft and his men were also free to move amongst the living, and the first thing they wanted was revenge. It was no accident that a trap was set for you in the village of Thousand Oaks outside of LASO Depot No. 7. Both Oswalt and Rycroft wanted you badly."

"That explains how I ended up in Tanglewood," John said. "Imagine all those people who died just so Oswalt and Rycroft could settle an old score. And how many more will die as they continue rampaging their way through Calvendar since they apparently can't be stopped? The wraiths could move on to another host even if chopped into a thousand pieces."

"That is true," I said. "There is no way of defeating such enemies with manmade weapons, which is why I bring you this."

I moved to the doorway where I had placed a parcel earlier and brought the package over as Ingrid removed the bowls so I could lay it on the table. The leather binding was carefully removed, revealing the most magnificent sword anyone had ever seen.

Approximately four feet from pommel to tip, the sword was slender with a delicate curve, both edges honed razor-sharp. Roses were etched the length of its silver blade, culminating in a golden guard wrapping the handle.

"John, I give you 'Thornblade.' It cannot be touched by evil, and when wheeled by a righteous hand, it will cut through any being, whether living or dead."

Johnathan picked up the sword, which immediately became one with him, pulsating divine energy with every beat of his heart.

"In light of Vennick's interference, I'm prepared to break a cardinal rule of nature and give you back your life. Take Thornblade and return to the land of the living. Find Rycroft, Oswalt, and every other abomination that escaped from Hell, and send them back to where they belong."

"I will accept this cause, if Ingrid joins me."

"That I can not grant."

"Can't, or won't?

Ingrid moved close to Johnathan and whispered, "You must go, John. So many innocent people depend upon you. Don't worry; I'll be here waiting for you when your task is complete." She gave him a warm, reassuring smile and kissed his cheek.

"Will you, at least, be joining me? A kolgarr can come in handy," asked Alcott.

"I cannot join you on this quest," I said, "not as Conrad, the man, nor as Adak, your kolgarr. But you will not be alone, for an ally awaits you."

***

There was a blinding flash of light, and Johnathan awoke, lying in the clearing where he had been tortured to death, a freshly dug grave unearthed next to him. He frantically began to examine himself, patting down his body; he was whole again, with no severed limbs, cuts, or bruises.

I must have been dreaming.

Then he saw Thornblade lying on the grass next to him. It had been no dream.

"Welcome back."

Startled, Johnathan whipped his head around to find his old friend, Bozwell Knoggs, sitting cross-legged, ten feet away.

"Crossing the veil and coming back again is quite the journey, don't you agree?"

"You're right about that — how are you feeling, my old friend?"

"I've never felt better, and look at this beautiful battleaxe Adak, I mean Conrad, gave to me. Her name is Shadow Slayer. I can't wait to put her to good use!"

"Perfect, because there is no time to waste; the wraiths we hunt have a head start."

"You're right; we'll have to ride fast." Boz pointed to a stand of trees where two horses were waiting. One of them was Tess.

Johnathan walked over and ran his hand down her long, slender neck. Leaning forward, he kissed her on the snout, whispering how good it was to see her again. Tess whinnied as though she understood all that had happened. "Let's ride.

As they picked their way through Tanglewood Forest, Knoggs asked Alcott where they were heading.

"We're going to LASO Depot No. 7 to meet with Marshal Fleming."

"Your presence is going to take some explaining since it was Spence and his deputies who found and buried you yesterday."

Once free of the forest, the two men spurred their horses into a gallop. LASO 7 was within an hour's ride.

It was still early morning when the Law Enforcement and Special Operations outpost came into view, but there was no sign of life.

Alcott and Knoggs rode forward cautiously. Dismounting their horses, the two prepared to enter the depot, readying themselves for the unexpected; Alcott pulled Thornblade free as Knoggs clutched Shadow Slayer in both hands. Together, they stepped through the open doorway.

The office was in disarray, overturned, and broken furniture scattered about the room. Huddled in the far corner were Marshal Fleming and three of his deputies; they were noticeably distraught.

"Spencer, it's Johnathan Alcott and Bozwell Knoggs. You've got nothing to fear from us. Come forward so we may speak."

Marshal Fleming did step forward with a raised sword in his hand.

"I don't know who or what you are, but you'll take no more of us. Now be gone, abominations; you're not wanted here, and we are prepared to fight to our death."

"Better you live to play with your grandchildren someday and leave the fighting to us. I'm sure Mary would prefer it that way," replied Alcott.

Marshal Fleming looked perplexed. "How is it that you know my wife's name?"

"Because we were all together the night you met her at the Raven's Eye Tavern," Boz chimed in. "You couldn't stop staring, and she noticed how you looked at her. Boldly, she sashayed crossed the room, walked straight up to our table, and took the tankard of ale out of your hand. After taking a sip, she smiled and asked your name. You could hardly speak."

"So, you know something about me; that may be nothing more than a cheap trick for a phantom."

"This babbling is getting us nowhere, and we're wasting precious time." Alcott slid Thornblade against the back of his arm; not a deep cut, but enough to show blood.

"There you have it, wraiths don't bleed. I hope the demonstration is good enough to reassure you. Now, can we speak on the matter at hand?"

Marshal Fleming turned to his men and ordered them to sheath their swords.

"Good." said Alcott. "Everyone grab a chair and be seated, for what I have to say concerns us all."

Alcott briefly shared the story of why he and Boz returned to the land of the living.

"Do we know how many demons and monsters escaped when this deity Vennick opened the door to the Underworld?" asked one of the deputies.

"What can we do to find them before they inflict any harm? And how do we kill them once found?" injected the two other deputies before Alcott could answer the first question.

Alcott raised his hands for silence.

"Regretfully, I don't have the answers to your questions. I'm not sure that anyone understands all the nuances of the situation. We will have to learn together, and no doubt there will be loss while we search for the answers."

"How can we help, John?" asked Spencer.

"First and foremost, notify King Bembridge as quickly as possible, for he is in mortal danger. Then, inform all the Law Enforcement and Special Operation Depots about what is happening. Tell them to keep this information to themselves; there is no use in causing mass panic among the public. All deputies shall keep their eyes and ears open for any conduct out of the ordinary, especially heinous crimes or unexplained events. Boz and I will be routinely checking in for the latest information."

"You mean like what happened in Thousand Oaks with our comrades?"

"Exactly."

"And, what exactly happened in Thousand Oaks? questioned Boz.

"Most town occupants were slaughtered, along with three Deputy Marshals who came to their aid. It is what I was investigating when Rycroft captured me, said Alcott."

There is still a pall that hangs over the village like a heavy fog," advised Marshal Fleming.

"Then, that seems like a good place to start our investigation," responded Boz as he looked to Alcott for reassurance.

"I agree." With that final word, Alcott and Knoggs headed out searching for evil incarnate.

***

As they neared Thousand Oaks, the air was pungent with the smell of death, and when they reached the village, it was void of life. The remains of dead bodies lay about the streets and within empty houses and commercial buildings. They had all been picked apart by scavengers. In the doorway to the Hardwood Tavern stood a stranger, staring in disbelief.

"I can hardly believe my eyes," he called out. "As I lived and died, it's the notorious Minister Alcott and Commandant Knoggs." He began to laugh as though he alone was privy to some cosmic joke. Still, he held his ground as Alcott and Knoggs approached within a few feet.

"Any idea who this guy is?" asked Alcott.

"Nope," responded Knoggs.

"I'm Jason Sinclair."

"Who?" questioned Knoggs.

"The stable boy from The Last Chance pub in Jadhar," he responded as though it should be obvious.

"Oh, I would have never guessed. He doesn't look so young any longer, more like a dried-out piece of jerky," smirked Knoggs.

"You weren't so smug when I helped Tobias kill you."

"You mean when you distracted me long enough for Rycroft to sneak up from behind like the coward he was; that's very brave of you."

"Fuck you. Dead is dead."

"Enough. What is it that you find so amusing, Sinclair?" asked Alcott.

"Can't you see the obvious? Two of the greatest champions of Calvendar, now nothing more than lowly ghosts destined to wander the countryside like a rudderless boat. Welcome to my world." Jason spread his arms and twirled about as though he was an emperor. "Hey now, just how is it that you two escaped the Underworld? Is the gate still open?"

"No, it's closed tight again, but we didn't have to escape the Underworld; we were never there. However, we were sent back from the Twilight," said Alcott.

"Sent back, by who?"

"You mean by whom? corrected Knoggs. It was a childish retort, but he couldn't help himself.

"Rather than who sent us back, the better question is why have we come?" said Alcott.

"All right, I'll bite – why are you here?"

"A wise man once told me you can't escape your destiny. Unfortunately, in this case, your destiny is one of eternal anguish. So, we've come to dispatch you back to Hell with all due haste.

"You're bluffing. There's nothing you can do to me in this world. Go tell your stories to someone who will listen." Sinclair turned to walk back into the tavern, which is when Knoggs swung Shadow Slayer in a low arch, removing his rotting foot at the ankle; he screamed out in pain, falling to the floor.

"Minister Alcott said you can't run from your destiny; I guess I just ensured it." Knoggs looked to Alcott, "See what I did there with that play on words? Now that's funny, John." Alcott just rolled his eyes.

Jason was writhing on the floor in agony, his severed foot beside him. "Well, Boz, the kid may grow a few more inches, but he'll never grow another foot. Ha! Now that's funny; you've got to admit it, that's funny." Alcott stood above the stolen corpse, grinning.

"Ya, that was funny; wish I had thought of it," responded Knoggs.

After the moment of levity, the actual interrogation started. "I have a couple of questions, and you would do well to answer me with the truth. First, is this the type of existence, for lack of a better word, that you envisioned when you threw in with Tobias Rycroft, and second, where can I find that sack of shit?"

"Go fuck yourself if that is even possible!"

"Seems the boy has grown a pair since we last met', said Knoggs.

Alcott pressed the sole of his boot against Jason's bloody nub. He screamed out in response. "Shall I have Boz chop off your new balls, or will you answer my questions?"

"I don't know how you're doing this, but why should I tell you anything? You told me you're here to send me back to Hell anyway?"

What if I could stop your pain and send you somewhere else? Somewhere you can find eternal joy and peace?"

Jason quickly considered his options. "All right, after we tortured and killed you, some of us decided to go our own way. Tobias and a few of his men wanted revenge on that bitch that cut the bridge out from under them at the Pillars-of-the-Sky.

"As for that crazy fucker, Oswalt, he only wanted payback by personally slitting the throat of King Bembridge. I just wanted to stop being Tobias's flunky now in death as it was in life. Last I heard, Oswalt was heading to Bembridge Castle while Tobias and his gang set off for the Pillars-of-the-Sky. That's all I know; I gave you what you wanted; now give me the peace you promised."

"I made no such promise; I merely asked, what if I could stop the pain and send you somewhere you could find eternal peace? — Actually, I can't do either of those things. You sealed your fate long ago, and your destiny is one of eternal agony."

Alcott pushed Thornblade slowly into Jason Sinclair's chest. He let loose his last scream before vanishing in a purple haze of smoke.

CHAPTER 29

DIVIDE AND CONQUER

After learning that Tobias Rycroft and his gang had split up, Alcott and Knoggs had no choice but to do the same...

(So writes Conrad Nightingale)

"Boz, swing back to LESO Depot No. 7 and tell Spencer what's happening. Have him send the latest information to King Bembridge, and then the two of you ride to Bembridge Castle as quickly as possible. The King will need all the protection he can get to keep Oswalt away."

"Got it; Spencer and I ride to Bembridge Castle, and where will you be?" Of course, it was a rhetorical question, but he wanted to hear the response.

"You know very well that I'll be heading for the Pillars-of-the-Sky. The Creel won't stand a chance against the specters of Rycroft and his gang." Alcott could see that Knoggs was about to protest.

"No argument, Boz. This is how it must be." Alcott rode off, leaving Boz mumbling under his breath.

***

Alcott galloped hard via Pennon Pass through the remainder of the day and night, stopping for brief intervals to rest Tess. He arrived just south of the Pillars-of-the-Sky as daylight broke. From his vantage point on top of a hill, Alcott could see the giant monoliths the Creel called home, silhouetted against the crimson dawn.

He could also see periodic breaks in the suspended walkways between the structures. That was not a good sign, and it could only mean the Creel were trying to prevent someone or something from passing. Based upon Jason's tricked confession, Alcott surmised it was Tobias Rycroft and the remainder of his gang.

He spurred Tess forward, giving her full rein, arriving at the base of one of the columns twenty minutes later. A dozen or more Creel bodies were spread out on the ground before him. From the condition of the broken bodies, they had fallen a great distance.

Above him, Alcott could hear Rycroft yelling his worn-out adage, promising long and painful deaths if the Creel failed to bring him and his men across immediately.

"Fly over to us if you can, or perhaps even wraiths have their limitations." It was the voice of Lord Trask.

Incensed and frustrated, Rycroft let loose with a litany of profanity. That's when Alcott recognized an opportunity. Cupping his hands around his mouth, Alcott yelled, hoping to be heard above the commotion. All went silent as Rycroft peered over his perch.

"Is that really you, Longshanks?"

"It is," came the response from below.

"Unexpected, to say the least. What do you want?"

"To join you up there."

"And why would I bring you up here?" yelled Rycroft.

"Because I am one of you now and know how to get across to the other monoliths. Bring me up."

As Rycroft walked over to lower the basket, his men protested. "It's a trick, Tobias. He can't be trusted."

"I trust no one, but I'm curious about this latest turn of events. Besides, he can't hurt any of us. So, let's hear what our new friend has to say; we've got nothing to lose."

Moments later, Alcott stepped out of the basket and stood face-to-face with his old nemesis. Rycroft looked him up and down.

"Grew your skin back, I see. You don't look any worse for wear." Rycroft laughed, trying to goad Alcott into giving away his true intent.

"By the way, how did you manage that since the rest of us have to jump from corpse to corpse?"

"You're about to find out!"

Alcott drew Thornblade from its scabbard and moved with purpose to confront Rycroft, who immediately shielded himself behind his men.

"I promise you a **QUICK** death and painful afterlife, rotting in the Underworld, and this time, there will be no escaping your destinies."

The sword pulsated its eerie purple glow as Alcott struck out in a fury, concentrating upon the minions first. He wanted Rycroft to bear witness and understand what was coming. Then, whirling the blade like a tornado, he cleaved the wraiths asunder. They disappeared in puffs of smoke, their screams echoing between the pillars.

Rycroft quickly processed the danger, and his instincts warned him to escape at any cost. He threw himself off the cliff, hitting the ground with an audible thud. Within seconds, his broken body stood up, and he began to move toward the forest.

Alcott glanced at the next pillar, where Lord Trask and other Creel stood transfixed. He gave his friends a quick wave and repelled down an escape rope as fast as possible.

Once on the ground, Alcott whistled for Tess; he mounted her while still in mid-gallop and swung her about-face. Rycroft was several hundred yards away, running on a broken leg straight for the tree line where he hoped to hide. Alcott spurred Tess, and she bolted forward, picking up maximum speed and quickly closing the gap on Rycroft.

As Tobias Rycroft looked over his shoulder, he saw Alcott raise Thornblade high. Seconds later, Rycroft's head hit the ground, his body incinerated, and instantly, he was back in the Underworld, where he belonged.

Alcott never slowed, instead riding at full gallop for Serpent's Gulch, the quickest way to Bembridge Castle; Knoggs may need help.

BEWARE

After receiving Minister Alcott's orders, Knoggs and Fleming immediately acted. A message was prepared and sent by homing pigeon; it read: "Beware, the wraith of Nigel Oswalt comes for you. Help is on the way. — Marshal Fleming...

(So writes Conrad Nightingale)

Knoggs and Fleming rode fast and hard. They had one advantage that Alcott didn't – they could trade out their horses for fresh mounts at several of the LESO Depots along their route. Under the circumstances, they made it to Bembridge Castle in record time.

As they rode into the city, nothing seemed out of the ordinary. People were in the streets going about their daily routines, unaware of the pending danger.

"Is it possible that Oswalt has yet to arrive?" asked Marshal Fleming.

"Anything is possible these days, but we mustn't let down our guard. Oswalt was a slippery bastard in life, and I don't expect he's changed any in death."

The two trotted on toward the castle, and nobody paid particular attention. They rode unchallenged past the towers, through the main gate, and across the drawbridge until they were well within the courtyard to Bembridge Castle. There, they were greeted by Captain Perkins, the newly appointed commander of the King's Impregnable Guards. Captain Perkins was well acquainted with Marshal Fleming but had never before seen Bozwell Knoggs.

"Well met, Spencer. King Bembridge expects you and asked me to bring you to him immediately upon arrival. However, he said nothing about a companion."

"Allow me to introduce Commandant Bozwell Knoggs of the Blackpool Penitentiary Sentries."

"It is a pleasure to meet you, Commandant, but I'm afraid you must remain here until the King clears it. I trust that you understand."

"It is Commandant Knoggs that carries a message of great importance for the King. Therefore, he shall accompany me."

"Not until the King clears him," Captain Perkins gripped the hilt of his sword as if to emphasize the point.

"It should be sufficient that I vouch for him!" snarled Fleming. "You are wasting time, and every second is precious. Now take us to the King at once!"

Marshal Fleming also grabbed the hilt of his sword. Captain Perkins quickly assessed the situation and reluctantly agreed to break protocol.

"The King awaits you in his private chambers." The three walked briskly to the northeast tower, climbed the steps, and continued down the heavily guarded hallway.

***

When they arrived, Captain Perkins knocked upon the door.

"Enter," it was the voice of King Bembridge, but he was not alone. Standing beside him was a distinguished-looking man dressed in a dark brown robe tied shut with a silver braided rope.

First, through the doorway was Captain Perkins, followed closely by Fleming and Knoggs. No sooner had the three passed over the threshold then Captain Perkins turned about, thrusting his dagger into the High Marshall's heart.

It happened quickly, but as Perkins moved to strike Knoggs, an eerie green light shot forth from the old man's fingertips, picking up Knoggs and tossing him against the far wall, out of reach of the wraith. The impact knocked Knoggs nearly unconscious.

Hearing the commotion, King Bembridge's Impregnable Guard rushed inside the room.

"Stay out!" ordered the King.

"But, Your Majesty," the guard began to protest.

"You have your orders, Sergeant. No one is to enter or leave this room without my expressed authorization. Am I clear!"

"Yes, Your Majesty." The door slammed shut.

"Back to the business at hand. You're a Druid, I presume?" questioned Captain Perkins.

"The name is Diack and know that this Druid is more than a match for you, wraith of Nigel Oswalt."

"You know who I am. I'm flattered. Nevertheless, let's put that hypothesis to the test."

Diack's arms rose, and he let loose a second blast, burning a hole into the corpse; Oswalt stood his ground.

"Well, so much for your theory. I've never killed a Druid. Do you die any differently than a commoner?"

Oswalt dropped his dagger and drew his sword. As he stepped forward, his advance was blocked.

"Ah, King Bembridge, paladin of the people, to the rescue as usual, but not this time."

The two swords clashed. Oswalt had never been as competent with a weapon as King Bembridge. Normally, there would be no competition. However, each time Bembridge struck forth, the corpse absorbed the blow.

"Why don't you try the lunge of death move that Alcott taught me?" Oswalt laughed mockingly. Oswalt held his sword in both hands and hammered down on King Bembridge, forcing him to his knees.

"Getting tired, your Majesty?"

A barely conscious Knoggs slid his weapon across the floor to King Bembridge.

"Use Shadow Slayer!" he shouted.

Bembridge grabbed the axe and fended off Oswalt's attack. The defensive move was followed immediately by cutting deep into Oswalt's side. Oswalt's eyes widened in astonishment as he screamed in pain, dropping to the ground.

Now, it was King Bembridge's turn to dish out the punishment. He stood above Oswalt, raining down blow after blow. Oswalt couldn't believe what was happening, but his face showed that he knew how it was about to end. In a fiery purple flash, he was gone.

All was quiet as King Bembridge opened the door to the hallway. "Sergeant, send for the doctor."

CHAPTER 30

MAINTAINING THE COURSE

It took several days of exotic medicine and regular rest to overcome the effects of Diack's magic, smashing him against the wall. Once back on his feet, Commandant Knoggs was invited to dine with King Bembridge in his private chambers...

(So writes Conrad Nightingale)

As Minister Alcott entered the room, Bozwell Knoggs and the Druid Diack were already with King Bembridge.

"Ah, the final guest of honor has arrived. Please come sit at the table and partake in food and drink."

The King was seated at the head of the table; as protocol dictated, the other guests filled in the empty chairs. Crystal glasses were filled to the brim with the finest wine in Calvendar as plates of hot bread, roasted venison, and fresh vegetables were set before the King and his guests. The dinner conversation remained nonchalant through a dessert of fruit and cheeses.

Finally, when all appeared satiated, King Bembridge changed the subject to more critical matters.

"Gentlemen, apart from John, the last time we were together in my chambers was not too pleasant, which is not to suggest he wasn't busy handling his burdens. John told me he had experienced a similar encounter with the wraith of Tobias Rycroft and several phantom gang members at the Pillars-of-the-Sky.

"As you can surmise from his presence here, he, too, was successful in dispatching these abominations back to the Underworld. A toast to our combined success."

Glasses were raised, and congratulations were passed around.

"I wish I could say that the danger is over, and things can return to normal; however, such is not the case. Over the past few days, I have pondered the miraculous return of John and Boz and their assignment to hunt down the demons and monsters who have crossed the veil into the land of the living.

"I have also carefully considered the portent of things to come, as revealed by our friends, the Druids of Thorsten. The pieces of the puzzle begin to fit. Unfortunately, it is not a good picture.

"Allow me to elaborate. While we fought the XaOrc to preserve and protect our way of life, unseen forces were at work to tip the scales in favor of chaos, and these maniacal forces are still at work. Now more than ever, we must be vigilant. How then shall we proceed?"

Diack was the first to respond, "The Druid Order has always walked a narrow path when serving all the races of Calvendar. My beliefs dictate that I return to Thorsten, but rest assured, whenever anyone attempts to pervert magic for dark purposes, the Druids will be there to shed light."

Alcott spoke next.

"I have served the House of Bembridge my entire life, and I have no regrets. However, I have been given a second chance to act as a champion for those who cannot stand for themselves. I will hunt down all the abominations that have escaped the Underworld and send them back to where they belong. This is my destiny until one day I am called by my beloved, Ingrid."

All eyes fell upon Knoggs.

"I, too, have been given a second chance to ferret out evil, but I lack John's strength. In the remaining days I have left on this earth, I want to spend them with my family. I want to embrace my wife and sleep by her side at night. I want to see my children grow and someday have their children. Perhaps I am selfish, perhaps even a coward, but I must be with my loved ones."

"Any man foolish enough to call you coward in my presence does so at his peril', responded Alcott. "You, more than any man I know, deserve happiness."

"Thank you, old friend." The tears began to well up in Knoggs' eyes.

"Retirement may be the safe choice, but I fear you will grow bored. Unfortunately, your job as Warden of Blackpool Penitentiary has been filled since your untimely demise. However, as it turns out, and it gives me no pleasure in saying so, the Kingdom requires another High Marshal. You can move your family here and take advantage of all that the city of Roderick offers in culture, education, and a strong community.

"Of course, the job comes with accommodations and a generous salary. Think about it, under the auspices of the Minister of Justice, whom I understand you know quite well," King Bembridge chuckled, "you can play an indispensable role in maintaining peace and stability throughout Calvendar. You'll also be able to coordinate with John whenever such needs arise. What say you?"

King Bembridge thought he detected Bozwell Knoggs blush if such a thing was possible for a bohkor.

"A chance to support the community while providing for my family sounds good, even if I must put up with John's contrite sense of humor. I graciously accept your offer, My King."

I trust the appointment meets your approval, Thornblade, Huntsman of Calvendar?"

"By the gods, Walter. As I've said many times, you love titles." They all had a good laugh.

COMING SOON

BOOK 2

OF THE

THE DRAGON OAK SAGAS

INSATIABLE

SNEAK PEEK. . .

CHAPTER 1

INSATIABLE

The meek looking old man and his girl companion walked unmolested through the streets of Thammarat. Hardly a person took notice, for everyone was far too busy wallowing in their self-pity . . . (So writes Conrad Nightingale)

***

"Vennick, I've known these people my entire life, yet look around us –– there's not so much as a casual acknowledgment of our presence here. The war has taken all the light from their eyes. The Xagada are but empty shells of their former selves."

"Does that bother you, Eleanor?"

"Oddly enough, I don't care what they think or feel. Does that make me a bad person?"

"Good and bad are nebulous concepts, a matter of perspective rather than reality. I intend to teach you how to discard the paltry thoughts of others, and when you can accomplish that with as little conviction as it takes to breathe, you will be truly invincible."

"Eleanor the Invincible, I like the sound of that," she smirked.

"Then together, let's set things in motion. Where would you like to begin?"

"First, let's ensure our house is in order."

***

Without further ado, the two picked their way through the city until they reached the house of Kayla Rycroft, the former Xantara of the Xagada Nation. Rocking on the front porch, in an almost catatonic state, was Gregor Yorick, her grandmother's faithful confidant and bodyguard.

Eleanor climbed the squeaky wooden porch steps and approached slowly. He didn't seem to take notice. Placing a gentle hand on his shoulder, she spoke his name softly, "Gregor." When he raised his eyes to look at her face, he was immediately reinvigorated.

"Ellie!" Gregor jumped to his feet and embraced the girl tightly. "Your grandmother and I heard you had been captured by a rogue band of orcs and sold into slavery. We thought you were lost to us. How did you manage to escape? Have you been harmed in any way?"

"I'm okay, thanks to my new friend here. Allow me to introduce Vennick." Eleanor glanced at her companion, standing just below the porch railing. His eyes were clear and bright, and he wore a sly grin on his weathered face. Gregor found the resemblance to Kayla Rycroft uncanny. He instantly liked the old man.

"You will learn how we escaped soon enough, but let's go inside the house for now. We need to talk." The house was just as her grandmother had left it; nothing was out of place. Gregor would have it no other way, even during these troubling times; preserving the integrity of the Xantara was his sworn duty.

"Gregor, I want your first-hand observations and impressions regarding the war. Spare no detail, no matter how trivial."

For the next few hours, Gregor told Eleanor and Vennick all he could remember, from the difficulty of forming an alliance with the orc, to the plan of attack, and the division of responsibilities. He was also sure to point out the utter disdain held between the Orc Clans and the Xagada Nation, especially how the orcs never missed a chance to mock the Xagada.

Lastly, he shared his recollection of the orcs' failure to implement the plan and then deserting at the battle's most critical stage.

When Gregor finished his accounting, Eleanor thanked him for explaining how things played out. As for Vennick, his true thoughts hidden as always, he simply stared blankly as though the most minor details of Gregor's report were commonly known.

***

The sun was beginning to wane. "It's time for some nourishment before retiring for the night. I don't know what provisions we have left in the pantry, but I'm sure I can find something for us to eat and drink," Gregor said.

"Allow me," responded Vennick. He passed his hand over the table, and a cornucopia of fruits, vegetables, cheeses, and meats appeared before them. A decanter of fine wine sat alongside.

Gregor's eyes widened. "**MAGIC**! That explains a lot. I take it that you're a druid. "

Vennick chuckled. "Not even close. My capabilities far exceed those charlatans, which will soon be the same for Eleanor."

"What exactly are you saying?"

Eleanor immediately took control of the conversation. "I have agreed to leave with Vennick and become his apprentice." Her tone was resolute; the matter was not subject to discussion.

"How long will you be gone?"

"The apprenticeship is twenty years," replied Vennick.

Gregor looked at Eleanor and spoke solemnly, "With your grandmother's passing, you are now the Xantara of the Xagada Nation. Twenty years is a long time for our people to be without a leader, especially in these hard times."

"**YOU** shall lead the Xagada while I'm away."

"You are asking a lot of our people. They are tired, hurt, and demoralized."

"I'm not asking," came her emphatic response. Eleanor rose to her feet and began to walk toward her old bedroom. Turning back momentarily, "Gregor, see that everyone is gathered in the main square by noon tomorrow, and one last thing -- attendance is mandatory."

***

Eleanor snuggled deep under her comforter; silent tears ran down her cheeks as her mind recalled the day's events. Vennick's words played repeatedly in her head:

"Good and bad are nebulous concepts, a matter of one's perspective rather than of actual reality. I intend to teach you how to discard the paltry thoughts of others, and when you can accomplish that with as little conviction as it takes to breathe, you will be truly invincible."

I will learn all that you can teach me, Vennick. However, there is nothing paltry about my grandmother, whom I love with every fiber of my being. I swear to cling to her memory and always consider what she would think of me.

***

Sunrise found Gregor darting through the streets, spreading the word regarding Eleanor's command to appear. From the disgruntled looks and murmurings, most people were unhappy with this youngster commanding anything from them, especially considering recent events.

Eleanor, Vennick, and Gregor stood in the pavilion at noon at the far end of the main square. No one dared be absent, whether because they were curious or scared. Gregor stepped forward, raising his hands, and the square fell silent. Eleanor immediately took his place.

"Like many of you, I have lost loved ones in 'The Cleanse'. My grandmother, Kayla Rycroft, Xantara of the Xagada Nation, took her last breath on that battlefield, defiantly spitting in the face of King Bembridge. She died refusing to give up on her dream that the Xagada would no longer hide in the shadows or be treated as second-class citizens in Calvendar. I share this dream and intend to see it come to fruition. Today, by divine right, I accept the mantle of Xantara!" A less than enthusiastic response came from those gathered; however, this did not deter Eleanor.

"Now, more than ever, the Xagada Nation must have a competent leader at the helm, for we cannot expect to navigate turbulent waters in a rudderless boat," she continued. The crowd remained unenthusiastic.

"Some of you believe that I lack the prerequisite qualities to assume the role of Xantara," she looked around at the sullen faces.

"I must admit, a part of me shares your concern, which is why I am going away for an extended period to hone my leadership skills. While I am away, I leave you in the capable hands of my second in command, Chancellor Gregor Yorick. The people began to stir, a few cheering while many more nodded in concurrence. She hoped for that response; the fish had taken the bait.

"Know this, good and brave citizens of the Xagada Nation, you would have certainly achieved Kayla Rycroft's objective but for the insubordinate, cowardly acts of our supposed allies, the orcs." The crowd was now committed. It was easier to blame others than to focus on one's own shortcomings.

"The orcs must be punished for their insolence! They must learn their place in a new order, not as our equals but as our SLAVES!" The crowd roared their approval.

"I intend to see to that personally," Eleanor yelled above the uproar. "It is not just the orcs, but all races of Calvendar that must accept the Xagada as their betters. If anyone disrespects us, then they will be taught to **FEAR** us, for we shall be resolute in our pursuit of superiority!" The crowd went wild. It took several moments before Eleanor could continue speaking.

"The Preservation Coalition drove us from their lands and branded us like cattle. They want us to be easily identified, and they want us to be ashamed. I say wear the brand like a badge of honor! Let it be the last thing they see on this earthly plane."

All voices raised in unison: "Eleanor . . . Eleanor . . . Eleanor," they chanted.

Then, right before their eyes, in a flash of eerie green light, Eleanor and the old man vanished. Silence immediately fell over the crowd.

DISOBEDIENCE IS NOT TOLERATED

Having been defeated, the Xagada's sentence of exile back to Eastern Calvendar was sealed with a brand of shame. As for the Orc Clans, King Bembridge had given the order to kill any orc on sight that dared to wander out of their homeland in the Sawtooth Mountains. Under such draconian resolutions, if you were stupid enough to have any business with orcs, you best be prepared to climb those forbidding mountains. However, they didn't climb; they simply appeared in a flash of eerie green light...

(So writes Conrad Nightingale)

Eleanor and Vennick stood at the center of an outcropping of enormous boulders, a natural amphitheater. Orcs spilled in from all directions. They didn't know why they made the journey; they were simply compelled to come.

Eleanor held up her hands, and the clambering abruptly stopped. All was quiet. The girl could sense their apprehension, a palatable mixture of curiosity and trepidation. As usual, Vennick was unimpressed, as though something of this magnitude was an everyday occurrence. He leaned in close to her.

"Keep in mind our bargain. I am with you. Claim what is yours, and it shall be."

As Eleanor lowered her hands, she was wearing a confident smile and began to speak softly, yet every orc could hear her as though she was standing next to them.

"Don't be afraid, at least not until I explain why I have come." Eleanor smirked; Vennick's power was coursing through her veins, and she was intoxicated. Regaining control, she continued.

"My name is Eleanor Rycroft, granddaughter to Kayla Rycroft, heir to the Xagada Nation and your new Queen. Maybe more noteworthy is the fact that your Queen is not happy.

The orcs were taken aback but also angered by the impertinence of this child's proclamation. Weapons were raised, and rebukes echoed down the rocky hillside. However, that was the best they could muster, for the orcs found themselves incapable of advancing upon the intruders.

"It appears there is some disagreement with my edict. Most unfortunate, for there is no place for dissent, let alone a challenge, in my realm. Allow me to demonstrate."

Out of nowhere, a cold wind swept down from the snowcapped mountains, and an ominous dark green cloud descended upon the assembly. Still unable to move in any direction, the orcs fell to their knees, covering their heads in their hands like children trying to hide from an imaginary monster.

When next she spoke, Queen Eleanor's words boomed like thunder.

"Olav Tyan, come before me!"

Putting on a brave face, Olav Tyan made his way through the crowd until he stood towering over the small girl.

SNORT... "Still no respect? Maybe another gentle slap remind you." HARRUMPH...

"Perhaps the same is true for you?" Queen Eleanor's tiny hand struck out like a venomous serpent, sending Olav Tyan head over heels.

Vennick strolled over to Olav Tyan and casually peed in the face of the unconscious orc.

"Wake up pig, your Queen isn't through speaking to you." Before Olav Tyan could grasp what was happening, he was magically thrown upon his knees before the feet of Eleanor.

Queen Eleanor bent down, grabbed one of Olav Tyan's tusks, and snapped it like a twig from his jowl. The orc screamed out in pain.

"You shall wear this tusk around your neck as a symbol of my dominance and fidelity to your new Queen. From this day forth, you, Olav Tyan, shall serve as Supreme Commander over all Orc Clans under the discretion of Gregor Yorick, Chancellor to the Xagada Nation. I caution you not to vex him, for he dislikes you."

Immediately, Olav Tyan settled down. The idea of being the Supreme Commander was worth the pain of a broken tusk.

"Supreme Commander Olav Tyan, while I am away, you have two primary objectives: first, ensure that orc women breed a new generation of soldiers, and second, build me a citadel the envy of any province. Nod your head if you understand." Olav Tyan frantically nodded his head in the affirmative.

"Good. Now tell me, who was responsible for commanding the orc forces at 'The Cleanse'? Do not lie to me, for like my late grandmother, I have ways of knowing the truth."

That is a lesson that Olav Tyan understood all too well.

SNORT... "It was Blox Nye, Your Majesty." HARRUMPH...

"Blox Nye, stand before me!" Nobody moved, for they were petrified with fear. It didn't matter. An eerie green light came forth from the sky, winding its way through the crowd until it lifted a lone orc and deposited him at the feet of Queen Eleanor. He groveled, burying his face in the dirt and crying out for mercy.

"Why do you beg for mercy? Have you done something that warrants my wrath?" Blox Nye mumbled incoherently.

"Speak up, you pig that walks on two legs!" demanded Queen Eleanor.

SNORT... "I led orcs to die in battle." HARRUMPH...

"What makes you think I care how many orcs died in battle? Tell me, what is your true crime? Speak quickly while you still possess a tongue, for I grow impatient."

Blox Nye was not stupid; he knew what Queen Eleanor wanted to hear.

SNORT... "I deserted Xagada!" he yelled out. HARRUMPH...

"Exactly. Now name the officers who fled by your side."

As Blox Nye spoke the names of the four remaining commanding officers, each, in turn, was picked up by the strange light and thrown to the ground before her.

"You have all broken your sworn alliance to the Xagada, leaving your brothers in arms to fend for themselves." Queen Eleanor spit on the ground.

"Your cowardice sickens me. Supreme Commander Olav Tyan take these traitors in chains to Chancellor Yorick. Tell him it's my gift. He will know what to do with them."

Eleanor looked at Vennick as if seeking his approval.

"That was fun," remarked Vennick. I knew you were special."

Then, miraculously, the two disappeared.

TO BE CONTINUED...

COMING SOON

BOOK 2

OF THE

THE DRAGON OAK SAGAS

INSATIABLE

www.ingramcontent.com/pod-product-compliance
Lightning Source LLC
Chambersburg PA
CBHW070642310726
48982CB00001B/376

9798992488159